£ 1· 50

FORGET IT

THE ALIAS MAN
MESSAGE ENDS
CONTACT LOST
YOUNG MEN MAY DIE
A WALK AT NIGHT
UP FROM THE GRAVE
DOUBLE TAKE
BOLTHOLE
WHOSE LITTLE GIRL ARE YOU (filmed as *The Squeeze*.)
A DEAD LIBERTY
THE ALBION CASE
FAITH, HOPE AND DEATH

By the same author
As Bill James: the Harper and Iles series

YOU'D BETTER BELIEVE IT
THE LOLITA MAN
HALO PARADE
PROTECTION
COME CLEAN
TAKE
CLUB
ASTRIDE A GRAVE
GOSPEL
ROSES, ROSES
IN GOOD HANDS

FORGET IT

Bill James

writing as

David Craig

This first world edition published in Great Britain 1995 by
SEVERN HOUSE PUBLISHERS LTD of
9–15 High Street, Sutton, Surrey SM1 1DF.

British Library Cataloguing in Publication Data
James, Bill
  Forget it
  I. Title
  823.914 [F]

  ISBN 0-7278-4744-9

Typeset by Hewer Text Composition Services, Edinburgh.
Printed and bound in Great Britain by
Hartnolls Ltd, Bodmin, Cornwall.

Memory is a great artist. For every man and for every woman it makes the recollection of his or her life a work of art and an unfaithful record.

Maurois

Author's note: This is a work of fiction. Although the general geography of Cardiff and its docks in the book is correct, some locations have been changed or invented. There is a Cardiff Bay development plan and a marina-style housing. Bute Street is still the main thoroughfare in the docks. There is no police station in it, though. There is no Toledo or Four Horsemen club. There is an ice rink in Cardiff, but no Cheald Meadows.

Chapter 1

Brade found that to watch a woman you had once loved make love with someone else could still bring pain. Up that a bit: call it agony. Not too many men would have had this experience, but police duty put you in rare spots. A detective did voyeurism of all sorts, of course. Of course. That's what the trade was about. You made a career as a Peeping Tom, and the professional term for observing Dilsom's ardent frame heaving and swooping, and Julie's clutching nails dig dull blood from each of his shoulder blades, was "close surveillance".

Brade could not recall ever being fondly ripped like that by Julie himself and, though he was fully clothed and unobserved, suddenly felt ashamed of his virgin back. Had he failed her somehow, not unlocked her the way this lad could? Regret and self-blame chewed at him. Possibly he still loved her. The idea startled Brade. It laid him open again. There had been nobody else since her, not really, but until now he thought he had seen off most of the sad, sad longings by his various sad, sad, distractions: just the usual methods. But, gazing now at the rather grubby soles of her feet, as they hung in the air above Dilsom, he knew all those longings were rushing back, if they had ever truly left. He wanted to push his palm lovingly over the line of her jaw, her cheekbones and the bristle of hair above her ears. He yearned for the way she used to talk to him – so head-on and unstoppable – and for the way she could read him, yet still stay loyal, at least until those black-edged, final days.

Christ, the gouging nails in Dilsom's back – as if she had to collect more of him than he was already giving. These two were on the floor near Julie's big repro-Victorian desk, both naked, their clothes higgledy-piggledy in and flowing out of a metal wastepaper basket, her vermilion and silver cravat the top item. Everything about them and the suave, chaotic setting said savage passion, and Brade felt himself trembling with envy. Although this would be fine quality carpet, suiting the fine job Julie had now, Dilsom's knees were sure to show wear and might take some explaining to his wife. As injuries, negligible, obviously. What Brade had to worry about, or try to worry about as a cop, was that in Dilsom's present position a man could not be more vulnerable to real, bone-deep damage, fatal damage. Dilsom was a hated, stalked, targeted man, but you'd never have guessed to look at him now. His eyes would probably be shut or fixed, rapt, on Julie's gorgeous face. He took no account of anything else in the room, eardrums probably booming only to the thuds of a hard-pushed, forty-three-year-old, adulterous heart, almost forty-four. This man had helped the State. This man had the protection of the State. Brade was it.

Although it was late evening and there seemed nobody else about, a few other media companies besides Julie's had office suites in this building, and they worked all hours. The street door stayed open till around midnight, or Brade would not be here. Luckily, he knew Danny on Reception, a salt-of-the-earth, helpful lad. And, also luckily, Julie's room was a booth in an open-plan space, its walls solid panels to half height, then glass. And luckily again, Julie had not locked the door to the firm's spread. Though they had no lights on, standing in shadow in the general office, Brade could see all it was necessary to see, and so would anyone else who might come stalking Dilsom. Contempt for security was written right across him.

Brade would go soon. He must not be found here. Dilsom, of course, would understand. Where he went, Brade was likely to go, too. Was ordered to. But Julie would not understand at all, and she could not be told. Julie would suppose some paltry, pervy, jealous nostalgia made Brade peep. Well, yes, a bit. He was discovering that. It was more than a year since he and Julie broke up, but, no question, the old, useless possessiveness tore at him now. Wasn't there something foully appreciative, even smug, about those floating feet, fat big toes erect, like a double thumbs-up? It sickened Brade to think she might spot him, confront him, despise and pity him.

2

But more was involved, too, and especially Geoffrey Dilsom's dangerous history and very dangerous, very secret present. Jesus, but how about this for pain, rising to agony: someone made love to your live-in girl, ex-girl, and the job said it was your main current duty to protect him, if necessary with your life? This was Mr Supergrass, retired. He was far from his former home, hidden away with a new name in a new community, untraced and untraceable. Or that was the hope. Nobody could be quite sure, and so Brade was given the chore of keeping a guardian eye for a month or two. It could not have been known then that Dilsom would strike up something satisfying with Julie. He had, though, and tonight, now, Brade began to wonder how seriously he should listen to his orders. Wasn't there a case for a little intelligent neglect, which might leave Dilsom exposed to one of those old-times'-sake vengeance callers who wanted him – perhaps more than one? Dilsom would be briskly removed from Julie's . . . well, from Julie's consideration, and everyone else's. It would be easy and entirely safe, for Brade, that is. After all, as tonight made plain, Dilsom did not mind leaving himself exposed. Couldn't Brade go along with that? A grass was only a grass.

But good Christ, he must sink such thoughts. They were monstrous, criminal, natural. Dilsom had to be preserved. Brade decided he would wait outside in the street, to see him safely away eventually, or longer than that. Dilsom was prized and must be cherished, and not just by Julie. No, by all those who looked for the victory of good over evil, who expected Brade and others in the police force to produce this victory and go on producing it, and who paid them to produce it: did not pay them enough, but enough to own them.

As to pay, when leaving Brade dropped a tenner to Danny. Their grand, solid understanding went back at least fifteen years and Brade knew as cast iron fact that he could rely on Danny's total silence about tonight's visit unless someone else dropped him another ten, or a bottle of Newcastle Brown.

3

Chapter 2

Brade waited in a doorway but Dilsom did not appear. Perhaps Julie had shown him a different way out. Perhaps they were still up there. God almighty. Could this be turning into a real, worthwhile relationship? She might be sweetly binding up his mental wounds. Sod that. Brade reckoned he was the one hurt. He often allowed himself short sessions of first quality self-pity these days, and nights.

He gave it until Danny closed the street doors, then turned his mind to remedies and drove the little distance to the pavements around the Toledo Club off James Street, still rap-booming away. Brade looked out for one or the other of the foreign girls he liked to take home occasionally these nights. Kerb crawling could bring grave trouble even for Brade, so he always parked a decent way off and walked. Anyone who saw him might assume he was working. Might. Yes, yes. This was his realm, was still his realm, more or less. This was the new Cardiff dockland. By night it kept a few murky traces of how it had always been – the girls, the gangs, the violence. And, by day . . . By day it looked transfigured.

Like almost every other dead port, it had a marina now, and a lot of bright, new, dinky-scale, cement-brick housing. Old warehouses had been gutted with imagination and turned into apartment blocks. There were the smart media offices like Julie's where young and youngish creative people called Bronwen or Jake, or Julie, arrived in the mornings by Audi or Saab or Senator, sporting great projects. They wore a hundred quid jeans or beautiful suits, and hatched cartoons and ads and newsfilm for Welsh language TV and the world. In the evening, they drove out again to somewhere leafy, leaving dockland to the night crew, and to Brade.

The changes came from the hugely puffed, hugely busy, hugely financed Cardiff Bay development, which would take what was once the world's greatest coal port and turn it into Bijouville for the twenty-first century. For now, today, tonight, it was still Brade's realm. Sometimes, though, or even more often, he felt it moving away from him, bought up by opportunist London money, opportunist US money, worthy European Community money. It might be for the best, eventually. Yes, it might, eventually. Resurrection, but as something different. Part of Brade's job was to make the whole area seem spruce and tranquil, by day and night, so that all this fine investment did not take fright and kept coming.

The girls he sought could be Italian or French or Dutch or Philippino. For most of them, Cardiff was their first stopping place in Britain. They were generally youngish, prettyish, knew hardly any English, except cash talk and sex talk and sickness talk. Brade did not mind this. He had plenty to say himself. The girls never stayed long in the city before pushing on to London, and there was a nice rate of change. Most of the tarts gave themselves fancy British names: so many people wanted to blend. The one he took home tonight was Italian and must have been kidded along by someone that "Boadicia" was a great choice, so for now that's who she was. He had invited her back two or three times before and found her delightful. Her English was the worst of all of them. She would do anything, and what he wanted her to do tonight was sit and listen. Not understand, listen. Definitely not understand. At *first* tonight, anyway, this was what he wanted.

Brade lived in a flat well outside the docks, and near Llandaff Cathedral. It had been chosen by Julie, and he loathed it now – jogging clerics at dawn, Rover-loads of worshippers, the miserable spire, grey and so fucking know-all, through the trees. He settled Boadicia in the big armchair and brought beer. Brade took his jacket off and put the 629 Magnum Smith and Wesson cannon and shoulder holster on the so-called coffee table, then sat down opposite her confidingly. For anything concerned with Dilsom he was under permanent orders to go armed with this eight and a half inch barrel. He was under orders to go paired with Glyndwr Jenkins, too, but

5

felt glad he had ignored that tonight. Some incidents were for private view.

Stretching out in his chair, Brade said: "Boadicia, what we've done, a few of us, is a wondrous act, yea even a Godlike act. Cardiff docks marina is suddenly the Garden of Eden. We've created a person. Well, no, it's better than God: we've created a *family*, though very dicey with the children, as you'll understand."

She nodded wisely. "Always you talk, Dave. What use?" She grunted, then settled back in the chair and half closed her eyes, feet in green and gold ankle socks crossed in front of her.

"You're privileged," Brade said. "Only a few people in the whole force know anything of this, and I wish it were fewer. Yet I spill everything to you. Well, I need to chat, that's a fact. I do miss talking things over. That was with someone else. Perhaps I shouldn't speak of her to you."

Boadicia said nothing. She stood suddenly, walked to the record player and put on an old record of *Somewhere Along The Way*, then began to hum the tune, standing close to his Magnum. She glanced at it, before deliberately turning away as though nauseated by guns. He used to share the feeling. But there was a new policing, just as there was a new dockland.

Brade said: "What we've created is a man called Dil – well, no, no I won't give it in full, even to you, secure as you are, Boadicia, just in case. It could have been anything. Simply a random bag of vowels and consonants to make a name, not too ordinary and yet not freakish. He's got to merge."

"Merge, I know. One of the girls."

"That's Marj."

"Ah. Her, a double dose."

"I heard."

"Sad. You say 'sad'?"

"Very."

He stood up and and switched off all but a wall light. Then he crossed the room to Boadicia and they danced very close for about twenty minutes in the middle of the carpet, covering hardly any ground, the style for a crowded nightclub. She kept her body a little distant from him, as if she knew he had a ton of chat to unload again before anything else, and she had better wait. The replay faithfully sent and re-sent the needle back to the start. He could almost soothe himself like this. Lovingly, he murmured in her ear, "Of course, he's been under this new name for months now. That's the bloody trouble. They start getting careless. In his case, cocky. When he's . . . well, call it enjoying himself, he forgets entirely that all sorts might be hunting him, with very bloody bills to settle. He's helped put a lot of people away, Boadicia, and brothers and sons and fathers and cousins and mothers and sisters and wives and girlfriends and one-time colleagues from the Elephant, Peckham, Lewisham, New Cross – well, from all over London – are vendetta-hunting his kidneys. You know 'vendetta'?"

"Ah," she replied. "Vendetta, yes. Bad."

"Bad. Grassing they never forgive. Grassing they kill for. It's understandable." He gave a small whoop of satisfaction. "But they don't know where to hunt. Again, we hope. He's been shipped to us and we guard him, remake him, blend him and his wife and his children in, far from his old haunts and one-time mates. Routine. I've done it before. No, not a specialist, I wouldn't claim that, but familiar with the problems. At least, the usual ones. Not how to manage the kids, for instance. Sorry? That's a fair question, Boadicia. Yes, certainly, there've been occasional, terrible fuck-ups."

Her head was against his chest but she pulled back and smiled at him, hearing the love word.

Brade said: "Oh, yes, they lost an ex-grass somewhere in the north of England lately – stabbed twelve times in what was wittily called a safe house. I just can't let anything similar happen here, not even if the bastard is screwing my . . . well, that's probably by the way. It *is* by the way. Has to be by the way. Society owes him – them – security, you see. They were our lifeline – police's information lifeline – and now we're *their* lifeline. It's reasonable. But, the things is, this sod lies to us – tells us he's passing his nights securely at home, when I know different – when I now know he's out having . . . out putting himself into appalling, unnecessary hazard. Absolutely unnecessary. This is a married bloody man, Boadicia! Do I want to spend half my time tailing him, for God's sake? Cardiff docks has a damn sight more than one ex-grass, and it all has to be policed, mainly by Dave Brade, plus Glyn

Jenkins. OK, OK, with some help. All right, I know, I'm shouting. When they first dumped him on us, the Yard did warn he was prick-led, but tonight went beyond. *Certainly*, I think once in a while of slick ways to get the bastard happily snuffed. Why not open a trail to him? Oh, Jesus, yes."

She seemed to respond to this name, glancing up again, this time with a smile that was holy.

Brade remarked: "I exaggerate when I say he could have been relabelled anything at all. You're quite right to protest. There were discussions and a lot of options considered. Obviously, the target has to feel comfortable with the change. And his wife. If they're not at ease the identity's useless. They'd draw attention to themselves through awkwardness. Well, you'd understand – why you chose 'Boadicia', for instance."

She recognised this word, too, and opened her eyes wider, as if he had called her and was going to shut up at last. She came closer. It did not feel as if she had anything on under her bit of dress. He liked this, but not enough, yet.

He said in a steady, teaching voice: "Yes, they might even forget the name in a moment of stress and revert to their real – sorry, their previous – one: of course, we forcefully discourage them from thinking of their earlier existence as the real one, because *this* is the real now. Fortunately their twins are only six years old and will soon ditch the old identity and all recollections from that period. We hope. Yes, we very much have to hope. It's tricky. As a matter of fact, there's an expert coming down to help on the kids' memories before they start the new school here and have a chance to talk to other pupils. At present we pay for them to have lessons at home. Before they go out to the classroom, their infant minds have to be purged by this psychology specialist from London. Sounds a bit chilling? I agree, but probably necessary. Probably."

There was a knock at the front door of the flat: three heavy, two light, then the same repeated. Brade tensed. In a moment, he broke from Boadicia and, taking his revolver and holster from the coffee table, hid them in a drawer of the bureau.

"The priest again?" she asked.

"His knock, yes."

"I like this priest."

"Good. One of the very best."

8

"And his friend?"

"Probably." Brade danced over to the door with her and opened it. Clifford Hale-Garning came in, carrying a suitcase and with a bottle of Emu tonic wine sticking out of his pocket: although in his dog collar, he had on an ordinary dark suit tonight, not the cassock. Brade left Boadicia again for a minute and and went to the kitchen. He found a glass and a cup and put these on the coffee table, then reclaimed Boadicia and resumed dancing. Cliffy sat down and poured a drink of wine for Brade in the glass and for himself in the cup, where it was easier to mask quantity. He drank his, refilled and drank that, then brought out Enid, his favourite life-size, from the case and blew her up by mouth. Always he insisted on this, spurning a pump. He said it gave him a kick to see and feel the doll come alive from his personal wind, which recalled the book of *Genesis*, familiar in his game. Many people were keen on creation. Also, Brade knew it gratified Cliffy that at sixty he still had the lungs. He produced some clothes from the case and dressed Enid in one of those foul, tweedy outfits he thought suited her. Then the pair stepped languorously on to the dance area.

"Come here often?" he asked Enid in a hot whisper. "I guessed there was a party again, Dave. Heard the music and delicious buzz of cheek-to-cheek woo through the floor. Boadicia, dear, grand to see you."

Brade said: "Sorry if we disturbed you."

"Picked up no words, don't worry. I never eavesdrop on intimacies. Disturb? I'm grateful for any interruption. Isn't this is the dullest fucking flat block I've ever been in, including Llandrindod Wells?"

"It's cathedrals. They cast a pall. P-a-l-l, not the Saint."

"Don't knock my bread and butter. But so lucky to be living right above you, Dave, and able now and then to hear blissful signs of hottish life and catch a whiff of rough desire." Hale-Garning crooned gently with the record for a while. The phone on the sort of sideboard rang and as they were nearest he lifted the receiver. "Dave's Place," he said and listened, a finger in his free ear. "You'll have to speak up – the music!" he bellowed. "Oh, just a little soirée." He covered the mouthpiece and turned to Brade.

9

"An officer? In a bit of a panic? Glyndwr Something? Jenkins?"

Brade and Boadicia split apart again and he went to turn down the record volume. He took the receiver: "Glyn? Problems?"

"I think someone's near the Dilsom nest. On the lurk."

"One? Or more?"

"Might be more. I thought one. Who the hell's with you, Dave?"

"I'll come down." He replaced the phone. "Must take you back, Boadicia," he said. "I've got to slip out, Cliffy."

"Serious?"

"Just an admin crisis. File missing at the nick. Perhaps more than one. But better take a glance before higher authority hears."

"At this time of night? Frustrating." Gloom shadowed his face at the loss of this get-together. "Look, Dave, do you think I could risk it back up the stairs to my flat with her like this? It's so, well, callous to deflate, then expect her to fill out bonny for me again immediately we're home."

"Yes, it's late. Nobody about. Pull her hat down further to cover the face."

Hale-Garning placed one arm around Enid's waist and put the half full bottle of wine in his case to carry in the other hand. Brade let him out on to the landing and for a few seconds watched them make their way upstairs to Cliffy's floor. Even from behind, they looked established, companionable – looked almost solid, although her feet were well off the ground.

Brade shut the door. He offered Boadicia twenty-five and she gave him back ten. "Only talk, dance," she said. He strapped on the pistol, got into his jacket and drove fast from Llandaff to the docks. He put Boadicia down near the Toledo then went on to the marina. But he could not find Glyndwr. Christ. Although the instruction was to work double, Brade and Jenkins would each drive alone past Dilsom's place at random times, looking for anything that might say trouble. How else could he be guarded? To watch him round-the-clock would give signals, finger him. The spot-check system was the best they could think of, and Glyndwr must have taken a spin

10

here tonight. Brade saw his car empty under a street light. He would have been investigating on foot whatever it was he saw. Why wasn't this sodding Magnum smaller, so he could transfer it from the holster to his pocket for readiness? Pulling a long- barrelled gun from a pouch was a damn slow, awkward job, no matter how easy Dirty Harry made it look. It might get snarled up in a pocket, too, though.

Public funds had gratefully provided Geoffrey Dilsom, who had once been Hector Vale, with a place in the expanding Cardiff Bay marina, alongside what was once the city's Bute East Dock. These smart properties lay just over the railway line from Cardiff's famous Bute Street and the former Tiger Bay, though that name was as taboo as Dilsom's old one now. The word "Bay" had been cleaned up, given a new rôle, just as Vale had, and so, for instance, some renovated old docks buildings had become the Celtic Bay Hotel. This whole previous wasteland shone as a chi-chi spread of properties and pleasant waterways. Putting Dilsom here followed a procedure proved nationwide. *Half* proved. You looked for a new community like the marina's, hoping the retired grass and his family would not stick out as strangers, since everybody here was a stranger. Until tonight, this seemed to work. Perhaps, as Cliffy said, Glyndwr Jenkins had panicked, though that would be untypical, very. Glyndwr was one of those whizz kids, but decent with it. He was the only Welsh-speaking black in the force – and probably in any police force anywhere.

Dilsom's house was just off Schooner Way. Brade parked in the private yard of the Spillers and Bakers one-time warehouse, now prestige flats, and also walked. Everybody knew – villains as well as police – that two cars together were more than twice as noticeable as one, and you never parked close, not even unmarked vehicles. It was almost 1.30 a.m. and he saw nobody. Dilsom's place was dark. He had a quick look at it, front and back, and spotted nothing wrong. The windows behind their ornamental bars and the doors all seemed to be intact and he could examine the kitchen through a rear window, neat and serene, a table set for breakfast. The builder had been told to put solid wood doors in the house, not the usual three-ply, and all the locks were superior Chubb. The house was double glazed

11

with shatterproof throughout at brilliant cost, plus more good locks for each window and a top class, sensor alarm system. Of course, none of it would keep out for five minutes someone who knew his trade, and anybody who came looking for Dilsom *would*. In fact, anybody who traced him this far would have every skill in the villain manual. Dilsom was aware of that, and Brade had once watched him smother a giggle when the special safeguards were glowingly listed for him by Raging Bullfinch at headquarters. Bullfinch, from his grand rank, oversaw this whole cover project. Yes, Dilsom had some winning aspects: the dark humour, wryness, spells of courage, spells of fatalism. Brade might have have liked him, *did* like him before tonight. One could put up with an ex-grass, but not an ex-grass who satisfactorily gave it to one's ex-partner in her fine career lair. Yes, that did seem to make it all so crudely ravenous, the splendid setting, the disregard of risk. Again Brade asked himself whether he had ever reached her so irresistibly? Perhaps. The triumphant times faded in your mind, and only defeats stuck. Ultimately, there had been quite a few of those. "Blub, blub," he muttered.

Brade stood still in the rear garden for a minute, listening and watching. Possibly during his earlier, heavy existence, Dilsom himself had successfully penetrated a little fortress like this house and dealt finality to an informer. Life's rôles could change very fast. Brade heard and saw nothing and now walked down to the side of the long, rectangular lake that used to be a dock. The whole development was brightly lit by goldfish bowl street lamps and, standing on the railed walkway at the edge of the water, he gazed about again, trying to spot Glyndwr, or anyone else. He made his eyes pass systematically over the lake's surface, working from one end to the other, searching for any darker, floating shape in the dark water. It was not so very long since High Life Vernon had been fished out of this ornamental pond, bullet-torn and dead, a baddish moment in the docks' endless gang tussles. Endless? The Bay scheme might really work the magic its creators promised, and make the old teams and their warfare obsolete. Not yet, though.

He spotted no floater and was walking back up towards Schooner Way when he heard the sudden rasping din of a high-performance car moving at fierce speed and still accelerating. He fished the Magnum from its holster and holding it at his side ran the few more yards to the road. Just before he reached it, a dark Escort went past, doing around 80 and making for the exit from the development into Herbert Street. As Brade stepped on to the pavement the car screamed away. Its driver appeared not to see him and kept his eyes ahead, so Brade could get only colour and profile and likely age: white, fair haired and hatless, mad Mohican haircut, delicate nose and chin, about twenty-five. He seemed to be alone. Brade felt helpless. You did not put 44 shells into what might be only a joy ride vehicle. Even in the States or France they would draw the line at that. He committed to memory the registration, but that would probably lead only to where the Escort had been stolen from.

Brade thought the car had come from beyond The Wharf pub and he began to run that way, the revolver still in his hand. He considered yelling Glyndwr's name, but held back. There were times when he yearned for the old police whistle: you could blow and receive an answering call, if your mate was capable of giving one. Glyndwr was not. Brade found him beside a big, decorative, metal barque fixed fetchingly in concrete at the entrance to Admiral Howe Gardens. He lay face to the ground, unmoving, with blood seeping down each side of his face and neck from what seemed like two deep head wounds. Brade crouched low by Glyndwr, took his wrist and could not be sure he was getting a pulse.

Chapter 3

A spark called Andrew Rockmain came down from some-where in the Yard to help with Dilsom's twins, six years old, almost seven. "What we try to do, very gently, is to adjust their memory," Rockmain said. They talked in Brade's office at the Bute Street nick.

"Adjust?" Brade replied.

Rockmain gave a great clatter of a laugh, rich in guilt, and so brilliant with spontaneity and sudden shame you knew he had run this pantomime many times before. "Sorry, Dave," he said. "I'm pissing about with words, yes. It's my salesmanship. Forgot I was talking to a fellow cop, alert to half truths."

Such reasonableness. Brade saw he was being managed. Rockmain would be trained to that. Every word was tech-nique: he would slip in some blatant bit of evasion like "adjust", to give Brade the chance to query it, and give himself a chance to apologise, to come clean, to put cards on the table, or seem to. This was supposed to make Brade feel they were equals, chatting frankly from now on. They were not equals, not in the dark area of Rockmain's special trade. "You mean, blot out memories?" Brade asked.

"Oh, you talk extremes. I suppose the first thing you think is 'brainwashing'." Rockmain made the word sound simplistic, but tolerantly, he said: "And fair enough. There's going to be an element of that."

"Of course there is."

"The memory is a very slippery, very fallible item, you know. Well, Dave, obviously you know. You're a detective. Witnesses give you demonstrations of that every day. Any psychologist will tell you, the memory doesn't simply record, it reconstructs. That is, it will make up stuff it decides it *ought* to have in its store, because it's suitable. 'Schemata's'

14

the technical label – that famous business of John Dean's Watergate testimony, where he was trying to tell the truth about what he remembered, but the White House tapes showed him to be repeatedly inaccurate, even on sequence of events."

"We force these six-year-old twins to reconstruct a different past for themselves?"

Rockmain was on the edge of his chair, looking wide-open, hopelessly frank, even confessional: "I realise it sounds sinister. Not the essence of their pasts, obviously. The autobiographical memory can't be mucked about with to that degree. It has its own invincible integrity – at least in a healthy subject. It will be inaccurate, yes, but it will also want to be 'true' in the wide sense, and often is. Dean got all sorts of important facts wrong, but his overall recollections pointing to a cover-up were right. As for these children, we could never alter their memories of, say, family atmosphere at home, the nature of the relationships between the two and between each of the parents. We can manipulate only details."

"Like place?"

"Yes, obviously, we need to reconstruct place for them."

"Place is a detail, for God's sake?" Brade yawned. "So, how did you get into this game, Andy?"

"Drifted. The way it happens? One *was* in straight detection. Then they sent me to university for a psychology degree."

"That's drifting? Why send you?"

He waved a delicate, modest hand in a small movement. "They decided I wasn't bad at interrogation. And at turning people around."

"Manufacturing grasses?"

"That's it. Midwifing, they call it. We call it."

"Did you deliver Dilsom, then?"

He twitched, offended by the stupidity. "No, no, no. We wouldn't allow that sort of link. It could be known – who talked him over. That would mean a possible trace to his new location and self."

"You keep looking over your shoulder?"

"They move us about. One won't be long here. Best to do this sort of work in very short sessions or one's own mind can start to wobble." His voice fell suddenly: "Either that, or shame could suffocate you, like falling in a cess pit." He took a gulp of air. Although Rockmain was slight, almost frail, and in pricey denim, Brade might have picked him out as police. That would be his fine, narrow-fit black shoes, the general watchfulness, his ability to listen and stay untroubled by long silences, and a polished semblance of believing quite a proportion of what you said. He must be about thirty-five, smooth faced, fair hair a bit long, maybe to proclaim the special, boffin status. On the other hand, you could see he did not expect to wow anyone instantly with his stuff – was ready for resistance to his smartarse knowledge and theorising and had put on modesty like a suit today, or like denim. The smile was deferential, not patronising and, when he first came in his body was arched slightly, like playing a courtier before the king in a costume movie. He had probably handled this sort of situation a dozen times, before – been sent into the offices of an alien police headquarters to order the locals what to do, while seeming only to cooperate and advise. Little Andy gleamed with tactfulness, guile and steel.

Chapter 4

Brade went over to the hospital and talked for a while to Glyndwr Jenkins in his private room. There should have been a permanent guard on him, in case someone came back to finish the job before he could say what he had seen, but Brade had been overruled. Glyndwr looked grand, the heavy head dressing unstained and glistening with special whiteness against his black face and brow, features strong and serene, his closed eyelids utterly twitch free.

Staff said this total motionlessness was normal for someone in his condition and should certainly not be taken as a sign that consciousness was gone for ever, irreclaimable, or – in their view even more unlikely – that life would decamp any minute. Glyndwr's parents spent hours at the bedside, but his father could not get more time off and Mrs Jenkins had driven him to his job. Although Glyndwr had a loud, live-in girl friend who also visited, she must be at work, too, so Brade and he were alone. It grieved Brade to think of Glyndwr's parents. Both docks-born West Indians, they had obviously wanted their boy to integrate well in Wales and make a go – hence the princely, nationalist first name, and his fluency in the Welsh language. Then this. Brade had told them it could have been anyone. And it was true. Did they believe it?

When pressed, and Brade pressed, doctors said Glyndwr might not come out of the concussion for at least a week. Or, it could be weeks running to a month, or "just conceivably" a month plus. They insisted definitely not as much as several months, though: measurable improvement had already taken place – admittedly not apparent to the eye or without instruments – and the pace of this would now increase and bring steady and assured recovery. Brade had been informed there were many instances where patients with worse head damage

17

came round after very long periods of seemingly unrelenting sleep and were fine: mind OK, morale OK, memory OK.

Yes, medics cited memory as a crucial part of good health, and Andy Rockmain identified it as a plague. Brade could not argue with either.

With Glyndwr, it was like talking to Boadicia, or one of the others. You spoke and they could not understand or answer. Brade rather liked this one-way transmission. "I don't know if it was someone looking for Dilsom or just a run-of-the-mill breaker and enterer, Glyn. I don't suppose you could care less now – a clobbering's a clobbering, whoever. The Escort tells us nothing. It had been stolen in the morning. I didn't recognise the driver. You're right – we've got a severe problem. If they've located him, do we close down the Dilsom identity, move the family to another force and let them start all over with new creations? Bullfinch says this would create a panic, and he knows plenty about that. His view is, you surprised a standard issue burglar in a prime break-and-enter target spot, the marina. I said, this would suggest local knowledge, so why didn't I know the burglar? Bullfinch replies, do I – i.e. me – presume to know every fucking burglar on this patch and perhaps he was only a beginner, with no form, or would he have got surprised and would he have turned recklessly violent like that? Obviously, Bullfinch is mightily pissed you went unaccompanied. I said I was to rendezvous with you there."

Brade sighed. "Of course, my own judgement on things may be a bit adrift because Julie's screwing Dilsom. You remember Julie. Media girl with a lineless brow, a degree in Japanese and fine green eyes, fine skin, lovely sense of humour and tearaway laugh, as long as you could keep her cheerful. And this was often possible, at the beginning. You can see I still crave her. Perhaps I'd like to see Dilsom freighted off somewhere else, out of her life. Things might pick up again between us. I need her – could do with the healthiness and fire she brought. I look elsewhere, but it's not the same, is it? Contrariwise, if Dilsom stays and has been spotted he might get wiped out at the next attempt and would still disappear from Julie's life, maybe more definitively. Tempting, I admit. I don't say make it easy for them, no I don't think I say that, honestly. But these are clearly resourceful people, Glyndwr. This is an operator who could spot you stalking him, turn it and get behind you and put in at least two head blows, very likely fatal as I read these lying fucking docs. This is talent, Glyn, and that lad might be only the pathfinder, so there could be other gifted people on Dilsom's alarmed doorstep very soon. He might easily be taken out of the running, out of the loving. Well, yes, that would be an appalling failure for us as police, but it would be a failure with some sweetness to it, possibly. Personally, to me, I mean. I do keep returning to it, as an idea."

A nurse came in. "I heard talking."

Brade said: "I was told it's a good drill with people in this state. Something might be getting through to them, no matter how far gone they may appear."

"Absolutely right. I talk to him myself."

"I'm glad. It's companionable."

"For me as well as him. You and I – we'll talk to him together one day when I've got more time."

"Great," Brade replied. "Yes. We don't always need replies to what we say, do we? We can fill them in for ourselves."

"Like a child with a doll?"

"Yes, like with a doll or—"

"He's quite a doll." She was in her fifties, bustling, plain, small, an auxiliary. "But nurses shouldn't say such. And are you police, too?" She was tidying up the bedside cabinet. "So, what happened – these terrible injuries? We heard it was a very special mission."

Brade said: "Every mission's special in our job. Like yours."

"Actually, one bedpan's much like another. We heard he was guarding someone – someone, well, yes, special."

"Sort of Princess Di, living in Cardiff docks, since the marriage breakdown?"

"Only what I picked up."

"Gossip's got a life of its own. Picked up where?"

"Around."

"He surprised a sneak thief, that's all."

"You caught him?"

"We will."

"So how do you know? Sneak thieves hit that hard? That efficiently? You ask me, these were blows to kill."

Hurriedly, she gripped Glyndwr's arm where it lay on the cover, like someone touching wood. "But he's still got a chance. Definitely."

"Sneak thieves don't like being caught. They can lash out, like anyone else."

She was leaving and stood near the door. "No, not royalty. The story is, a transplanted supergrass."

"It gets richer. Glyndwr would smile."

"They exist, though, don't they?"

"And finish in jail, not a folly property on the marina. Although they talk, grasses are still villains. That's how they have something to talk about. Perhaps a few years lopped off for cooperation, but that is all."

"I thought deals were done, new identities provided. I thought police needed big informants – couldn't work without them."

"Very, very occasionally need them. We always prefer above-board methods."

"Oh." She seemed startled.

"What?"

"Now I *did* think I saw Glyndwr smile."

Chapter 5

So, it was crucial to reach Julie fast and warn her Dilsom might have been pinpointed despite everything. If vengeance arrived from London and found them the way Brade had found them, Julie would be as exposed as Dilsom. For Dilsom to be exposed might be fine with Brade – yes, might, might – but definitely not Julie. You could say there was an overlap of targets. She was Dilsom's salvation.

But, of course, it could not be spelled out to her like this. She still must not be told who Dilsom was previously, and why he pulled peril to him as well as women, the sod. She must not be told either that Brade knew she had something going, and certainly not *how* he knew. Paul Pry. Christ, there were so many things he wanted to say to her and must not. Brade walked to Julie's office in Mount Stuart Square and asked Danny at Reception to intercom properly and announce he would like to see Ms Tamitte.

Danny said: "Why not just go straight up, Dave, as—"

"I couldn't do that. I always like to follow procedures."

"Ah, I know it, I know it. A stickler."

After ten minutes Danny's buzzer went and Brade took the lift. "Dave, this is wonderful," she cried, standing at the door of her room to welcome him. They kissed cheeks. Jesus. Her vermilion and silver cravat was on an old fashioned coat-stand, with the cream silk jacket of her suit. Somehow, that cravat went to his soul, it was so brilliant, so skittish, so discardable. He sat down in an easy chair which put his feet about a yard from where her head had been on the heavy, blue carpet the other night, possibly shag pile. She did not go behind the big desk, but took an easy chair herself, opposite Brade. Apparently, some executives dispensed with desks altogether these days, and she would be up with fashions.

Julie was smiling, though with a touch of wonderment to see him there. She had on a wide-sleeved, off-white blouse and looked as she almost always looked – like a woman he eternally wanted but who had eternally signalled she might one day elude him. Her smile generally held a ton of goodbye as well as the bits of hello. Even when they lived together he felt he was on a timed contract. You accepted that with someone as beautiful as Julie. She used to sing Japanese laments now and then and he would get the feeling they were for him. "Is this official or friendly?" she asked.

"Friendly. Well, and official: you still work on my patch, you know."

"I hear tales of your exploits. All good, as ever."

"So, how are things, Julie?"

She bent forward a little and roughed up her hair with one hand in that way she had, to show suavity bored her, even in this bigger job. "Business? Or sex life? Oh, I see, sex life. Comes and goes. How about you?"

"Little time. I'm hopelessly busy. Now and then I might manage a dance and so on."

"Dance, where?"

"Oh, you know, small places."

"Intimate."

"The old tunes, not disco junk. *Somewhere Along The Way* – that vintage."

"You really find girls who go for that? I mean, young enough? You've met someone nice? Or hired?"

"I like a bit of an amble around the floor, not too many people present, and a pleasant chat. And you? Something steady, heavy?"

"Very busy, likewise. I seem to spend a lot of time in the office."

"Yes. Well, it's comfy. You should see mine."

"We have to fight for work. The slump. It's easing, thank God."

"I heard. But you do all right? Your own room now."

"The goldfish bowl. Dave, I feel less private than when I was out on a general desk."

Brade gazed carefully around at the upper walls. This would

22

be standard glass, not the double strength in Dilsom's windows at home. "I worry about you, Julie." It came out sounding like he was a granny for God's sake, and he sexed it up: "I don't want you damaged – any part of you."

She closed her eyes for a second, obviously trying to work out what this meant. Perhaps she feared he might try to talk her back to him. Feared it? Did she prize her freedom from him that much? He longed to try to persuade her, but would not, not now. It might confuse things. After all, this was about her life. Then she said: "Well, I worry about you, too, Dave. You're not still into porn, are you?"

"That was only interim."

"You need the three dimensional."

"Exactly. But, Julie, all sorts around here now. I'm telling everyone to be careful. This is part of a little security tour. What I meant – friendly *and* official. The docks could always be rough, but now a very unknown and possibly diabolical social mix. The marina, and so on."

Her features tightened. He recognised the sign. "I don't understand," she said.

"In the old days, docks villains were notorious. You just counted the face scars. These lads were easy to deal with, or avoid. Now it's different. Higher calibre. Top grade suits, fine shoes."

She was quiet for a minute. Then she hissed: "Jesus, Dave, you're saying stay away from everyone from the marina? That has to be crazy. This is a star development. Hundreds of properties. One of my bosses lives there."

"I'm saying look very carefully. Don't take those face values any longer. You know people, someone, from the marina, then? Apart from this boss."

"I don't ask their address." She went back in the chair suddenly and snapped her fingers "eureka" style. "This is because your side-kick, that really grand black lad, was near-mortally thumped. It *is* only near-mortally? I heard a whisper about that. Sorry, Dave. And it might have been you? Yes, I do worry. But probably you don't believe this."

"Glyndwr doesn't really come into it. Bigger matters."

"Dave, the story around is – probably total cock-and-bull

– he was engaged in something sensitive. A kind of minding, but very – yes, very, very sensitive."

"You're right, total cock-and-bull. A routine outing that went wrong. There are exceptional hazards over there, though, and they could spread this way."

"Exceptional how? And you're briefing everyone like this?"

"Everyone who might be at risk."

"What's that mean?"

Brade gazed about again. "Yes, you're very much on view here."

She looked about, too, and then jerked her head back and sat forward, crouched fiercely over her closed knees, eyes hard on his face. So many times before he had seen that sudden swoop into anger, legs tight together like an eternal exclusion order, and had never worked out how to cope. Dilsom would probably just punch her face. But she was not marked, so perhaps he never angered her. Or possibly she knew what she would get if she turned rough, and so didn't. "On view? Dave, has someone been talking to you?" She still stared. Then, unravelling the situation slowly, she said: "Yes, someone's been talking to you. That bugger on Reception. An old fink of yours, yes, bought and rebought."

"Talking about what? I told you, this is general advice I'm giving."

"Christ, I'll scalp that sod, Danny."

"Danny's nothing to do with it."

"He's on the blower to you, saying Julie brings a friend back after hours some nights? It's diseased. You're working out some rancid jealousy again, are you? You don't let go, regardless. 'Beware the marina people.' My God!"

"Have you got a friend from there, then?"

"Mind your own fucking business, Dave."

Brade waved towards the general office outside. "They can't hear, but people will see you're in a rage, Julie. Not good."

"I'm not having some bloody doorman snoop on my private life."

"Please, don't bring him into it. Danny's not involved."

"What do you drop him? Ten? Twenty?" She was staring at the carpet, near Brade's shoes, recollecting. "Now, wait a minute. Oh, my God, you mean he watches, reports? Thirty, then? More?"

"Julie, this is a perilous square mile, that's all. Can't I worry about you, love?"

"Cut the 'love', will you?"

Chapter 6

Andrew Rockmain stood and went to the magnetic display board, which stood on an easel. From a box he took three metal strips and fixed them on the board, like a rectangle but with one end open. "This is our memory, Dave," he said. He brought some letters from the box and made the word "Past". This he put inside the rectangle. "What we keep in our memory," he said: "recollections, correct or otherwise, about the past. But now, watch." He took another handful of letters and made the phrase "More Recent Past". He pushed this phrase along the surface of the board from the open end of the rectangle until it bumped against the first word and began moving it. The vertical line of the rectangle was shoved aside and, as Rockmain continued to push the new phrase, that first simple word, "Past", was edged right out of the rectangle until the space was occupied only by "More Recent Past".

"Thusly," Rockmain said, rejoining Brade at the table, "our more recent recollections drive out the older ones." They were in one of the big briefing rooms at headquarters in Cathays Park. "For example, Dave, the kids went to a circus when they lived in London. I can really work on that. Entirely shatter their recollections of it." He had discarded denim and was in a wide-shouldered, greenish suit today which seemed liable to curl around his slight, unpoliceman-like frame and eat him up, like the tide with a sandcastle. "And, talking of wild animals, you'll know the cockroach experiment."

"Might have missed that," Brade replied.

"The very one which proves that, if the memory gets new stuff to store, older material is forgotten, lost . . . well, as on a computer's memory." He pointed to the board. "Or like that. There's the famous yarn about an ichthyologist – a fish professor, to you."

"Oh, everyone knows that one," Brade replied.

"Who said that each time he remembered a new student's name he forgot the name of a fish. Similarly, these cockroaches showed that forgetting is not just the decay of what was remembered, but can actually be induced. First, scientists made the insects remember to avoid a part of their cage by giving them a shock each time they went there. Then they divided them into two teams. They let one lot continue normal life activities and confined the others to a small box where they were idle. When they were all returned to the cage only those from the box remembered to avoid the dangerous part of their cage. Why? Because their memories had not been loaded with other material while resting. They had no 'distractor tasks' – the jargon term."

Brade decided to go fully scrupulous and said: "Dilsom's twins are cockroaches?"

Rockmain twitched his little lips, maybe to show he was stung, or signalling he had heard similar quips a thousand times.

"You'll give Jeremy and Anita plenty of new memory material to swamp what went before?" Brade asked.

"OK, an unfortunate, demeaning choice of creatures. Roaches are not people, and one always expects this kind of sentimental objection. The experiment has its validity, all the same. Why we remember better after a sleep, for instance."

"Jesus, you won't stop the kids sleeping?"

"Of course not. Our aim is to do the most good, with the least harm." He squirted out his stuff now, no longer putting points apologetically as in that first meeting. Special knowledge and the scientific flam clothed him like body armour. "Not the sort of mentally destructive process you associate with interrogations in a police state, forgive the term. Benign. Wholly for the benefit of the subjects and the general polity."

The door opened and Raging Bullfinch, wearing uniform today, joined them. Both stood. Brade did the introductions. "I'll just sit in and listen," Bullfinch said. "Ignore me." Approvingly, he gazed at the blackboard. "You've been simplifying things for Dave, have you?" Bullfinch had his nickname from a tendency to panic and storm when the

27

stresses came, flapping agitatedly about dropping blame over everyone of lower rank in range. Today, though, he seemed wonderfully calm and genial, neat in his olive-green garb for some ceremonial do.

They sat down. "Andrew's been telling me how he intends to help Dilsom's twins integrate with the new life, sir," Brade said. "That's supposing the family still stay after the attack on—"

"Oh, yes, I haven't changed my mind," Bullfinch interrupted. He jutted his jaw to signal consistency. "Terrible about Glyndwr, but I really don't think we should read too much into it. Is he going to pull through, Dave? Of course. Their skulls are known to be – We can't go shutting down an expensive and elaborate operation on such debatable evidence." Bullfinch shook his head, only once, decisively, finally. "How would we look to the Yard, to the Home Office? Like yokels. We let things run, no fuss. Why I'm against a bedside guard, Dave. It would suggest some unusual significance to the attack and to the work Glyndwr was on. Yes." He swung back to Rockmain. "Integrate, Andrew? Fascinating."

"To do with their memories, sir," Brade said. "Apparently, they were taken to a circus at Lewisham by their parents. Andy will focus on that. Make them believe they never went."

"Memory's such a puzzle," Bullfinch replied.

"Andy's got it taped, sir."

"We start from the observation that people – including adult, intelligent people – can be terribly unreliable at putting remembered experiences in the right location," Rockmain said. "Football fans will recall being at some epic game – talk about whom they went with, where they sat – when they actually saw the game on TV or only read about it in the *Sun*. They're not wilfully lying. They wanted to be part of the experience and their memory does a creative kindness and lets them believe they were."

"All right, Andrew, these kids are young," Brade replied, "but they're bright. Suppose they have accurate memories of the place where they lived – not just the circus visit, but actual geography. You're saying smash these memories so new, bogus ones can be built?"

Rockmain held up both hands in a surrender parody and

grinned weakly. "These are rough terms – 'bogus', 'smash' – but, OK, yes, along those lines."

"It's for their own good, Dave," Bullfinch said.

Rockmain also nodded the once. He had lowered his hands and now flung out his left palm, as though about to pat Bullfinch on the back for perceptiveness. He did not go through with it. "For their own good, and beyond, sir. Primarily, it's for the good of the father, of course, who has, in the view of society, done well by us through his help as informant. An attack on him or his family is an attack on order and legality – as much as an attack on a police officer. We three get paid to protect order and legality, so we protect him, by every means."

Bullfinch again jutted his jaw out proudly.

"This is a man to whom society is in big debt," Rockmain said. "Part can be repaid by money, job, house. Hence, he's here. Society also owes him safety, if it can be got and maintained."

"Must be, will be," Bullfinch remarked.

"Plus, obviously, to give him safety is in society's interests. We bring him in and supply a new identity – an established procedure with grasses."

"A skill, a duty," Bullfinch remarked.

Rockmain nodded. "Adults can see the need for that and will cooperate in creating it. They'll ditch their local accent, learn a fictitious past. Children? No. The change is too much for them to manage alone. They'll always be liable to give away facts about their past – including place. If that happens, their new identity is in peril. If theirs is, so is the parents'. And if we ignore this we ignore our debt to reward dangerous services with safety."

"But how do we start?" Bullfinch asked, straight-manning keenly today.

Rockmain said: "Basically we get their parents to help them recollect events from their London time, but do it by locating these pleasures here, in Cardiff. We might get mum or dad to say, 'Tell me all the interesting things you remember from the circus, Anita, Jeremy. Try and picture it all in your head. Remember? Of course you do: those two big tents in Cheald Meadows.'"

29

Astonished, Bullfinch whispered: "Cheald Meadows being in the town centre, here."

"Right. Where touring circuses set up, I believe."

"Of course," Bullfinch replied.

"The kids will wear that?" Brade asked. "Really?"

"First time it will shock them. And the second. Yes, naturally, they'll reject it. We work away at it, though. The parents insist it was at Cheald and go on insisting – give circumstantial stuff about the journey, the parking spot, the layout of the Meadows, the river nearby. These location details have to become the cues, you see. Eventually – if we do an effective job – when the children begin to re-see the circus acts in their heads and list them they will inevitably make an association with this locality. What's more, they'll believe they're doing these retrievals for themselves, which ensures they're more valid. The vividness of their recollections of the wild animals and trapeze stars will be superimposed on the field here, on the geography here, and this will take on a similar vividness, a similar, as it were, authenticity and graphicness."

Brade said: "I like the 'as it were'."

Rockmain pressed on: "We have to fix the children in this setting. Memory will always struggle to endorse our present idea of what we are. It will recall or create a past not necessarily as it really was but one that suits us as we see ourselves now – because the past made us what we are, or think we are. On the face of it, memory is about the then but has to serve the now and produces material that fits the now."

There was an ordinary wall blackboard in the room, too. He went to this and drew a matchstick man. Alongside he sketched a mountain, a lake, and some capering animal, perhaps a deer. He put three lines coming from the matchstick man's head, like thought beams, to each of these items. Then, inside the matchstick man's head he wrote "Poet". Rockmain turned and addressed Bullfinch and Brade. "As you'll, of course, know, Wordsworth became our great Nature writer. He decided he would explain to people how he got to be like this, and wrote his autobiography, a poem called *The Prelude*. What he did in that was recalled or imagined all the bits from his childhood which he thought turned him into the kind of writer who could write about all these bits in his childhood.

30

Just a self-proving circle. I don't need to remind you of what Maurois says, I'm sure: 'Memory is a great artist. For every man and for every woman it makes the recollection of his or her life a work of art and an unfaithful record.'"

"Wordsworth makes a change from the kind of drawings we usually get there," Brade said.

Rockmain took a few paces, as if wanting to stride about a lecture platform or the Lake District. He arched his body forward, though no longer in the seemingly servile way of before. "What we do for starters is build a strong, new self for the children so that when they delve into the past they will search for matter relevant to themselves as now – *as now* – that's the crux. To create this 'now', we ensure they get a powerful sense of the new locality – loyalty to the school, neighbourhood, town football team, ice hockey team, town beauty queen. The present self becomes emphatically a part of the new geography and memories of the old are drastically weakened then lost. It takes time, of course. And what we have to keep in mind during the delay is that the physical dangers to this family – the bullet and knife dangers – will be high. It is important to begin at once, and intensively. Possibly, this appalling assault on a colleague proves the urgency of things, though I do realise, sir, that its nature is unproven."

"Quite," Bullfinch replied.

Rockmain said: "Generally, when we remember, so-called, we only recall certain very salient, general matters, and we fill in the rest – construct it – just because it seems in harmony with these major elements. Usually, this constructed material is reasonably close to what actually happened, though not absolutely. In this way, we think we're getting a solid version of the past."

Now, he smiled sadly, again like someone conceding he's been rumbled: "Which, of course, in the case of these children, Anita and Jeremy Dilsom, is exactly what we must prevent. Imperative. The more solid their past seems to them, the more readily and comfortably they will tell their tales from the past to friends. They're kids from the big city." Again the missionary voice took over. "We must suppress these tales, then. We have to make areas of the children's past

31

intolerable to them. Yes, intolerable." He struck the table a small, frank blow. "We do it by swiftly and decisively undermining the validity of key items – e.g. the circus. If these are shaken, everything else collapses, too. The children then become uncertain about that whole region of their previous life, uneasy when talking about it or – better still – when only on the point of talking about it, and will learn to steer very clear."

"Like cockroaches," Brade muttered. Then louder he said: "No pushover. These are bright kids."

"Well, yes," Rockmain replied. "Naturally, I've looked at the dossier. That's fine: the cleverer the better, because the mental failure when it comes will be more total. These are youngsters who've come to prize and rely on their brains."

Bullfinch said: "And if the brain seems to let them down—?"

"They're lost, sure. Yes, indeed, we'll have hit them where it hurts most." Rockmain lowered his head and grew a little huddled inside the suit's green acreage, seemed to become reflective. "We'll need great parental help here. Fortunately, we can always count on that. In all these operations, mum and dad see what's at stake – their skin and the kids' – and they eagerly cooperate in chameleoning. But, as to the children, first we must discover and isolate what they remember best – discover what's stuck in their little heads from the past. Then, as with the circus, trusted adults – parents, primarily, but also myself in due course – will tell the children – repeatedly and jointly tell them – that these 'true' memories are wholly or partly false. Combination and repetition are the essence. This treatment, given ten or a dozen times on children's power of recall, has a catastrophically unsettling impact."

That seemed to thrill Rockmain. He sat up erect again. His voice shook and he made as if to strike the table once more, but held back, possibly suddenly ashamed of his enthusiasm for the scrambling of a child's psyche. "It brings disabling doubts about the version they have of their entire early life," he said. "They are then forced to a choice: decide that the parents can't be trusted or that they, the children, themselves are wrong. Very few kids can admit the possibility both parents are haywire. That would be a chaotic scenario, like thinking both pilots are pissed. It would present a vacuum, or worse.

32

If we work sweetly, the children quite soon become unwilling to attempt further mental trips into the disputed parts of their past. This is our first aim."

Brade muttered: "My God, it's *The Manchurian Candidate* technique.

"This is *not* brainwashing," Rockmain replied.

"It would be absurd to say so," Bullfinch remarked.

"OK, Dave, you obviously want to ask whether this could do them long-term damage mentally." Rockmain blanked his face. Perhaps there was anxiety and even pity in it for a second, but they were swiftly hounded off. This apparent weakness might have been another part of the performance – an attempt to humanise himself and his trade – or it could have been something real surfacing for an unguarded second. "No denying it. Yes, we have to gamble. But, Dave, isn't our problem that these children might meet very short-term, even very immediate, very physical, damage, possibly death, and so might their father and mother, if inconvenient sections of their memory are not quickly erased?"

"Priorities," Bullfinch declared. "Flesh and blood. The now. Yes, this is our métier."

"Quite, sir," Rockmain said. He recovered matter-of-factness. "Then a bit later we might well be able to make use of some of the best known aids to memory. Take mnemonics – those word or letter systems by which we remember difficult material." He wrote ACE on the board. "Mnemonics are the way school kids might use that word to remind them of the first three prime ministers after the war: Attlee, Churchill, Eden – ACE. Now, what does one see at a circus: clowns, horses, elephants, acrobats, lions, dogs of the performing kind."

"C, H, E, A, L, D," Brade said. "Cheald Meadows."

"Oh, sharp old you." Rockmain wrote the letters in big capitals. "The parents suggest the letters of the place name as a prompt. You see, if the children know where the circus happened they can remember the acts. In their heads, circus and site become one."

"When you say they 'know' where the circus took place, what you mean is they *don't* know?" Brade asked.

"What is 'know', Dave? Who really *knows* anything?

We feel sure of this or that, would say we *know*, but new information comes along and we find we didn't *know* at all. The sureness was an illusion."

Bullfinch said: "Nature of knowledge, a deep study. Epistemology?"

"What one has to do is gravely shake these children's belief in what they thought they knew, and supply substitute material. If we're very, very lucky this is a possibility. It's not easy. Some of these ploys are rather old hat, based on passé theories of what memory is and does. But I do think they might suit here." He turned towards Bullfinch. "I have to make a snap decision, sir. We're pressured."

"Very much so," Bullfinch said. "I'm riveted, absolutely. Yours is a truly intriguing game, Andy."

"Truly," Brade said.

"Dave can be hopelessly narrow," Bullfinch replied. "Sort of knee-jerk humanism."

Chapter 7

"This is a fuck-up, Derwent," Barty Linacre said. "We find him, we lose him."

"Rick couldn't do nothing else. I can't see it – what else he could've done."

"So what else could I have done, Barty?" Rick asked.

"Nice echo. Months of work locating him gone. They'll move him again now," Linacre replied. "Maybe already. So he disappears – Yeovil, Manchester, Liverpool, Edinburgh, anywhere. What they call 'merging'."

"They might," Derwent Cole said. "But they've spent a lot recreating him, plus family. Look, it's months of work, for them, too. He's only a grass out to grass. They could think, sod it, we done our bit: this fink can take his chance. Finks they use and sort of protect, but not love them. Police think they're slime, too."

"I ring the hospital re this black," Linacre replied, "playing some far-flung relative, so concerned and putting on the Carib, and they say comfortable but still unconscious. Comfortable. Which means not right at that moment climbing up the wall through agony – or doctor talk for he could die any minute or go eternal vegetable. Either way, they'll be looking hard for who hit him. What the hell you use, Rick? Not just a cop, this is ethnic cop, so they got to show exceptional effort, for TV and the papers. To slam black fuzz with a wrench, Rick, I mean, but . . . well, Christ. The *Mirror* said he's called Glyndwr, or however you say it. I ask you, this is a name for a black?"

"Some like a touch of history. They can't trace Rick."

"They can't trace me, Barty," Rick Cole echoed. "The car leads no place, except its owner. I switched after ten miles."

"But you said one saw you," Linacre replied. "Maybe two."

"What I said, Barty, one *might* have got a glimpse half of half a second when I'm leaving. God, I'm doing eighty, crouched down so I can't *be* seen. It's dark. He's running up from the water, bent over by the weight of that piece in his hand, face nearly at his feet. Can he do a photofit from that?"

"Never," Derwent Cole said.

"The black worries you, Uncle Bart?" Rick said. "Don't. I'm behind him. He's out before he hits the ground. He didn't see one thing."

"Ricky, he saw something before or why's he tailing you?" Linacre replied. "Maybe studied you all angles."

"Anyway, he's not in a talking mood, is he?" Rick said. "Might never be."

"One of the problems," Linacre replied. "You could've brought his notebook, couldn't you? Your details might be in. Nice teeth and that fucking ridge haircut."

"This is Nowhere Land cops, Barty, not the Met," Derwent said. "They don't know Rick."

Linacre emitted a tired laugh and said the police would work back, that was all. They'd ask themselves or ask the Met who was most likely to be stalking Hector Vale, or whatever his new name was.

"Dilsom," Rick said. "Geoffrey Dilsom."

"Which brings them to families in this bit of South London he done dirt on. Which brings them to everyone close to Brydon Maurice Cole, into twelve years at Long Lartin – his dad, Derwent, his brother, Rick, and his uncle Bartholomew."

Derwent Cole said, "Not so simple. There was a stack of hurt families. Vale alias Dilsom shopped a legion eventually, as was famous. The police wouldn't know where to start."

Linacre said: "Only one lad looks like Rick looked in the Escort."

"They didn't see me," Rick Cole replied. "On my granny's grave I swear."

"She's not dead yet. This boy with the artillery in his hand hears the car?" Linacre asked. "Of course. You're doing eighty. That's a lot of engine noise in the middle of the night. He's paying real attention."

"Past the top of the street. A fraction of a second," Derwent replied.

"Rick's a pretty profile," Linacre said. "Memorable. Takes after you, Derwent. He knows you're white, he knows you're not sixty or twelve, he knows you're blonde, no beard or moustache, a neat nose. One idea now is, get that fucking haircut repaired. I don't know how, not with such a mess. Wig? Go skinhead? How you messed up, I don't understand, Rick. This is from using a kid, Derwent. Didn't I say? OK, your boy, but still a kid. How d'you make a show like that, Rick? A wrench. So crude. So hasty. I mean, the job is to locate the property, no intrusion, no attempt on him. An address. But you bring half Cardiff's police, and give them time to sign out weaponry. What you doing there? Firing flares, playing ice cream chimes?"

Derwent Cole said police nurse-maiding what was known as a supergrass *emeritus* would be tooled up continuously even in a place like Cardiff.

"They're cruising, that's all," Rick said. "The black guy – just randoming around the area."

"What we told you to look out for, Ricky, boy," Linacre replied. "This is not one for a helmet: door sentrying like Downing Street. This is them keeping a constant eye, but casual. Your father, myself, we both mentioned subtlety to you. And more than once."

"Not anything *I* did to make them spot me. He had luck, that's all."

"But there's two. Maybe more," Linacre replied. "How'd they get so organised?"

"The black obviously called aid," Derwent Cole said. "They're twenty-four hours geared up for trouble, knowing the hunt could arrive any time."

"Yes, that's why we said subtlety. What I got against grasses, they take all the joy and spice out of our business, make it measly."

Derwent replied: "You're looking at the down side only, Barty. You got to remember Rick did trace this bugger. Honour where due, that's all we ask."

"I just did what you sent me for, Dad," Rick said. "No call for medals."

"Trace?" Linacre replied. "Look, there's trace and trace. Our friend in the DSS did the real work, bless her. Sees the name change papers and gives you the whisper, Derwent. Well, not gives. No. Pricey. Without her we'd still be right in the dark, searching Leeds or Blackpool. Talking of luck, will she have that sort of chance again? She likely to get a squint at the next new identity they give him now? I doubt it. And we got to shell out again if she did?"

"We only got the general area where he was going," Derwent Cole replied. "He still needed pinpointing."

"Not easy," Rick said.

"This place was a long way away Barty. This was a whole principality. Rick don't know a soul there, but still comes back with all the details."

Linacre said he'd never take anything away from Rick and what he had done, no way. Of all his nephews and such Rick had the genuine wisdom. But then to screw it all up, so they were back where they started. Or worse if the police traced him. This was what was hurtful."

"Think of it this way – the police, they screwed up, too, Barty, thank God," Derwent Cole replied. "Are they going to put it around they let someone get so close to the target and then missed him? How they going to look to the Yard? Like Nowhere cops, woodentops. They make this public and someone's élite balls are in the mangle after all that cost and effort, a nice house with special fittings, someone high. My view is, they'll hush this up, let him and the family stay and pray it was a one-off: hope the Escort lad will've been scared by getting spotted and stay scared, no return. My view, we're doing extremely passable or better. My view, Rick brought back a fine dossier – this house layout, the roads, and the report he might be already fixed up with extramarital, as par."

"But how're we so sure of that?" Linacre asked.

"Coming back very late," Rick said, "and then a shouting match in the house."

"Just like old times for him," Derwent Cole said.

"You must've been stuck very near to hear yelling. That why you got spotted, Rick? You proclaiming yourself in some hotted-up, hot car right alongside the house?"

"This shouting went a mile," Rick replied. "His wife's seen it all before: she's ready with full volume."

But Linacre asked was it right to say from one late home-coming, Dilsom, who had been Vale, was banging a woman? "This a bit of a leap, Ricky?"

"Maybe more than once he's late, but I'd only just found his place," Rick said. "And he turns up, and straightens his clothes so careful before he goes into the house, making sure he hasn't put his trousers back on back to front."

"How close to the house you lying, you can see him putting himself to rights?" Linacre asked.

Derwent Cole said: "If he's out late and he's like he always was it will, incontrovertible, be pussy, won't it, Bart? He's called Geoffrey now, but inside his pants this is our true Hard-on Hector."

"But they're turning him into someone who's not like he always was," Linacre replied.

"Police can't corral that chopper," Derwent said. "Find this woman and we could have him unchaperoned, unprotected, arse baying at the moon, away from the house, no security bars, no alarms or Fort Knox doors."

After a brief pause, Barty Linacre said that well, maybe, yes, it could be like that. Possibly they could still salvage something. "But do him on the job and the girl's also likely to get—"

"Can't be helped, can it, Barty? She's screwing a grass, even if she don't know it's a grass, I can't fret about her."

"That's unfeeling, Derwent, cold," Linacre replied. "Dilsom, yes – to be wiped out, a duty, obvious duty. But the woman don't owe us."

"Always tender, Barty," Derwent Cole replied.

"Fair, that's all."

"Well, we'll take care, won't we?" Derwent Cole said.

"Can we find her?" Linacre replied. "Where'd they do it?"

Rick said: "I think I could—"

"You're not going back, not anywhere near," Linacre said. "They're waiting for you. You're all lit up, boy."

"Barty's right, Rick. You done well, but we can't expose you now. I know you want to be out in front. Naturally – he shopped your brother. Your brother, my son, we're both hurt so deep, Rick. But you got to stay back now."

"And, look, when I said this black could be dangerous if he wakes up one day, that don't mean I want him seen to by you, Rick, so he won't ever talk," Linacre added. "That's not what I'm saying at all. They'll have some watch on him at that hospital, because it's an obvious one. They'll be expecting you, because you read in the paper he's not dead despite a banging and could do a picture of the Escort lad if he surfaced. Killing someone in a hospital bed, that's not on, Rick, not our style. A bunch of flowers hiding the Luger, that's *The Godfather*, not the Cole way, the Linacre way. You sure you understand that now? I don't want you going solo again."

"He understands, Bart."

"You sure you understand, Rick?"

"Of course I understand."

"Me and your dad will reach the grass. If he's still there. If there's a girl. If the law don't turn up on the doorstep any day, tracing a speedster in an Escort."

"They'd have been here by now," Derwent Cole replied.

Linacre said that to blow him apart in those conditions would also be a kind of support statement for marriage faithfulness.

Chapter 8

Dilsom said: "Why I wanted to see you, Dave is – what I know is a tricky request – but whether I could have a piece, sort of urgent?"

"A piece?" Brade replied. He had been expecting this. It was reasonable.

Dilsom said: "You know. Armament. Did you think I meant a piece of arse? Those days are over, and nights."

"A gun?" Brade gave a small whistle and finally gently shook his head. He wondered if the pleasure he took in refusing had anything to do with wanting Dilsom wide open to whatever came.

"This black hammered nigh unto death, Dave, in the next street, this is one of your best boys, I know it. This is the boy I met with you at the start, my security, a gem, named from Welsh history. I saw it in the paper. This is very, very close, Dave. If they take out one of your people, I'm next. Don't I need self-protection?"

"Oh, it's just docks blacks get ratty if one of their people joins the police."

"You're telling me he was done over by local talent?"

"Grudge job, or surprising a burglar. Did you see anything?"

"Me? How would I? Home all night, as scheduled. Would I walk the streets late in unknown country? But they're looking for me, Dave. I must have fire power. Look, I want to do the right thing and ask for it official, not go private. I'll act absolutely straight now."

Brade would swiftly fix a meeting with Dilsom whenever he asked, generally one-to-one, though sometimes including Dilsom's wife, Carmel, and the twins. Today, it was just the two of them. Carmel certainly had a body and great grey-blue eyes, but she came from a long-venerated Peckham family that naturally regarded all police as filth, and the eyes gleamed with hate if they turned on Brade. He did not mind too much when she and the children were absent. Of course, Carmel's family would also regard Dilsom, like any recruited fink, as filth now, and possibly Carmel, herself. An extra reason for her to loathe police.

"I can't give you a gun, Geoffrey. And don't try for yourself. We'd bring charges. There's no need. We can look after you – *have* looked after you."

"This boy was lying blood-soaked, deep concussed, at Admiral Howe's flagship. He was looking after me?"

"That's not related."

"Oh, come on, Dave. You got anyone for it?"

"We will."

"No, they're back in London, setting up another visit, the one to count. That was pathfinding."

"You're safe, Geoff. Keep decent hours, set the alarms."

"Well, of course. Max cooperation from me. Look, don't take offence, but down here you can't understand what they're like, South London teams. These are iron. They won't be stopped."

"I'll stop them," Brade replied. For a second then he had a recollection of himself seen in the mirror at home, dancing with Boadicia, Cliffy and Enid close. At those times he might not look like a civic rampart. "They're the same as anyone else – the same as any other villains."

"No. It's all bigger, darker, there."

"I'm sure. But first they've got to find you."

"They've found me."

"When we can talk to Glyndwr we'll learn more."

"*If* you can talk to him."

"The hospital says not long."

For Dilsom's safety, the meetings had to be secret and on remote ground. They could not use his house, or the Bute Street nick, or Brade's flat or Glyndwr's place, in case of tracing. Were they all crazy, though, these fine precautions? This was a target who stayed out late and stripped down to his vulnerables in an office open to the street. Anyone could have him, anyone, anyone. Nice idea?

42

But the old-time rituals were necessary, to show willing and for the log. .

Glyndwr's girlfriend had a lovely, elderly, widowed mother living in the Canton part of Cardiff and, for a monthly retainer slipped her in notes by Brade, made one or two rooms available whenever needed. Of course, people's mothers might talk, maybe especially the mother of someone as loud as Glyndwr's girlfriend. People as loud as Glyndwr's girlfriend might even talk themselves, and this girl was management in the Wales Tourist Board, so could do it bilingually. No, the arrangement was not perfect but Brade reckoned it about as good as possible. You could only worry so far for a grass, and especially this one.

"Not even a hint of who they were, Dave? No sighting? You give me a description and I could say who. We all knew each other. Like a livery company? Just age, black or white, missing fingers or teeth, clothes, scars, hair."

"Nothing. Anyway, how the hell could they find you?"

Dilsom laughed, his voice tight. "Fifty ways, and you know it. Look, there are routes into even the Chancellor's private affairs. My name change – there's papers, bound to be. Who sees them? Dave, can I say this? – you scare me. So fucking blasé." He put a hand over his mouth for a moment, prim about cursing in someone else's decent home. "You don't know what you're up against. These people are dedicated. Their pride's involved."

"Just take basic precautions and leave the rest to me," Brade said. "Follow your agreed routine, try not to be out late, and especially not late alone or in situations where you could be off-guard."

"Well, Christ, would I? But—"

"Such as not caught preoccupied."

"What's that mean?"

"We've handled this kind of exercise before. I've never lost a grass yet. Famous for it. They'd have to be so talented to locate you here."

"They *are*. Hate makes them intelligent."

The little room where they sat now was comfortable enough. Mrs Canter-Williams supplied a genuine cup of tea with Welsh cakes, and side streets gave plenty of parking well clear of the house. On the wall were three oak-framed, black and white photographs of what appeared to be a church outing by coach to the countryside. The clothes and hair said late 1950s, perhaps a Whitsun treat: there were marquees visible behind the smiling groups in their frocks and open necked shirts. Brade thought he had identified their hostess, a very pretty woman in her twenties then. She was standing on the coach steps, near to what might be the minister, in mufti, a man much older and the only one wearing a tie. He looked fired up by the spirit or something. Whenever Brade had a chance, he studied these pictures. They consoled him with their sunny aura of simple, old-time niceness and their continuity. Yes, continuity above all: if you were trying to build a phoney past for somebody, a real and respectable past came to seem beautifully solid, and there might be nothing sexual about her closeness to the man in the tie. Anyway, her husband had been a minister, and the house was still full of his heavy books, so perhaps if there was a relationship it had worked out.

"Geoff, I've told you, that green phone on the upper shelf in your place, away from the kids, is direct to one of our operators. You pick it up at any time and speak for instant contact. Or your wife."

"So, these operators—"

"Know nothing. You're a voice. They start a procedure, that's all. They've no idea where you're ringing from or what it's about."

"Don't know where I am? So, if I need help?"

"They're immediately in touch with me or—?"

"Or the black cop. But the black cop is sick and sinking."

"I—"

"That's why I must have some bullets, Dave."

Mrs Canter-Williams, grey, a bit stately and dressed in old, goodish, brown and beige, knocked and asked whether they needed any more tea or Welsh cakes and had a few words about the damp problem in Edwardian properties. Brade said he and Dilsom were fine and needed nothing. It troubled Brade that he might expose her and this good place to a vengeance troop. Despite his show to Dilsom, he did fear the London people, recognised that they were something different. These days, he was conscious all the time of large scale, metropolitan evil moving in to the city, and was not always sure he could cope. Most of it followed the big money for the Bay redevelopment. Everywhere, big money brought big villains, jungling for their share – London, New York, Chicago, Rio, here. And now there was Dilsom as well, attracting injury or peril to great, home-grown people like Glyndwr, Julie and Mrs Canter-Williams. After a moment, Mrs Canter-Williams left the room.

Dilsom said: "As I see it, if the black's gone, you'll bring in someone else, or leave me unguarded for longer spells. You can't do everything, Dave. When all this started you said four, maybe five, in your outfit knew, and vital to keep it limited. Agreed. But now, I think about all these operators on shift and the replacement for your hurt friend. Plus this learned lad, Rockmain, who's doing things to the kids' minds and wants us to help. Yes, brings them to this house and wants us to mess up our own children's grey matter with him – and, of course, no choice, really. We sit in that other room and can hear him here, chopping slabs from their memory, hear him convince them they've been half mad and only he can mend their little heads. It all means more and more are in the picture. I get famous. No stopping it. Someone's going to stick one of those blue plaques on the marina house soon – 'Geoffrey Dilsom who was Hector Vale lived here'. I say lived, not lives. I'll be history, too."

Dilsom had a good, unmarked, almost sensitive face, and Brade could see how it would pull Julie, and women generally – the kind of face Brade could willingly visualise at the barrel end of a hitman's Browning. Women would think that someone with looks like this was just made to spot their special qualities and get addicted to them. There was no touch of crudity anywhere in his features and no touch of shiftiness either, not in his eyes or the working of his lips or his grin. Brade noticed that, even at her age, Mrs Canter-Williams saw Dilsom had something, and she would listen eagerly whenever he spoke, a wondering smile in place, her eyes fixed fondly on his, her big, round head winsomely to one side and nodding now and then with approval. She was flirting with him and, all credit to Dilsom, he pretended to respond, dug out most of his ladies' man stuff, joined in the game. He had consideration, if you took time to search. He would really be best out of the way.

Always Brade had found visiting this house disturbing, and today more than ever. It was not just the mixed pleasure and concern sparked by those pictures. Brade would respectfully nibble Welsh cakes and go through these chats with her about house maintenance or Tesco prices or Lloyd George or Shirley Bassey's early Cardiff days, while all the time trying to make sure the butt of the Magnum never edged into her sight from under his jacket, and that Dilsom sat away from the window and said nothing to reveal the terrors romping beneath his creaky charm and miniature jokes. Whatever happened to Dilsom, Brade did not want it to happen here. Today, to add an extra pain, when Brade looked at him he saw as well as the good, loose-cut, grey-green suit, those passion punctures on his shoulder blades, and his heaving back and buttocks framed by Julie's fine legs and jubilant bloody feet. Christ, did she ever ask where he had been?

Brade said: "Now, Geoff, promise me you'll pick up that green phone if you see the least thing. Don't wait for it to develop. Don't kid yourself you can handle things alone. Don't feel ashamed of looking for help. What I'm talking about is someone seen repeatedly in the street or near, but who doesn't seem to have a place there. I know, I know – this is elementary to someone from your kind of life. But I'll get it said, just the same. This could be man or woman, obviously. A girl can handle a surveillance. Then, vehicles. Anything parked for a while with someone in it, and especially more than one in it, especially a man and a girl. People know that two men in a waiting car could be trouble. They see it in cop shows. So, these days gangs do it mixed. Don't expect the vehicle to be parked front-on to your place. It's easy and less obvious to watch from a car's back window and in the mirror. You give us a call and we can look at a vehicle like that in three minutes."

Dilsom stood and went and stared at the outing pictures. Brade found himself looking at the back of the jacket to see whether the claw blood had come through in two patches, but no. Dilsom was overweight yet pretty nimble, an inch or two taller than Brade. His gut and neck bulged and the trousers

46

of the smart suit looked tight on his thighs. Perhaps he ate for nerves. "We had photographs like this at home, you know, Dave."

"Yes?"

"You can't credit it, can you?"

"Why not?"

"Because of what you think of me," Dilsom said.

Brade did not rise.

"Rubbish, from a rubbish family," Dilsom said.

"No, I don't think that."

"We had good excursions, neighbourhood excursions and all of it when I was small. With decent people. We were well liked. My parents were well liked. I mean well liked by these people, these decent people, entirely decent people." His voice cracked on the "entirely" and fell away. It seemed genuine.

"Of course. It doesn't matter, anyway. Our job is the future not . . ." – he waved towards the pictures – "not whenever. We're producing someone new, someone who'll fit in with decent people again, will be as decent as they are."

Dilsom came and sat down. He sipped some of his untouched tea, which must be cold now. "So what's my identity, anyway, Dave?" he asked.

"As I say, we're making one."

"I mean my real me, my self."

"Is this philosophical? Religious?"

"OK, your job is to look after my body, not the soul."

"Souls are tricky."

"I've switched, turned, so what in God's name am I? Is this two people? Vale who was crooked, Vale who isn't. And now we make a third; Dilsom."

"A trinity? Everyone changes," Brade said.

"Turns inside out?"

"Paul was Saul. Kinnock was unilateralist. Churchill was a Liberal."

"Dave, I put five people away who used to be friends."

Brade said: "You came to see that what they were doing was wrong."

"I'd done the same myself."

"You learned the opposite. You were smart."

Dilsom sat with his eyes shut for a full minute. "*He* was smart. He took me to pieces, and then put me back as someone else. One of Rockmain's lot."

"When they're bringing someone over, even the best interrogators can only use what's already there. That's what I'm told."

"What you're saying is, I'm a born turncoat and grass?"

"You're bright. You're human. You came to recognise what was wrong. Evangelists see it all the time."

"I came to recognise I could go down for twenty-five years, too."

"Yes, that's what I mean – bright."

"You think I'm shit, don't you, Dave?" This time he did not screen his mouth for the language. "Turncoat shit that's been flung your way?"

Brade said: "Law and order largely depend on your sort. I'm law and order, so I respect you. Anyway, that's the word, isn't it?"

"What?"

"Turncoat. It's only your coat. You're you inside."

"I don't know what's inside, Dave."

"Someone hooked on self-pity, psychobabble, shame, greed. Just like me, or Glyndwr or Bullfinch. Is this why you called the meeting, Geoff? You needed a confessor?"

"No, I need a gun."

"Don't fret. If you're a trinity they won't know which to hit."

"The crucifixion party did."

"He was betrayed."

"Right."

Dilsom left first today. Brade talked a little more with Mrs Canter-Williams and paid for the coming month. "Such lovely children, his twins," she said.

"Yes."

"And they were so friendly and cheerful. At frist."

Chapter 9

"Dawn?"

"Angela, that you? Oh, that you, Angie, love?"

"Well, yes."

"You sound like you're not sure."

"It figures. I've got a new name. It's the new me you're talking to."

"You sound like the old you to me."

"Well, only to you, then."

"Angie, where are you?"

"Name of Carmel."

"Christ, kid, where did you get that?"

"Off of a list."

"Couldn't you do better?"

"I don't mind it. I can't give you the rest, Dawn. Not the second name. We're not going to be in any phone books."

"Look, I've been desperate. Wanting to call you."

"No, you can't. Not at present. But I'll always be in touch. Dawn, love, could you try it?"

"What?"

"Try it, please – call me Carmel."

"Oh, God. I've got no sister called Carmel."

"No, but I must get into it, and hearing you say Angie again, it upsets me, Dawn, sends me back. Nice, but it's wrong. We've all got to try – the twins, him, me. It's so tough for the twins. I mustn't let them down."

"Does he know you're ringing?"

"Nobody knows. This is a pay-phone. But I'm on a card, so no rush."

"But, I mean, where are you, Angie? All right – Carmel. Jesus, who's called Carmel these days? Couldn't it have been your other Christian name? I like Sophia."

49

"They said not allowed."

"Who?"

"You know – the protection. They've got this drill they go through with people like us. It's what's worked with others. Completely new names. We've got to play it their way. They're our safety. They're our money. One of them seems all right. I look hate at him – habit – but he seems all right, really. Well, the habit's out of date, I suppose."

"Yes, they're your friends now. But, I mean, where are you?"

"Better not say. Not at present."

"Just general. I don't mean the street. South, north, east, west, an island?"

"Not at present. It could get easier in a while. I'm not even supposed to phone, which is why this street corner. We've already got some trouble, Dawn. A cop hurt."

"Still in London?"

"Even standing in a phone box like this, I feel so open."

"What trouble?"

"If they look for him. For us. It's possible they've got a trace. Some leak? Dawn, what do Dad and Mum say about us, him, what he did? You been to Peckham lately?"

"Mum won't talk about it, not one word. Not with me. Well, she knows we're close, you and me. Dad? He asks if I'm in touch. I said no, which was dead right till now. He won't talk about him, won't say his name even, but you, that's different. He can't write you off, Angie."

"Carmel. He's got a new name, too. Geoffrey."

"I won't tell Dad you've got a new name."

"He'll know. He'll know how it works."

"Well, not that name, anyway. Dad has a snarl, but he won't write you off, not ever. So, what trouble?"

"A lot will be looking for us, Dawn."

"Yes, that's going to happen. Listen, Dad says he heard Linacre and the Coles might be. That crew. Their Brydon shopped, wasn't it? But they're in the dark about finding you, him. Are they in the dark? Dad says so. But are they going to tell him? What trouble? You've got real protection, Angie?"

"Well, give them my love. I mean, both, including Mum. Including Mum, Dawn. Say I'm fine. Say I'm sorry."

"Are you fine?"

"The children."

"What, love?"

"It has to be like this, Dawn. Because of the children."

"And him?"

"He takes to it better than the rest of us. You know what he's like, bouncy."

"So, he's got a woman so soon? Christ, though."

"You know what he's like."

"God, how do you—?"

"What do I do, Dawn? All this – somehow it makes me more tied to him. So many things in him I hate, but, yes, more tied than ever. And they're making the kids part of this place, blocking out the before, and maybe it's working. I can't clear out with them. They couldn't handle another change, more stress. I could be wrong about him – a woman, I mean, or women. What he says is he's out late trying for a weapon, that's all. This is possible. It is, really, Dawn. He thinks we're on toast here and has to be able to defend us. But he doesn't know the local supply scene, and obviously he can't come back up there for a piece to the usual people. The word would be out so fast. Anyway, nobody up there's going to help him now. So, to get armament he must find the right people, in a club down here or like that, and then build some trust. It takes time before they'll deal. That's his story."

"I can hear the sod say it."

"He's got no faith in the protection. These are out of town people. They don't know the way it is. He's scared. He didn't used to be bad like that, but he's scared now. He puts on the gloss, but he's scared."

"Oh, Angie, cut loose from him, love. Nobody's hunting *you*. Why stick?"

"Carmel."

"Fuck that. It's Angie I'm talking to. It's Angie I'm frightened for."

"For the moment, I'll stay."

"That could be too late."

"So you will give them my love, say I'm all right?"

"Don't go."

"I'm jumpy, so long in a glass box under lights. And wearing a yellow jacket. I'm like the sunrise."

"Angie, you always look great in yellow. You've got smart shops?"

"I've lashed out on quite a bit. It's a relaxation."

"Oh, look, myself, I've just bought a – But, listen, if I had your number I'd never tell a soul – not Ian, not anyone – and ring only when you were sure you'll be alone."

"I suppose because I know he needs me."

"What?"

"Why I'm still with him."

"Christ, he's the fink of finks, Angie!"

"And I haven't asked you anything about you and Ian and the baby. Next time."

"Angie, now don't ring off. Carmel. The card going? Just give me the box number. That wouldn't lead anywhere. I don't know one out-of-town code from another. Honestly, I wouldn't try to find out."

Chapter 10

Brade was good on faces, but a side view in the dark and seen only through the window of a car doing eighty was a poor offering. He studied a sheaf of pictures sent down by the Yard to meet the description and at the end still had a shortlist of thirty. Probably nearly half Britain's crime was done by twenty-five-year-old men with fair hair, ridge-cut, and the other half by twenty-five-year-old men with dark hair, ridge-cut. At the hospital when he called on Glyndwr, Brade found himself tensing up two or three times a visit, hand on the Magnum, thinking he glimpsed that raw barbering and the profile.

Brade disliked the room where they had Glyndwr. A general hospital was wide open, and had to be. For Glyndwr, you walked up one flight of stairs, along twenty yards of corridor, first right into the foyer of the ward, first right again into his room which had walls of opaque glass. It could not be easier. Brade would have preferred him on the main ward, where he would be in view, and so would anyone who called on him. Even a room a bit nearer the ward would have been an improvement. As it was, somebody could slip in from the corridor, have complete privacy with Glyndwr and be away again in less than a minute, perhaps unobserved. In London they would hear he had survived and not talked yet, and would want to make sure he never did.

Brade had been to see a hospital administrator and asked if Glyndwr could be moved on the quiet right out of the place to one of their convalescent homes, as his precise location had appeared all over the media. But, of course, the administrator said Glyndwr was regrettably not convalescent, no, indeed not, and had to be near a theatre, the skull experts and special equipment. Yes, oh yes, he was definitely improving, but could relapse and a move might be detrimental at this stage. The hospital would have no objection to a continuous guard for Mr Jenkins, and would not that be the best compromise? It would, but Raging Bullfinch did not see it that way. So, as a further compromise, Brade spent all available time sitting with Glyndwr, the Magnum aboard, though the hospital need not know that. Brade had asked for calls about Glyndwr's condition to be monitored and recorded. However, the administrator thought, also regrettably, that this would not be a warrantable intrusion by the hospital, unless Glyndwr were demonstrably in danger: that is, if he were given a police guard. "To be blunt, Mr Brade, you must not expect us to do your dirty work."

"Why not? We do yours," Brade replied.

"But I'm confident you'll be all right," he told Glyndwr. "Their target is our friend who shall be nameless, even new-nameless, and they won't spare energy looking for you. They'll probably be getting daily bulletins and will know you're still well submerged, so why should they fret?"

Glyndwr's mother had gone down to the entrance hall of the hospital for a smoke and a coffee. Brade was alone with him. The bandaging gleamed antiseptically, as ever. If he was getting better, it did not show, still did not show. Glyndwr's features had the same uncrackable serenity which was there yesterday, last week, last month. His long eyelashes lay spread in full, unnerving relaxation like a sleeping child's or a corpse's.

"It's easy to start thinking of these people as if they were as organised and resourced as the old KBG, Glyndwr," said Brade. "In fact, they're some slapdash, injured remnants of a scruffy South London gang. Anyway, I'm continually here, as you can see, so to speak. This might entail leaving our friend a bit exposed, but he knows how to look after himself, I should think. Then, as we've said, some would ask why not pull off all protection. If he was wasted, Julie might want to come back, so I wouldn't be alone in that sodding, unsellable, church-blighted flat. But, of course, our friend is in my charge, and I half believe, or even more than half, that I'll do my best for him, regardless. In some ways he's—"

54

"I trust you will, Dave," Jenkins said. "In fact I know you will."

He lay as before, eyes closed, in grim, frozen peacefulness, and yet the words were so exactly bloody Glyndwr – that poncy "I trust", and then, over and above that, the Balliol-trained, fart-arseing, high-flier quibble of the whole fucking thing, "trust you will", "in fact, know you will".

Brade hissed at him: "Have you been awake the whole time, you sod?"

"Not the whole time, Dave. I come and go. One can observe very well from this situation. People are so off-guard. There's a nice little nurse who on her own initiative tries to get me erect, as a sign of returning vigour and focus. I fight and fight it and so far I win, which depresses her, I think, but it's pleasant enough. And then would I ever have heard you talk of getting a love rival knocked off through complicity, if you'd thought I was listening? That's degenerate, you know. You obviously need me back there, looking after your soul. Not long now, Dave."

"Which nurse?" Brade replied.

"I don't think she'd be interested in you. This is a medical experiment."

He still had not opened his eyes. "Jenkins, I'm going to—"

"We might be able to work out something pretty useful, Dave, if the world keeps thinking I'm still in a coma."

"Useful?"

"The lad who hit me might come looking, mightn't he? In case I wake up and talk."

"You as bait?" Brade said.

"Along those lines."

"Noble."

"I think so."

"The medics will know you're faking," Brade said.

"Eventually. But we might be able to get somewhere before that."

"This would be beautiful for your career," Brade said. "The quiet bravery and craftiness."

"Yes, I've thought of that."

"But to prolong the worry for your mother and father," Brade said.

"They'll understand, in due course. They know about duty, Dave; brought me up to it."

"I don't really like—"

The door opened without any knock and Brade turned urgently to face it, resisting the pull to put his hand on the Magnum, but very ready to. Julie, in a tremendous, businesslike pinstripe jacket and narrow black skirt said: "I rang the nick and they told me you'd probably be here. Dave, I thought I heard talking. He's come out of it?" Despite the formal clothes, she looked wonderfully young, her pale skin fresh and unlined, dark hair cropped very short to give full sight of her tidy features and soaring cheekbones. The smile was half in place – that hello, goodbye smile – but the way she stuck her head forward said a grievance, or it always had in the past. To Brade she seemed altogether loveable and unarguably a plus for any man.

"No, no change," he said. "Regrettably. He's still utterly blotto. But every day I tell him what's been happening on our patch," he replied, "hoping he might stir. You know how promotion-obsessed the bastard is – compensating for his underprivileged background and the race bit. I talk about people passing him on the ladder while he's laid out here sleeping. Rage and envy might bring him round."

"One-way transmission, like with the porno mags." She came into the room and sat on the other side of the bed from Brade, in the chair generally used by Glyndwr's mother. "Dave, I spoke to Danny. I meant to scalp him for snooping on my love life. And then with some persuasion he tells me it was you yourself up there that night." She rushed this bit, as though embarrassed and wanting to get through it. "I wondered what the hell was going on. What had happened to you, so you had to shadow me, doing a what-the-butler-saw? I knew you had your kinks, but this was . . . well, real pervy, Dave. It's over, you and me. Totally. I really believed you'd accepted that." She tried to smile again, some pity, some brick wall, plenty of venom.

"Totally? No, I can't accept that. Won't. Do we have to discuss such things in here?" Brade gazed at Julie across Glyndwr. Anger shone in her face and her eyes went savage. It did make a brilliant change from Glyndwr's impassiveness.

"He's not going to tell tales, is he?" she said.

"People are in and out. His relations."

She frowned – showed concentration: "And then I thought, no, you wouldn't hang on to the hope it could all start up again. Not really like you, Dave. Not to that degree – not so you'd come sniffing around my office at night."

Brade stood and went to the door. He looked along the corridor for Mrs Jenkins. He wished she would return, but no, not yet. He returned to his seat.

Julie said: "So then I started wondering if – Dave, the stories about what happened to Glyndwr pile up."

"I've heard them. All balls."

"Definitely protecting some prominent ex-grass, as I get it."

"It's balls, Julie."

"And you come to see me at the office with warnings about new people. Mystery. But suddenly, what I start wondering is, whether it's not me you're tailing but Geoff." She gave a sad grin. "Wow – one big shock to my ego."

"Geoff? This is a man you're seeing?"

"You were doing the seeing. You enjoyed that?"

"If I knew what we were talking about, I—"

She smiled a laugh, but not much of a one, one that made her sound jinxed and scared. "Dave, listen, in confidence – is my Geoffrey Dilsom this retired grass? That's why you're so damn near him, and incidentally near me. He's a target? I'm in love with an alias man?"

Jesus, the terminology was cruel. "In love? Is that right? You really love him: not just an adventure?" He knew his voice had fallen into misery. And wasn't it great to have Jenkins earholing all this? "Glyndwr was looking at a simple burglary."

"Christ, this is Julie you're talking to, someone *you* were in love with once yourself. Not a newspaper reporter to be fobbed off. Don't I deserve to know?"

She had begun to shout. Mrs Jenkins came hesitantly in and Brade said: "Julie was just trying to rouse him with a real yell. She's a good friend."

Glyndwr's mother went and peered closely into his face. "Was there any movement when you did it?" she asked them.

"I thought possibly," Brade replied at once. "A flicker. Julie has started avalanches."

"A flicker? Yes? Yes, yes," Mrs Jenkins said. She gave a very small, very reserved, grateful smile to Julie, then turned back to gaze at Glyndwr, her face still near his. In a moment, she bellowed at him, louder than Julie had, only inches from his ears. After a short pause, she repeated it. She watched and after a while lifted one hand to touch his closed eyes gently in turn, as though wanting to help them into a response. She was quietly weeping and some tears struck her wrist and skidded on to the folded-back sheet, making a string of faint marks across the whiteness, like small roof leaks through a ceiling.

Chapter 11

"Len?"

"Who's this?"

"Len, if you don't want to talk, to talk to me, bang the phone down now. It's OK. I mean it."

"Christ, this is—?"

"Right."

"This I never expected. I thought—"

"We've got new names, Len. Did you know I had a wife called Carmel? Nice? They're working on the kids, too."

"You're not in London, are you?"

"Could I be, Len? I mean, *could* I be?"

"So, where?"

"It doesn't matter. Maybe it's better you don't know. I mean, better for you as well. Maybe people there ask you if I have been in touch? As good old mates, Len. They're bound to have an eye on you."

"They're looking. Some of them are looking, I got to tell you that. Well, what would you expect? The *ones* you would expect."

"They been giving you trouble?"

"They don't give me trouble. I couldn't help them, anyway. If I wanted to."

"What I mean, best you don't know anything."

"So why you ringing?"

"I need help, Len. Something through your dealership. An item. But you can say no. I should think you'll say no, and I'll understand."

"Can't the new friends give you help, then?"

"Up to a point, but not that, clearly."

"What point? Anyway, why did you have to do it? I wouldn't believe it – not till it happened, till it was the

59

actual court. I was so sure you'd come all right, eventually. How?"

"Thanks, Len."

"Thanks? How thanks? You fucking did it."

"Thanks you thought I couldn't. That's a friend. Me, I thought I couldn't, too. Sometimes even now I don't believe I did."

"You did. Here they believe it. And in Long Lartin."

"Don't I know? But these lads who took me over, they're so smart, Len. OK, I'm smart likewise, but they do their leverage, none better. They keep coming back and coming back. They do such promises. So guess my new name, Len. No, not Judas."

"It better be good, that's all. You know what they're like here. They won't forget. They get insights."

"Why I'm ringing."

"What?"

"I wouldn't if I didn't have to – sort of drawing you in. That's how you'll think of it, bound to. You'd rather forget me. But how do I look after myself, Len?"

"I say again, they'll do that. Your new friends. As I understood, this is standard."

"They make a bit of a show. Do they care? I need self-help, in case I'm cut adrift, left alone. You know. This is for backs to the wall, Len. We've been there together. Like that, but just me now."

"What, you haven't got something? Didn't you hang on to something? That's basic."

"How would I, Len? This is a new house, new furniture, new nearly everything. It's all gone through their sieve. They're watching me like I'm their treasure."

"Well, you are."

"Sort of. All right."

"No local supplier?"

"There must be. But how can I? This is a far away place. Who do I know? Why I'm here. Do I stop someone on the street and ask if he can fix me up with something heavy? Or in a club? Who am I talking to? And then the ones I ask could wonder who they're talking to too, and they start digging. Which is what we got to avoid."

60

"We? That's the new friends and you?"

"I don't want people asking where do I come from, who do I know, why do I want it, who am I afraid of and why? All that. You see the point, Len? Look, I've got money."

"Well, I expect so. They look after you. Not just the house."

"Some from them. Yes, the mortgage down payment. Plus, some left from old outings."

"They let you keep it?"

"They don't know.

"Switzerland?"

"As good. But it's got to be ready, so closer. Maybe I have to buy someone off in a rush one day. Not kept in the house, though."

"You think I'll come looking for it?"

"I was always fair with you, Len."

"I don't say different."

"Don't think I don't know this is asking a lot. For something satisfactory there'd be a real payment. This is not just for me, Len, this is for the four of us."

"Does she know you're calling?"

"This is a phone box, on a card."

"Wise."

"Oh, all right, I know at your end it's different but—"

"I don't think I got listeners."

"I'm being careful."

"We're both being careful."

"What I'm worried about, Len, I bumped into a girl here. The way it happens, you know. Richly mutual. This is not something cheap but in a smart job, Vauxhall Senator on the firm, and with high-grade presence."

"So, what's it like there, wherever you are, for spare? In general."

"If you stick at it, give a decent smile, like anywhere."

"Right. Everywhere they're seeking warmth and so on."

"I do think so, Len. It's not just flesh with them, though partly. Their emotions are important to them, and they want these duly appreciated, that's all, which I for one find totally understandable. Going through the desk drawers while she's

61

getting a pee, there's a sweet picture of her with one of the, well—"

"One of the protection? Jesus."

"The main protection. I mean, this is a really sweet picture, a definite familiarity or more. A day in the country or something like that. You see what I mean?"

"He knows about you and her?"

"These people get to know, even the ones here."

"They do. So, this is something still going, her and him? How old's this picture? She look the same or him? Are the clothes 1980s, say? Older? It could be the past, couldn't it?"

"It's not old. It's sort of almost now period. They're not younger."

"She's running you both, then? This one's like that? Some of these in big jobs these days, they keep busy all round, like only top stars used to, Marlene Dietrich. Infection? To them it's standard risk, like a ski slope leg bust."

"I mean, if the stuff starts flying and he knows I'm having moments with his girl is he going to throw himself across me selflessly like that Rufus in the JFK car, 1963?"

"No, Rufus Youngblood was with Johnson."

"Sorry, Len, you being into history."

"But I read you. In cock conflicts who fights fair? as Plato said. You going to stick with her regardless?"

"It could be too late. If he knows."

"Seen any signs people this way know something? I'm talking about your location."

"Maybe one sign."

"What?"

"Yes, maybe one sign."

"But I can't know?"

"It would say the geography, Len. It's been in the media. Geography is what you don't want to be burdened with, I still say."

"But if I could provide something?"

"You mean, how deliver? Not parcel post. I'd come some-where for the transfer. Not there. I stay out of the Smoke. A motorway caff? Somewhere like that. Some no man's land. Your exes met and lavishly, clearly, Len – record the mileage. On top of purchase price, I mean. And a decent meal together, if you could face that. I hope so. It would be great to see you. A decent talk."

"You'd trust me?"

"What?"

"To turn up."

"If you said."

"To turn up alone."

"I thought it all over before I rang, didn't I, Len? I had to wonder, I got to say that. And then I said, no, Len wouldn't do something like that. Not something evil."

"Not Judas on a Judas? Some would say—"

"A duty. I know."

"Some would say you can't Judas on a Judas because with a Judas anything's right."

"Well, I've got to trust you, Len, that's all."

"So, if I could – any special requirements? Don't talk names, just guidance."

"I'd trust your taste on that, too. Something that would look after me. Not something minor. Not something for a handbag. If this protection I'm supposed to get is standing back, wanting my sex drive pulped, and the rest of me, I've got to be able to do it all solo, Len, meaning probably fighting off more than one."

"No question. It will be a posse."

"I'd need power. I know this is cost, but don't worry."

"Have you thought if you're holding something like this, or more if you use it, you could end where you don't want to be above all, i.e. in jail, because they'll be really waiting for you in there and they'll know you whatever your name is now?"

"This I thought about, too. It can't be helped, Len."

"You're not going to give me a number to reach you."

"In case one of the kids picks it up."

"All this coming into my home instead."

"Gratitude is what I'll always feel for this, Len. And never one quibble re price, believe me."

"Call Saturday after *Grandstand*."

"Yes, gratitude for ever, Len, and on behalf of her and the kiddies, too."

"This is *which* 'her'?"

Chapter 12

Rick Cole decided he would not take another Escort to go down to Cardiff. An Escort was just what police would expect. They would not expect exactly the same Escort because that would be back with the owner, but police with their dossier minds thought you had your pattern and you always stuck to it because you could not move off it. Around that marina they would be looking for another top-range Escort and maybe at the hospital. Police were like Dad and Uncle Bart, they thought a youngster could not think and did not know about the subtle. Thus, the thing to do would be to take something powerful enough, but solid and mid-management, maybe continental. He liked the idea of a big Peugeot. He also liked the idea of something sexier than a wrench as armament, and thought a 9 mm Parabellum Walther might do. Uncle Bart did get things right now and then, and, with Dilsom giving it to a bird somewhere, this would be a first class moment for a round in the back of the head, if he was on top – like a mercy shot with a hurt horse. It would be bad and unnecessary if the bullet went right through and smashed the girl, say in the open mouth through fake ecstasising or declaring love eternal, but this was the kind of risk girls took with someone like that.

Of course, his father and Uncle Bart had told him he must not go there, no way. They said this from kindness to him, and he felt grateful, but you could not spend your life listening to the aged, could you? Or there would never be progress, so fuck them. You had to think *for* people like that, this was the point. As people grew old they sometimes went confused. They could not see the shape of a problem, not totally. They might start all right and be noisy about it and so sure, but they would wander. You helped them then. You ignored what they said. You came back with your victories and put them in front of people like Dad and Uncle Bart the way a big-game hunter came back to the tent with dead tigers. Uncle Bart and Dad were scared that killing the cop would brisk up the police all round and make the real job harder. Which it would, unless it – both jobs – were all done fast. What they did not seem able to understand, though, was that the black and Dilsom were the *same* job now. What good if you killed Dilsom-that-was-Hector and then the black cop came out of the coma and said his piece about what he saw? Wham. Police would be on the doorstep five minutes later, and Brydon's sentence would start to look slight. Uncle Bart and Dad could not see as far into a situation as this. Vision was going. They saw what was right in front, and nothing else. Sad, really.

In the old Cavalier that he used for around the town, Rick Cole drove out Greenwich way to see an armourer called Len Everdon. This was going to be tricky. Everdon's name was about as a great provider, the way these things *did* get about if you learned where to listen, but Len did not know Rick Cole. People who dealt guns were very cagey, and Rick Cole realised that to Len he might look just like a kid from anywhere, with this haircut, and liable to shoot his mouth off, not just a gun, and bring all kinds of come-back. Rick Cole did not want any armourer used by Dad or Uncle Bart. Someone might feel it was his duty to get on the phone and give the word that young Rick had come buying and must be thinking of some perilous outing. Fuck-up. Dad and Uncle Bart always used Grenville Hollings from New Cross way. It was some sentimental connection going right back. He was cheap, but Rick would keep away from him.

Len did beautiful supplies and fairly reasonable, including foreign, like the Walther as well as the Starlight from Spain. He lived in a tiny dump of a place in a real shit street and drove a worse wreck than the Cavalier. This was Len's cleverness. He made the funds, all right, but he never showed it. The dynasty would be rich one day with all he must have piled up. So, Rick Cole knocked on Len's basement door and waited. This was the thing about Rick, he believed in head-on, no messing. What Rick had been told to look out for by people who dealt with Len was his high-rise adam's apple and great,

1928-style suits. You wanted to be sure you were talking to the right person if you asked about good, man-stopping handguns. When the door was opened, Rick looked for these two signs and said: "You must be Len Everdon."

"Why?"

"You won't know me."

"Maybe."

"I heard your name," Rick Cole said.

"And address."

"This would be a simple business matter."

"Or maybe I do know you," Everdon said.

"Oh? How?"

"I do myself shortlists of who might show. Called forward planning. A brother away?"

"A couple of things to put right," Rick Cole replied. This was the trouble with Everdon, or with any armourer – they always knew too fucking much. Because of the work, they lived half inside God knew how many teams. They were told requirements, and could see results in the media. Everdon had such a business that probably he even supplied Hector Vale with items, when Hector Vale was still in a career. When Hector Vale was still Hector Vale. Everdon was about fifty with these watery grey eyes that seemed right for the adam's apple.

"Look, Rick – it's Rick, yes? – look, Rick, this kind of turmoil I try to stay out of." He had the suit on but was barefooted.

"Which kind?"

"People stalking for grievances. It's a difficult trade, from my point of view. Do I take sides? You see what I'm saying? Someone gets blasted, so the family comes after not just the one who did it, but the supplier. Not what business is about at all."

"Can I come in?" Rick Cole said.

"Usually by appointment."

"Some urgency, Len."

"I try to keep a decent home here," Everdon replied.

"I've heard that. Like an oasis."

Everdon stood aside. They went through two long, grubby passages and then up a short flight of stairs into a wide, light room with French windows that looked out on to a conservatory which must have top-class heating for the plants because a great looking girl of about twenty in a struggling orange bikini was playing in there with a small baby, throwing a big, all colour ball to it over and over. They were both laughing like this was the greatest game since Strip Jack Naked. The conservatory and this room they were in looked a treat. It was winter, but the flowers they had in that conservatory seemed great, so neat and tall.

"That's a friend of mine and our dear child, Crispin," Len Everdon said. "This is why I said about an appointment. We were having what we call our little 'relax time' with Crispin."

The girl looked around and waved and grinned at Len. He waved back. That brown suit was of such grand, thick, old material it must have been tough work to get his arm up. Rick Cole said: "This can be as quick as you like, Len, if you want to be back with them."

"I heard some shambles Wales way," Everdon replied. "This is what I mean – chaos everywhere. I'm out there in the conservatory, having family pleasures with Delphine and Crispin when the door bell goes, and I have to put my jacket back on in case of business, which apparently it is, and suddenly I'm dragged out of a period of peace and gentleness into – well, into what? You could say this is very disturbing, Rick. You look so bloody young."

They sat down. The room had a lot of this lovely bamboo and cane furniture with bright cushions, and some art on the walls, not just paintings, but like plaques, with faces and vehicles made out of buttons and bottle tops and pieces of wood and tin. "You know French windows are the easiest way ever into a property don't you, Len?" Rick asked. He pointed at a couple of the creations. "Someone could be away with all these and into Sotheby's."

"People know me here, esteem me," Everdon replied. "My French windows will be respected, I think." The adam's apple went right up with true pride then.

"I thought a Walther, Len."

"Walther, Walther, Walther," he replied, like some nursery rhyme, and laughed a bit. "Everyone talks Walthers. It's

James Bond, even all these years after. You go hunting down there and as I read it now you've got two to deal with. One of them's an acquaintance of mine."

"I wondered."

"Which would not count at all. I deal. Business is about dealing, not sending postcards, Rick."

"Or whatever you like," Rick Cole replied. "I mean whatever you recommend. If not a Walther, I'd be happy with anything you picked."

"You wouldn't expect me to keep any of these articles on the premises. Crispin about. Baby fingers everywhere, believe me."

"Tomorrow? Later today?"

Everdon stood and went and fetched a big, black glass pitcher and a couple of black cups from a bamboo table. He poured some drink out with bits floating, it could be fruit or jug crud from years back, but Rick drank and smiled. "Build you up," Everdon said. "I don't ever ask for details about work to be carried out. Not my rôle, Rick." He raised his hand like the sign of peace in a cowboy film.

"Right," Rick Cole replied. "Thanks, Len."

"Am I right this is two, one possibly in a hospital bed nicely comatose?"

"Often what starts as one job can branch out," Rick Cole replied.

"Contingent."

"So, tomorrow? Later today? Later today would be better," Rick Cole replied.

"Cash."

"That's all right."

"Price is five hundred. I might be able to knock a tenner off."

"This will be a piece plus—"

"This will be everything you need for the kind of work you have in mind, Rick. This evening. I'd like to take you out to meet Delphine and our Crispin, but—"

"Give them my very best."

When he left, Cole thought he'd have a drive around some nicer areas with golf courses and bigger hotels in case he could see a Peugeot 605 parked. This outing to Cardiff would definitely be a challenge but he thought it was beginning to look a happy prospect. He wanted to please his father and Uncle Bart, but please them in a style he personally picked, not them. As a matter of fact, Rick considered the two of them had not been too bad about that business with the black; it could have been worse. Sure, they shouted, especially Uncle Bart, with personal insults. That might have just been nerves, though. They had their problems, which you should try to understand. A son and nephew owed them that. That's what family meant.

He drove through Norwood and around Sydenham, but without spotting what he wanted. Undoubedly, although Dad and Uncle Bart looked older than Cliff Richard, they had some good things to them, both, but not as many as they thought. That was the point. They were not too exact in their thinking these days. At this age, they needed something that told them they were still on top and could handle things, no slip-ups, even though fading. Thus, the easiest way for that was have a go at somebody less elderly who made a mistake, and then say they would still have to do the job themselves, regardless of having the scene buggered up. This would be the famed old firm back on the streets, putting everything right. So, hoo-fucking-ray, etcetera. What *they* called a mistake. Mind, it would have been a bigger mistake to get caught by that cop, and the whole thing blown before it started. That way the family might have two lads doing time instead of just Brydon, both on account of Hector Vale, now Dilsom, who would still be laughing in his villa, when he wasn't having it off outside.

Near Dulwich Common, he noticed a good, newish black 605 in the yard of a private old people's home and parked and walked back. Just as he arrived, though, a glossy look-ing quiffed type about sixty-five, wearing a navy and gold track- suit, came out from the home, climbed in and drove away. Rick Cole kept walking, looking casual. That was all right. The tracksuit would be the owner, no question. Big car, class hairstyle. He had so many paying ancients in there he had to buy the tracksuit to prove he wasn't one of them, yet . . . That car would be back when it was needed, tonight or early tomorrow. He was probably off to look at another of his branches and pick up the cheques. They paid by the week in these places, because of life expectancy.

When Rick reached home, Uncle Bart started again about Cardiff and what he called "this fucking, fucking mess." To Rick Cole it did not seem to matter much any longer. He knew things were so nicely in hand. He could have a little private laugh at Uncle Bart and even at Dad.

"Look around for something small and easy, something close to home, Rick," Uncle Bart said. "Try to work up from elementary outings."

"I can't go along it was so terrible, what happened down there," Rick's dad said, "but Uncle Bart's probably right, Rick. It would be an idea to get your confidence back on a nice, local task."

Fuck confidence. Rick Cole knew there was nothing wrong with *his* confidence. But these two? Anyone could see it gave them a real tonic to bleat superior about the attack on that cop, especially Bart Linacre. The thing about Uncle Bart was he almost believed he could handle anything. So much noise and neck. Mind, he did not have a son in Long Lartin doing twelve, only a nephew. Admitted, he thought a lot of Brydon, but still he was only his uncle. Whereas Brydon sent down for so long had really knocked the bounce out of Dad, and the way it was done, the thorough grassing by someone so close, Hector Vale, brought such sorrow. Of course, grassing almost always was by someone close or they would not know enough to grass, but it still went through to Dad's heart. Dad believed in community, and grassing ripped community to bits. Grassing pissed on community. Uncle Bart would get angry about it, too, but he did not have the full, close agony. Uncle Bart hung on to all his loudness and push, despite being nearly sixty. He thought whatever piece of life he was in he ran it, and he thought people would realise straight off he ought to run it. As soon as you talked to him he was giving orders.

"Could you do us sketches of all the areas we'll need to know?" Uncle Bart said. "Think you could handle that much?"

"Of course he could, couldn't you, Rick?" Dad said.

"Dilsom's house, approach roads, the spot where he bangs this piece of extra. Or don't you know that? Christ, Derwent,

70

we'll be starting this from bloody scratch. Ah, well, we can do it. Somebody's got to."

Give the bugger another fanfare. Uncle Bart was hard, no question, but another reason he did not like this attack on the cop was undoubtedly he hated to see the young moving to the front and handling things their own way – showing anyone difficult they would get dealt with, such as that black. The thing was, Uncle Bart could be bloody difficult himself. He was a gem sometimes, yes, but he could also get in the way often. Deep down, maybe without really knowing, he could be thinking that perhaps one day he could rate that kind of attention himself, if he did not ease off the fucking push and noise. This could be why he wanted to make a slapping like the black cop look stupid. What he was saying was, "Grow out of it, Rick". But what he meant underneath it and maybe not realising was, "Don't grow so fast, Rick, you might do my head next, you young sod", widely known as the subconscious.

"No idea at all where he does his extramarital?" Uncle Barney asked.

"I told you, I wasn't around long enough to tail him there."

"Jesus, Rick, you're all fucking haircut, boy."

Rick didn't say anything, but what the hell did this balding old bastard know of hair modes? 'Ridge' he called it, like a tent or some slab of mountain, and like he never heard of Mohican. This was a mode you'll see every day on rock stars, soccer stars, top boxers, fashion kings. It's *the* mode. All right, not Prince Philip, but people at the top, all the same. What people like Uncle Bart go on about is it's like army haircuts in the Second World War, clippers high on the back and sides and just a top layer so no room for lice, they say. Of course, they're too young to have been in that, but they've read a war book between them and they just want to sound like they've seen it all before, I-was-thereing again, and getting in something dirty about it like lice. Of course, when you look at it in depth, this is family – you could not get rough with your uncle, your mother's much cherished brother, especially someone so hard as Uncle Bart even at his age, hair growing out of his ears, but he ought to watch his rough old mouth, and he could be come up on silent from behind, hard or not, like that officer or worse.

This second trip to Cardiff would be moving the job up a league, of course. When Rick went down there earlier it was just to confirm and get all the details for Dad and Uncle Bart – house location, Dilsom's car and how they ran the new lives, him and the family. It was what Uncle Bart called pathfind, which was also a word he had picked up from a war book, the planes that went first to flare the target. He and Dad would have been coming down later, star pilots, with their payload. Just reconnaissance was Rick's job then, but to put things right and let them know he was not some kid nobody who ballsed up everything he would have to do more than that now and end the cop and then Dilsom in person.

It would soon be time to go over to Len Everdon's again. "What you so jumpy about?" Uncle Bart asked.

"I thought I'd just have a scout around – for the kind of openings you just mentioned. Local."

"Openings come from information, not scouting around."

"I haven't got any."

"Of course you fucking haven't."

"How do I get some?"

"How does he get some, Bart?" Rick's father asked.

"This takes patience. Exactly what kids are short of."

"I might have a scout around," Rick Cole replied.

In the Cavalier on his way back to Len's, he thought over the future a bit, and the past. The officer in hospital would be simple enough. A pest. It was necessary, of course it was. He would even have admitted that to Uncle Bart, if Uncle Bart was not such a mouth and could be reasonable for a couple of minutes. But to clobber that lad had been extremely needful, and no "fucking, fucking mess". In fact, Rick Cole still considered it had been a really fine half hour when he took out the officer. Just before, on that night, there was good confirmation he had found the right house because the grass's Angie, or whatever her name was now, came to a bedroom window with the light on behind her and pulled the curtains. He knew her from far back, parties at Uncle Bart's place and in The Rendezvous when all were such colleagues. Hector Vale had been a real, great lad in those days, everyone said. Gifted was a word often used, and ruthless. This was why it seemed so bad when someone like that went over. Dad was right – it did make you think the whole community could be rotten and coming apart.

Of course, they would have told Angie fifty times not to go to an uncovered window with the light behind her but she would forget or she did not believe it mattered. It mattered. Then walking away back to the car, he had got a sense of this black in a suit on the other side of the street behind him, coming along at a real relaxed pace, the way they were trained to for melting into the background and looking everywhere except at him. It was so good that at first Rick had thought it was just one of the locals on his way home. These days, blacks could do all right and have suits and places on a marina, and especially in this area, Cardiff docks, with its age-old tradition of blacks, and good luck to them.

That night, Rick Cole had not gone straight back to the car, though, because of this saunterer, and did a bit of a sightseeing tour of the marina on foot. This lad stayed with him, now hanging further back, still melting, or trying to. Eventually, after a very swift move down a side-street and returning through another, he came out behind the black boy, who was near a handsome metal model of an old times navy sailing vessel, stuck in concrete on the ground, to get the spirit of this marina and the various historical oceans. He was gazing down towards the dock water, and you could see from the back of his neck he felt remarkably puzzled, having duffed his tailing.

Many might have gone unprepared when just looking at a house, but to Rick it had seemed important to take the wrench in his trenchcoat pocket. Luckily, the black lad did not wear a hat with his suit. He did not even try to turn around to look, he did not have time. Maybe it was not really worth worrying about him in the hospital, if he had had no glimpse. You could not tell, though, and if you could not tell you had to think it could be the worst and do something about it. Yes. Something about it was that nice 605 and whatever Len Everdon came up with tonight, if he was not too busy with the bikini and bloody Crispin. When Dilsom was dead before Uncle Bart and Dad had even moved maybe Uncle Bart would learn to shut up. Maybe he ought to.

Chapter 13

In the car, Rockmain said: "They call me Andy, that's all. And you'll be Dave, Dave. Informality, familiarity, friendship, induced trust – they're vital. And, in any case, obviously we can't have them talking at Sunday school or wherever about someone called Mr Brade. That's a famous name in these parts, I hear, and so respected, obviously. But famous and respected as a cop. People would ask, how come they've got a cop friend, these kids? They could get stalked. They could lead. We edit their heads, Dave."

"Andy, what do they think *you* are then?"

"A mate, I hope. One who gets on really great with them," Rockmain replied. "Why I want you to come today – to put your noble mind at rest. I know you worried about their little brains, their little psyches. I come over sinister to you, yes? Don't apologise. I'm used to it." He chuckled. "Sorry, I'm not really laughing. It's quite a legit anxiety. But no cause for it, let me assure you. These are really sharp, delightful children, as you said from the start. They pick up the directions I'm giving them so fast, Dave. Well, you'd expect them sharp, with a father like that. But where does the niceness come from?"

"Mrs?"

"Yes, she's nice enough, I suppose," Rockmain said. He giggled briefly.

"Dilsom can be charming."

"Sure. Must be able to switch it on. Ask the women he screws. Famed for it."

"Yes? I hope he doesn't try it here. It would make surveillance difficult," Brade said. "I don't fancy voyeuring." One thing Brade was never going to do was tell this slick jerk about Julie. But this slick jerk was trained in psychology.

Would he pick up Brade's areas of special sensitivity? Yes, Andy was sinister all right.

"We have to spy on all sorts of activities, don't we Dave? Part of the trade. Be brave. The thing about Dilsom in the old days – well, girls like generosity, don't they? And he's always thrown the money around. He's seen plenty of that. Very big bank van and bullion jobs with no convictions or loss of earnings. Of course, there *would* have been a conviction last time, but he talked instead. So, Jason Soames, big Brydon Cole, Tommy Thomason and so on are inside instead."

"And they've all got fanged pals and relations."

Rockmain turned and smiled sweetly at him: "Hence my glorious, devious job, Dave. But it can't be just the money that brought Dilsom women. Some of them are well-off, utterly unslaggy – decent background, even in top careers. You'd be surprised."

No. "Women can be a puzzle." Brade had had two years with Julie, and never really known her properly. She followed her feelings. This was fine when her feelings led her to Brade. Later, they stopped doing that.

Rockmain grew excited. His voice soared, became almost boyish – fluting, semi-triumphal. "With the children, it's been possible to turn the change process into more or less fun. That can happen sometimes, as long as you've got kids with a bit of brightness and vim. It's really beautiful then, like striking a cricket ball just right. Their doing, entirely, not mine. That's what I mean about reassuring you. Sometimes these exercises have troublesome aspects, oh, deeply, I do concede – even breakdowns – but not with this pair."

"The mother?"

"Is pleased, too. What else, Dave? She knows it's progress. Carmel, yes." He chuckled a bit again and looked out of the side window, away from Brade who was driving. "Now and then in these exercises, I admit, one might get a warm situation."

"Oh? You and the mothers?"

"It can happen. It's recognised in the manuals." He turned back, more at ease with book theory. "Think, Dave: a mother sees her kids respond well to another man – someone other than their father. This can be important on its own. Her relations with the husband/partner could be rocky, anyway, in view of the kind of existence he's pushed her into, the kind of man he's likely to be. I mean, lies as one of the norms of life, possible violence to her – even probable. But it goes beyond that, obviously. This other man is actually helping create these kids – or, at least, recreate them. And, in a sense, he's improving them, too, isn't he? He's turning them into kids from a normal, decent family, not a villain's brood. View this work as a sort of missionary function, Dave. It can set up quite a bond with the mother, you see."

"Kind of back-dated conception. And so they want to go to bed with this magic missionary, do they? Is it happening this time? Dilsom's wife's been giving you the—?"

He switched his gaze again. "Yes, it can happen, Dave."

"She's quite a picture."

He yawned. "Believe me, I do everything I can to keep it neutral, neuter."

"Then all this racy denim."

His voice turned weary and hard. "I hate the whole notion of involvement. Look, my task, obviously a very positive task, is to mould something, make something, whereas that sort of situation is wholly disruptive, destructive. These families are already under huge stress. Obviously, one has to be on guard – regard it as a risk of the job, but always to be countered, rebuffed, though with kindness."

"Like gynaecologists. As risks go, not as bad as getting your head shot at. Though that could come later, if you were pillaging Dilsom's lady."

"Oh, one could cope with Dilsom. Me, you – we're surely used to villains, active or retired, Dave. After all, a small word of geography dropped among his old chums and he's wide open and on the revenge menu, yes? He'd know this very well. Does that sound monstrous in me, Dave? Possibly . . . Perhaps you couldn't imagine giving an ex-villain away to villains for sexual reasons."

Jesus, was this smart object smart enough to sense the way Brade's mind lurched sometimes?

"This job can coarsen one, Dave. But the problem with Carmel is nonexistent. I'm just not interested in her, don't let myself get interested in any of them, not even when they look like her."

"Wise. And I expect a jolly fellow like you is more than all right for that sort of thing elsewhere, anyway."

"Professional, professional, professional. That's what I must always be, Dave. Who'd want a slice of their grimy culture? And don't tell me the wives aren't part of it."

"Would I?"

"On the other hand, one must obviously keep a good, continuing relationship with the mothers. Mutual confidence, affection."

"But with your clothes on."

"It's tricky, yes, the balance."

When they arrived at the house, the twins and their mother were sitting with Mrs Canter-Williams in the little lounge where the happy outing pictures hung on the wall. Seeing Rockmain, the children jumped from their chairs happily and skipped to greet him shouting, "Andy, Andy!" He was carrying a large suitcase, but set it down and did that arching of the back Brade had noticed first time they met. Today, though, it was not to show humble, but so he could get down to kiss each of them on the cheek. Afterwards, holding hands, they did a wild, capering dance in a circle, first one way, then back, Rockmain loudly singing the old number,

"Here we are again,
Happy as can be,
All good pals,
And jolly good company."

His teeth shone and Mrs Canter-Williams beamed. "Didn't I tell you he would be here, children? They've been very worried, Andy." She left to make some tea in the kitchen.

Brade watched it all, as he was supposed to watch it all. He grinned in that benign, half daft way the Chief would, or Raging Bullfinch, when photographed by the local Press presenting a charity cheque.

"Plus I've brought you a new friend, kids," Rockmain said. He ended the dance and the three of them stood in a line facing Brade, still holding hands, like three quarters of a

77

joyous family. "Children, this is Dave. Dave, this is Anita and Jeremy Dilsom."

Rockmain spoke the changed name without a tremor. He had flair, this lad. Brade watched the two young faces for a wince or a smile, but saw nothing there except the usual indifference of kids meeting an adult. Brade took a couple of seconds to glance at their mother, who was sitting near the glass-fronted bookcase, its shelves full of heavy blue- and black-bound theology books, many in Welsh. The Rev Canter-Williams was exactly the kind of MA, BD name you saw on chapel notice boards in South Wales. No wonder his daughter had turned out so bilingual and noisy. When the children and Rockmain were dancing, Carmel had smiled, too, but Brade did not know whether this was from real joy to see the children's excitement, or because she had to make the best of things.

"Dave's brand new to this city, kids," Rockmain said. "Really, I ought to get you to tell him all about it."

"Well, bits of it," Jeremy said. He was round-faced, dark haired, a little defiant looking, like his mother rather than Dilsom.

"Yes, bits," Rockmain replied. "The best bits. Tell me which is the best bit."

Jeremy went into a long think about this. He seemed to be really working at it.

"Where the circus was?" Rockmain asked.

Anita laughed and nodded: "Oh, yes. We could tell him about that".

"And where was it?" Rockmain asked.

"Cheald Meadows," she said, nodding her head, hard this time, as if afraid of argument. She was dark haired, too, her face leaner than Jeremy's, sharper and more thoughtful, her small, brown eyes troubled, to use Rockmain's feeble word. She did not look like either parent, nor her twin. There was a good future in this child.

"You missed a great circus in Cheald Meadows, Dave," Rockmain told him.

"Perhaps next time," Brade said. "If I'm around. What did they have there, I wonder?" Jesus, he was falling so naturally into Rockmain's slippery art.

Jeremy smiled, welcoming a cue, and ticked the items off on his fingers slowly. "We saw clowns, horses . . . yes, clowns, horses, elephants, acrobats, lions and dogs – dogs who did tricks."

"Sounds great," Brade replied.

"Didn't we, Mum?" Anita asked.

"What, love?" Carmel Dilsom replied.

"See all those things, all those things in Cheald Meadows? That's where, wasn't it? So Dave can find it if it comes back and he wants to see the clowns, horses, elephants, acrobats, lions and dogs who do tricks."

"That's right," Carmel Dilsom said. "Cheald Meadows."

Anita pondered. "Well, I think it was Cheald Meadows, Dave."

"Of course it was," Rockmain said. "Where on earth else, Nita?"

"If Dave went there because we told him and it was not the right place," the girl replied, "he'd be so cross we told him wrong." She frowned, very concerned, and blushed. Now, it was as if she feared saying something absurd or ill-willed.

"Sometimes I do think it was somewhere else." Shamefaced, she put a hand over her mouth for a second but said, "Well, yes I do."

Rockmain had a merry laugh. Perhaps this came out of the manual. "She's terrible, Dave. Sometimes I swear she doesn't know what she thinks, that's a fact, isn't it Jeremy?"

"She gets things mixed up," Jeremy replied. He tutted for a while, despairingly, like an old man.

"I'm afraid you do, Anita," Carmel said.

"Sometimes I think you'll forget your own name next," Rockmain said. Joke, or cold challenge to the child? Rockmain was grinning, a grin short of humour, heavy on bluff.

Anita grinned too, but looked a bit frightened again and lost. "My name?" she replied.

"Sometimes, you're such a dreamer, we're scared you'll really forget your own name," Rockmain said. "You'll think you're Little Red Riding Hood or Sleeping Beauty."

She snapped her answer: "That's silly, Andy. Of course I won't."

"Good. Because obviously I'm not the handsome Prince," Rockmain said.

"Obviously," Brade said. "One of those poisonous toadstools?"

"Oh, thanks," Rockmain replied, with another good laugh.

Anita's voice had become dogged, empty, defeated. Brade shuddered, and told himself not to, then told himself again. What Rockmain did was crucial, was life-preserving. "But sometimes I think – I think I remember, well, some other name," she said.

"What, not Anita?"

"Oh, Andy, yes, Anita, of course. But my other name."

"Your other name's Dilsom, isn't it?" Rockmain replied. He pointed to Carmel in her chair. "This is Mrs Dilsom, I believe." He put on a very formal voice, like an interviewer. "Tell me, madam, are you Mrs Dilsom?"

"I am, indeed," Carmel said.

"And the dad is Mr Dilsom?"

"Correct."

"And do you have two children?"

"I do indeed."

"Would you please inform us of their names?"

"Anita and Jeremy."

"Yes?"

"What?"

"No other name?"

"Well, Dilsom, of course. I'm their mum."

Rockmain turned to the boy. "And you're this girl's brother?"

"Yes."

"Called Jeremy?"

"Yes."

"Jeremy what?"

"Jeremy Dilsom."

Rockmain started the dance with them again, grabbing their hands, this time singing something he seemed just to make up, tuneless and loud. There was no end to him.

"By the blood and the bones of the Great Tiddly-Tum,
All little girls get the name of their mum."

80

"You're so nutty, Anita," Jeremy told her, when the dance finished again.

"Running away," Anita replied, gazing at Brade.

"What did you say, love?" Brade asked.

Rockmain said: "Now Dave, you talk to Mrs Dilsom while I take the children into—"

"Andy, are we running away?" Anita asked, turning to him.

"Running away? I don't see you running," Rockmain said. "Dancing, yes. No running. Dave, do you see anybody running?"

"Why we come to this house. And our name," Anita replied. "Daddy's running away?"

"We visit this house for a little party. Mrs Canter-Williams brings us these grand Welsh cakes. That's why Dave wanted to come. Find out what the Welsh eat. He really kept on at me for an invite."

"Yes, indeed," Brade said.

"When?" Anita asked.

"What?" Rockmain said.

"When did he keep asking you?"

"All the time," Rockmain said.

"But you said he doesn't live in this city," Anita replied.

"I mean by telephone and even letter."

"Well, you don't live here, do you, Andy? I mean, not always," the girl replied. "You don't talk like here. Sometimes I think . . . Sometimes I think you talk like people in another place, another place where I used to live. I don't know what we're running away from."

"Nothing, love," Carmel Dilsom said.

"She's thinking about fairy tales again, I believe," Rockmain said. "Escaping from the wicked witch, probably."

"Do you know him, Dave?" Anita asked.

"Andy? Of course," Brade said.

"Really know him, who he really, *really* is?"

"Of course."

"A man who dances in somebody's room. Dances in the sitting room," Anita said.

"I do that all the time," Brade said.

"You're just saying it," Anita replied.

81

"Of course we know each other," Rockmain said. "Would I bring someone to this party if I didn't know him?"

Anita groaned. "Oh, of course you would. Who is Andy, then? Who are *you*, Dave?"

"First she's not sure of her own name, now ours!" Rockmain yelled, laughing even louder. For a moment he looked as though he would restart the dancing. But then he must have sensed it would not work again. Or perhaps he remembered his timetable. "Now, Dave," he said, "I'm going to take the children into the other room and show them pictures of famous people from this city, so when they start school they'll be best at all the lessons on the place where they live. You can talk to Mrs Dilsom for a little while." He picked up the suitcase.

Mrs Canter-Williams came in with a tray, and the children gathered some mugs and cakes for themselves and Rockmain before they went out. She pulled out a couple of small tables from a nest and put a mug and some food on each for Carmel and Brade. Then Mrs Canter-Williams left again. Brade said: "Your Anita's very intelligent."

She put her eyes on him momentarily, and the automatic, inbred hate for all police was there, as ever. But perhaps she felt isolated or anxious. Perhaps both. At any rate, she seemed willing to talk. "So-so. Jeremy's the real brain."

"Oh?"

"With Nita, what you see you get. But Jeremy plays along, looks right through. Nothing too . . . nothing too, well, what Rockmain would call obvious. See how Jeremy hung back about the circus? He's learned that people like Rockmain must be told what they need to hear. People like you, too, I expect. At this stage of the game. But he knows he mustn't make it sound pat. He's worked it all out for himself. He's got a future, that lad. Me, I do everything the way Rockmain wants, no sabotage. I can see it's a safety thing. We're helpless."

"Your daughter's—"

"Poor Anita feels she has to come clean. Takes after her dad, you see."

"A nice quality."

She nibbled at one of the Welsh cakes. "Police live by it, I know – I mean, by making other people come clean. But I love her, so I'll soon help her ditch the habit, or she'll get hurt more than her share." She paused and seemed suddenly to decide she could risk going a bit deeper with him. "Brade, if I took them away from their father would they be at less risk? Would *I* be, come to that?"

"Who's been saying this to you?"

"Would we be?"

"Leave him?"

"People wouldn't come looking for the children and me, as long as he was not there. These London teams are not like that. Not even the worst of them hunt women and kids. Not even the women and kids of a grass. Vengeance is personalised." She had kept her navy topcoat on in the house, but loosened it now. Underneath she wore old jeans and a grubby, high-necked sweater. Her round, surly, nearly beautiful face signalled despair and not much else. Had Rockmain really spotted more for himself there, or was that just Rockmain? With no success, Brade had tried to detect some signs of longing in her for Rockmain while he was in the room just now. Maybe he lacked Andy's ability to read people.

Brade said: "Carmel, these are early days. There are problems, of course. But you're a family. I'd hope you'd stay together. That's one of our objectives."

"Sure, you've got a business plan for us. Meanwhile, he fucks anything that moves here."

"I know he used to be a bit like that."

"He's adapted to the new location. He's putting it some-where. At least one somewhere."

"Hardly likely, the restrictions he's under," Brade replied as firmly as he could.

"What restrictions? He worked out in a week how to beat those."

"I doubt it."

"Look, pardon me, but he's used to dealing with the Met, who have some very clever animals."

"We haven't?"

"Don't they have to send someone like Andy down to help you?"

"He's a tradesman. It's like calling the plumber."

"Great. The plumber's stopping leaks from my kids."

There were loud, team-support yells from the other room: "Car-diff, Car-diff, Car-diff!"

Carmel Dilsom said: "Clever? I heard you've got a boy in hospital, likely to snuff it."

"People in the Met never get hurt?"

"Well, you worry me. Worry Hec . . . Geoffrey. He's not sure you can look after him, us. So, why do I stay? All this carry-on, Mrs Canter-Williams, dear Andy, you, my crazy new name, the hot chance of acquiring something grave in my bed, as always, or even more in this kind of area."

"My impression and Andy Rockmain's was that he has genuinely changed. He knows he must. Understands the hazards."

"Balls."

"Anyway, Carmel, *could* you leave him?"

Her eyes lost their flintiness and went sad for a couple of seconds. "Ah, you're not so stupid, are you?"

"I told you, we have our clever animals, too."

"It would be tough, yes. I still want him, want to be with the idiot. There have been great, raw times. Between jobs, between girls, he's mine."

"There won't be any more jobs – not those kinds of jobs. Nor girls. And I know he needs you."

She stared at him, her face full of mixed hope and disbelief. "Know it how?"

"I talk to him."

"He says that? Honestly, Dave? Honestly, Brade?"

"I'm used to sorting out what people are really saying behind it all."

"Oh, police second sight. We've run into a lot of that."

Brade said: "If you ditched him, all right, people might not come after you and the children to do damage, but sure as sure they'd come after you to ask where he is. And if you wouldn't tell them—"

"Of course I wouldn't."

"No, I didn't think so."

Again she stared. "You *did* think so? Christ, isn't that like police, though?"

"What I'm saying is, if you wouldn't tell them – well, that could bring damage, couldn't it?"

84

"They'd have to find me."

"There's three of you. Difficult to drop right out of sight."

"There's four of us here."

"But we've got a properly worked out drill."

"And they've still found us."

"We don't think so."

"Oh *you* think so, Brade. The people above you might not, or might not want to admit it." She pushed three quarters of the cake and all the tea away from her. "Yes, it might be safer apart from him. Definitely cleaner."

"If there's another woman involved, I could look into that. This would be entirely a security consideration. He's putting himself at hazard. I say again, if it's true."

"Nothing stops men like him. You know that, really, don't you? They'll always get it somehow. They have to. I don't know how things are with you sexually, Brade – you married, or . . .? Anyway, you must have come across career rams like . . . like Geoffrey."

There was more shouting and laughing from the other room. Rockmain sang something else, not anything Brade recognised, perhaps a sports fans's chant. More laughter followed, Anita's happy voice prominent.

"Oh, Rockmain's very able, no question," Carmel said. She shrugged, as though writing off the children to him – you made your deals and lived with the terms. For now, at any rate. "Well, I can't really ask about your sex life, but if you've got a long-time, serene thing going with someone, no, perhaps you wouldn't understand about Geoff. And congratulations: lucky lady. How it is? You *have* got something serene, steady? What's her name, then, Brade?"

No, nothing serene. Nothing at all at the moment, except an occasional docks whore. It had never been serene with Julie, either. He glanced around the vestry-cum-front room. Quaint situation. He felt – *almost* felt – he would like to talk to this hostile woman about things as they had been with Julie. Weren't they linked, he and Carmel? She loathed him, or at least loathed his species, yet, without being aware of it, dear Geoffrey had given them the sort of connection both would rather do without. Yes, if Brade had talked to her about Julie and the past, he would have said he was not interested in serenity. Julie could not have provided that, and did not try to. While it lasted, she was warm and loyal and demanding and clever, and these must have been the qualities he wanted in her. What she wanted from him he had never been clear about. Perhaps *she* had needed serenity. Once in a while, he could offer some of that. He regretted no part of the time with her, except letting her persuade him to invest in that fucking church-shadowed flat. Julie put her half into it, but when they split had asked him to buy her out. Because the break-up had been so charmingly civilised, he agreed.

"We could certainly find out if there's someone else," he told her. "That would be an entirely justified piece of surveillance. To do with safeguarding his life, not snooping."

"Pillow talk? He might cough his identity to her?"

"Simply, we don't want him anywhere we're not aware of. And going regularly, possibly at night. That's advertising for a lie-in-wait."

"So, they *have* located us."

"In case they did."

"Do you mean you haven't tracked him on one of these outings?"

"Why I'm so sceptical."

"And you're supposed to be this clever animal."

"I'd know if he was seeing a woman. Women. Believe me."

"People who say 'believe me' are unbelievable. Then there's what's happening to Anita," she replied. "Rockmain creating someone else, twisting her into someone else. Me, I have to help him twist her. Jeremy has to help him. I'm supposed to enjoy that?"

"You're sure the *boy* can cope? Anyway, not to *enjoy*. Just wear it. It's crucial."

"I don't know if I can, Dave. Brade."

"Dave will do. You don't have to put up with it for long. What do you think of him?"

"Andy Rockmain? Am I going to tell you? Talk to one cop about another?"

"I wouldn't—"

"Talk to one cop about another?"

"I'd never—"

"So you can compare notebooks?"

The children and Rockmain came back at a rush from the other room, laughing and shouting. They moved with bent-legged, lunging movements across the carpet, as if ice-skating, and carried miniature hockey sticks. They all wore skaters' helmets and red and green sweat shirts over their other clothes, with the name of the ice-skating team emblazoned in white, Cardiff Devils. Rockmain threw a matchbox into the middle of the room and the three of them went for it, rapping their sticks on one another's, fiercely battling for the puck, Rockmain snarling like a team talk.

"We are the champions!" Anita shouted.

"Andy's going to take us to see them play, if that's all right, Mum," Jeremy said. They stopped their game.

"Well, of course," Carmel replied.

"Car-diff, Car-diff, Car-diff!" Anita yelled.

"I'd really like them to learn to recognise all the players and store that in their memory, Carmel," Rockmain said.

"Andy's got autographed pictures for us," Anita said.

"When we go we might meet some of them," Jeremy said.

"So it's important to know whom you're talking to," Rockmain replied. "Try to memorise really well, kids."

"Car-diff, Car-diff, Car-diff!" Anita yelled.

"In the evenings, just before they go to bed, if they could spend a little while studying the names and the pictures, Carmel," Rockmain said. "I mean, really studying, familiarising. And the nicknames. Yes, just before they go to bed. Over and over. This will be real fun for them – won't it, Nita, Jeremy? These boys are towering local heroes, part of the folklore – fun, yet also, well, much to the point."

"Yes, I understand," she replied.

"It's important," Rockmain said.

"I said, I understand."

Brade still read no yearning for Rockmain in her voice, yet Andy did not seem the sort to imagine. An imagination might improve him.

"Of course you do, Carmel," Rockmain said. "Now, Dave, in case you want to come, too, do you know where the ice-rink is?"

"Not yet," he said, seeing this was expected.

"It's easy, Dave," Rockmain replied. "Just past Cheald Meadows, as a matter of fact."

"Yes, just past where the circus was, Dave," Anita said.

"Yes, just past where the circus was, Dave," Jeremy said. "Ask someone. Anybody will be able to tell you."

Although he disliked the flat, Brade went home there now and took from the sideboard fruit bowl his copy of *The Great White South* by Herbert G. Ponting, official photographer with Captain Scott's expedition to the South Pole in 1910–11. He often sought backbone in this volume when some part of his job made him feel truly shitty. Recalling the heroism of those explorers – a doomed heroism for five – Brade was almost always bucked up. It delighted him to know that men could do the supremely decent thing now and then, or at least then. He felt an especial bond, because Scott's ship, *Terra Nova*, had called at Cardiff en route to load donated coal. Tonight, using Rockmain's own subtle skills against him, Brade needed something to push from his memory the detail of that necessary work with the children earlier. He turned to a page near the end headed "Had we lived . . .", a phrase from Scott's last letter, recovered with his body. He read, and read once more, "Hereabouts died a very gallant gentleman, Captain L.E.G. Oates." It was the inscription on a cross where the crippled "Titus" Oates deliberately hobbled to his death in a blizzard, afraid he was a burden. This sentence always overwhelmed Brade. He would weep at the horrible, fancy correctness of "hereabouts". He also dwelt on the words, "gallant" and "gentleman", trying to plumb what they signified and wondering if they had any meaning these days. Did gallant gentlemen help hammer the mentalities of a pair of six-year-olds? Were gallant gentlemen even likely to be in Brade's kind of work, nursing a supergrass, occasionally thinking of how to get him slaughtered by proxy?

On the way back to the flat, he had considered looking out for Boadicia or one or two of the others, but had decided on a read instead. Perhaps thinking about the times with Julie had disabled him a bit. In any case, he would not have been able to risk the preliminary dancing. In this mood he did not want Cliffy and Enid here, seeking more gala times and slow foxtrotting in that grossly romantic, over-close style. Thinking of the inscription and Captain Oates, he decided there was no gallantry in making it for money with a teenage tart far from home, and not much gentlemanliness. Jesus, how was it he would fall now and then into these tedious, moralising fits? He turned back in the book to a more cheerful chapter about snow petrels, before sleeping alone again.

Chapter 14

So, for the trip down to see the black cop and Hector Vale, or Dilsom as he had to be called, Rick Cole avoided Escorts and took the L Peugeot 605 from the car park of that grand home for old people at Dulwich Common. The thing was, there shouldn't be need for flash acceleration, and the 605 could build to a cosy motorway speed. He would not have minded an executive style Citroën or Mazda, but the Peugeot was what was offered, so convenient. The important thing was to get to South Wales fast, or Dad and Uncle Bart might be there first. If those two did Dilsom they would be like kids with gold stars from teacher, especially Uncle Bart, and Rick would hear nonstop the details of their greatness, which had brought a golden win, regardless of cock-ups by others, such as him. This would affect Rick's career for years, like Cecil Parkinson or the cricketers who went to South Africa. Also, if they arrived ahead of Rick and did Dilsom but not the cop, there would never be a chance at all to do the cop, because the whole town would be alert after a killing like that. Which meant that if the black cop came out of his long blink eventually and described who and what on the night of the wrenching, Rick Cole could qualify by description for the charge of doing Dilsom. It would not have been too bad being locked up for fifteen for something Dad did, maybe – yes, maybe – but what Rick Cole could not stand the idea of was going down for something that fucker Uncle Bart pulled.

He drove around the marina once early in the day, to get the layout in his head again. This car would not be noticed there at all. It was just the right kind for someone living on a smart marina or thinking of buying a property and doing a tour. The thing he did about his haircut was he wore a hat, as simple as that, too simple and obvious for Uncle Bart, of course. Rick had bought two, both trilbies; one navy, one brown. He could wear one or the other, get a change, confuse. He had on the navy one now. It did not look too bad, racy but old-fashioned, of course, like a Cary Grant movie. At first he had wanted to use a couple of fun caps with the big peaks, but they would not be right for a Peugeot 605 and might get more attention than his haircut. He did not go past Dilsom's house, only the end of his street slowly, twice, with time for good glances. What Uncle Bart said – subtlety – was right enough. Sometimes he had sense. It was just the way he said things and kept on that was a kidney stone. You would think nobody ever heard of subtlety until he brought it into being, like inventing the zip. Rick could not see Dilsom's car outside the house.

He passed the model of that noble old sea vessel near where he had reached the black officer with those blows. He liked working in pleasant surroundings, such as Dulwich Common or this pricey marina with its brave toy sailing ship. Probably Uncle Bart would think he should be reminded of a mistake and feel ashamed when he saw that spot again, but fuck Uncle Bart. The thing was, that had been subtlety, no question, to get behind someone like that, someone alert in all directions looking for him. This boy must have been bright to get into CID against all the usual police race prejudice, and that thumping had not been a pushover. Uncle Bart said the black cop was still alive, still trying to sleep off the wrenching, and Rick would take a trip next to look at the hospital. Admitted, that attack had been partly crude as well as subtle. It was a clobbering, and the only way out of the situation that night, whatever Uncle Bart said. This time it would not be like that for the cop or Dilsom. It would be subtle all through. As he drove out of the marina, Rick took one hand from the wheel and touched the good shape in his pocket.

What Len Everdon had come up with was not the Walther, which he did not seem to think much of, but a 9 mm Ruger P-85 automatic for £490. Even with the ten off, this was at least a ton more than you would pay in any gun shop, yes, but was Rick going to buy one from a gun shop and be on a register? No thanks, even if ordinary gun shops had Ruger P-85s. This item was a stopper. There were thirty rounds included, which left room for an error or two. The butt magazine took 15, and that seemed a healthy number for a neat gun not eight inches long altogether. Rick pulled into the hospital car park and switched off. He gazed at the building. It looked possible, as any hospital would. Soon he must go closer, on foot.

At Everdon's house the second time, Rick had been able to hear the girl and Crispin upstairs, but they did not appear. Len, in that same suit, had given him a good chat about all the technicalities, such as high-visibility sights and a sliding safety catch, but Rick Cole was going to be very near and did not want to know about safety, not for the cop or Dilsom. He gave Len £200 down and would come up with the rest in two or three instalments, when he had time for some ordinary local jobs already sketched out. This was another good thing about Len, he did HP Grenville Hollings and Eustace wanted it all up front, in case you got hit or taken using the gun and couldn't complete. Also, people said Eustace always talked about weapons like they were pedigree pups which it hurt him to have to sell, and he stuck another hundred or more on so he could be sure these items were going to nice homes, well-funded clients. Eustace was no class at all, a real dropping, but he thought gaudy and acted up. Rick heard half the stuff he sold was rubbish and some of the rest traceable.

Anyway, Rick Cole had decided to risk it with Len although he was once close to Dilsom, or Hector Vale then, as he admitted. The thing was, with that kind of face and clothes, Len had to have his own way of doing things, that was plain, but he was also so solid in the community. He had real status there, plus the community gave him his business. So, was Len going to be in touch with someone who shopped his customers, a filthy grass like Dilsom? They used to be close, but Dilsom used to be close with many, and they all wanted him dead now. Somebody who grassed became a different somebody and not the somebody everyone used to know and have respect for. Obviously. Dilsom now, Vale then, when he was decent.

Len said he had selected this weapon carefully, based on the requirements Rick outlined, like getting clothes made to measure. This gave a nice personal feel. Yes, Rick was nearly sure Len would never give a warning. Probably he did not even know where Dilsom was, how could he? Locating him had been a very private and very subtle matter. Yes, subtle.

Chapter 15

Dilsom was sure he would enjoy this meeting with Len Everdon. There were risks, but not too grave, and they were the kind of risks he used to know something about. Good God, in those days, this would have looked like no risk at all: routine. How could it compare with stopping a bullion wagon or stalking a bank delivery van? But, obviously, all that would be when he was Hector Vale. Had he become something smaller, feebler now, something behind ornamental bars on a marina? God, did he really fret and sweat over a meeting in a services? Although there were times when he did not mind being his new name, or even his new, spruced-up self, it was the other one who had had all the happy, front-line and head-line status. Class was what he radiated then. All right, class of a special sort, but class all the same. So, there was bound to be some nostalgia. You could not just ditch a life, regardless of what Dave Brade said, or Rockmain said. That status and class used to bring the girls, many of them really thoughtful and genuinely interested, though very young. They spotted it, this special status – by instinct, really. It was not just that he had the cash to throw around, though that did help. The cash was part of that class and status, it was not the class and status itself. Now, though, money no longer came and went like that, and he needed good luck to meet the kind of women he wanted. Those he did manage to strike up something with were mostly older. They could be possessive, distant, bossy, and post pill, for fear of thrombosis. This executive type, Julie, for instance. She was lovely and in touching need of comfort despite the big job, but he did not get near to understanding her. Oh, there was some love sadness behind her, of course, but a sadness she tried to hide and which she never talked about, as if he could have no entitlement to know.

Dilsom arrived at Membury Services on time, around 10.30 am and habit and training said sit about for a while in the car park trying to pick out familiar vehicles, familiar faces, reassessing the geography. He did not listen to this advice from himself, though, but left his Orion and immediately walked towards the restaurant building. This he considered vital. He had to show he trusted Len Everdon, relied on him not to bring a London vengeance party, or send a London vengeance party. Probably, Len was watching from somewhere, and he would take it as a sick insult if he saw Dilsom hang about full of nerves in the car, as though fearing a trap. It would pull Len down to . . . yes, pull him down to the same level as himself, a betrayer. You could not suggest this about a stalwart like Len, about someone with a reputation like Len's. That would mean nothing meant anything. The world would be chaos.

The meeting itself had status. Any contact with Everdon brought that. His turkey cock adam's apple and skinniness could not spoil it, nor the of-yore suits he used. He sold great guns. Once he agreed to cater, you were certain to get something new, something no-trace, something perfect for the type of work you had in view, plus sufficient good quality ammo. Len understood technology, kept up with developments, and had sources that could always find what was asked for. He knew what a model and a type of bullet could do and would advise free. He brought in overseas arms, such as naturally the USA, but also Germany and Spain, even China. Some said he spoke languages and could discuss with foreigners things like locked-breech construction. This was flair, but no bullshit. Other dealers put on they revered guns and would talk about them like art or a vintage. How much it grieved them to part with their weapons! And the price went high to ease the wound. Len did none of that daft stuff. He was a shopkeeper and he sold. Another thing, even if he hated you and yearned night and day to see you finished, he would never sling you a dud. It was pride.

And here was dear old Len sitting at a table with what looked like a glass of iced water in front of him. If he had been watching the car park he must have moved back fast. Alongside the glass stood a large, cardboard Easter egg box, purple and gold, sealed at the top, and decorated with the words in yoke yellow, "Eggciting, Eggstremely Eggstatic, Eggstraordinarily Eggshilarating", and a wide scarlet ribbon and bow. It was only the second week of January, but perhaps Easter fell early this year. Anyway, you could never be too soon with a gift, and the box certainly jollied up the table.

Len was facing away from the restaurant entrance, staring across the room at nothing very much, or nothing that Dilsom could see. The back of his narrow head and the thin neck were unmistakeable, and the long, bony hand which held his glass. It was like him to seem uninterested in arrivals and full of calm. Although Len had a face like shrapnel, he always kept his behaviour smooth. You would see better clothes at a day centre, yet poise was something Len never failed on. That stuff about sitting with your back to a wall and facing the danger point he'd think purple.

Dilsom went in a semicircle around some tables so he could make the last part of the approach from in front and not startle Len, if Len could be startled. This meeting would put Dilsom back in touch with South London, though at a wise and maybe safe distance. Leonard Everdon, the urgency, the gun talk, the cost talk – all of it would signify a proper professional matter, which to Dilsom signified South London, which signified a tonic. Driving to the services, he had felt really hale, free for a few hours from that out-of-town littleness and flatness he was forced to live with these days, so as to live at all. This meeting was only a survival ploy, but it reminded him of the preliminaries to some big, productive job. It carried a thrill.

All right, there were also the routine anxieties about being spotted away from home, his new home, and now the fresh, darker anxieties about being set up by Len, possibly acting for the community: yes, he might have brought some of them. Dilsom did what he could to survey the room, without making an obvious thing of it. He could accept these stresses. Stress came with the career, operator turned grass. In those previous times, he had arrived for half a dozen conferences more or less like this, where you walked into a room, approached a table, which might be just a room and a table, or might be a target area. You did it, because that was the requirement and if you did not do it, the business, whatever it was, could not take place. He did it now. In any case, for Len today there would be stress, too, supposing he played straight. After all, Everdon was dealing with a grass, and grasses grassed to police. To him it could look like a joint wheeze by South Wales and the Met to land one of London's smartest armourers. No, no, no – *the* smartest, by a furlong. Grenville Hollings and Eustace meant well but no education, no calibre, you could say.

Dilsom sat down. "A real treat, Len, to see you again. You're looking rosy."

"I can't talk now, Hector."

He said it straight, matter-of-fact, without any attempt to whisper, as though without need of secrecy and as though saying something he had agreed with others. This suddenly terrified Dilsom and he wanted to turn at once and look properly where Len had seemed to stare just now. Christ, it had been mad after all to come, mad and arrogant. He longed to grab the Easter egg box and pull out the goody. That was the point with Len, it would be in fine killing order even if bait. Somehow, though, Dilsom sat still. "Not talk? Why, Len?" he muttered.

"I can't, that's all."

"Where are they? God, Len, who?"

Everdon sighed. "No, I mean I *won't* talk to you. On account of me, me only. Nobody's here. You think I'd bring someone?" The sharp, red face grew sad and even sharper. If he dropped hard forward suddenly, he'd cut the table in half like an axe. Yet Dilsom had heard some women went for Len. Wasn't there a chic, regular partner these days, even a child? The story was Len had a warm side and a nice jokiness late some evenings.

"Won't talk?" Dilsom said.

"Conversation with you. I can't."

"But, you *are* talking. I thought a meal, Len. No rush."

"Well, yes, I'm talking to say I can't talk."

"We talked on the phone."

"And that's enough. Not now."

Dilson gazed into the blank, brown eyes. "Because—"

"Of course because. You've gone, Hector. This egg is £490. No VAT," Everdon replied.

"That's not too extortionate. Not eggstortionate! In the circumstances."

"No, in the circumstances it's not. The circumstances are

you can't go anywhere else, and especially not to your police friends. I offer confidentiality at every stage, and so on. Ruger P-85, 15 magazine, 9 mm, thirty rounds. Pay any way you like. As usual."

"Up front." Dilsom leaned forward and whispered hard at him. "You won't talk and yet you brought the gun. I mean, why did you come the distance, use petrol if—? Well, you wouldn't do it just for a sale, Len. Not you, not just for money. Not just for five hundred, anyway."

"I'm a trader, that's all. Traders trade. Traders go to where the customer is. I'm on nobody's side. Hector, I don't want to know who you are now or where," Everdon replied. He touched the Easter egg box. "This is part of the past. It commemorates. Standard price, with a tenner discount for previous business. I'd do the same for almost anyone. Have done the same."

"Yes, I see." Dilsom heard the underlying message.

Everdon said: "We go to the self-service queue for meals. Get the money on to my tray then. You're carrying fifties? Say put them between two pieces of bread? In a serviette? As you like. Pay separately for the food."

Dilsom could sympathise. He knew what Everdon saw when he looked at him. "Len, shall I eat at another table, if I sicken you? Take the egg now? Pay and get out of your sight, in the circumstances?"

"No, we'll lunch together after all the journeying. More companionable."

"But no talk?"

"I can't."

Everdon ate the meal slowly and during his main course, eventually took Dilsom's money from between two slices of granary and put it uncounted in his jacket pocket. Dilsom finished first and sat watching him with fondness. Len ate his sticky pudding and custard, drained the glass of water and left with real dignity, the 1920s style stripey suit helping somehow. Even in a service station anyone could sense that this man had weight and almost integrity. Weight was vital in his game. Dilsom gave him five minutes, then picked up the Easter egg box. It also had weight and this comforted Dilsom as he went to his car to drive home.

Chapter 16

To try to put a few of his anxieties on hold, Brade asked for a meeting with Raging Bullfinch and walked up from the docks office to headquarters in Cathays Park. It was a grimy winter's morning, with a bit of fog and a bit of snow crowding each other, but all the rebuilding and transformation around brought Brade some genuine joy as he strolled. New life everywhere. Brade felt lucky to be part of the resurrection. Give it ten years and this could be a totally reclaimed area – no pushers' wars, no pimps, no punters' knives, no whores . . . well, they would be findable elsewhere. Brade told himself he might be watching the rebirth of what used to be a brilliant city, the world's coalopolis. That fine glory started to go in 1913, when the Admiralty switched war ships to oil, the bastards. But now here was a 1990s revival, starting where the town had always been at its greatest, the docks. Glancing right from Bute Street towards all the smart development at Atlantic Wharf, he recalled that Burt Lancaster film with half the same, ringing title, *Atlantic City*. That was a story about a man and a town coming triumphantly back from the near dead. Now and again in that film you'd glimpse a notice on some building they were doing up: "Atlantic City, you're back on the map again." Well, same here. Of course, a lot of rough crime in that movie, all the same.

By the time he reached Cathays Park, some of his optimism had gone. This would be in part from the prospect of closeness to Bullfinch, of course. On top of that, though, in the thickening fog and snow, all those huge, Edwardian, white Portland stone buildings of the civic centre looked like blank mausoleums. Suddenly, it had become the kind of weather when Brade liked to be cosy at home reading about Ponting's grand photo opportunities in the South Pole.

The lights of the offices and university looked dim and yellow and defeated from anything more than a few yards. And the Welsh Office seemed less of a beacon than it billed itself. At moments like this, the new year began to feel like most old years, tricky, demeaning, tilted gently but unmistakeably towards muck-up.

Brade would have preferred to write his worries down, on record, in case things went bloodily wrong and blame was officially apportioned, after the way of police forces. In this instance, it would be apportioned by Bullfinch and those above on anyone but Bullfinch and those above, after the way of police forces, and probably especially on Brade. Wasn't Bullfinch called Bullfinch from his flair for fluttering about in panic and dropping trouble on others?

Or was Brade being paranoid? Most of the anxieties he brought to this meeting were about himself rather than Dilsom, and they were so sinister and private he would never put them in a memo. Not that he would be speaking about them, either, come to that. He would be asking for more men to guard the former grass. Yet did Brade really want them? How could he write or say to Bullfinch that in his sounder, professional moments he feared not doing enough to protect Dilsom because an evil, yearning part of him wanted Dilsom dead? How did he explain that this evil was impossible to douse for keeps when he had actually watched Dilsom with – Well, was he going to spell that out for Bullfinch? On balance, Brade decided he must do what he could face to face, never a pretty prospect.

"We ought to keep someone near their house permanently, sir, at least for a week or two."

Bullfinch had a fine, lucid, reasonable style to him, a goodly, man-management style, and this would always persist right up until panic actually swooped and sank notched claws in his balls. "I recognise this is a major concern of yours, Dave, and greatly appreciate that you should have made it such a major concern – the care for our clients – and I'm certainly going to take it on board, you being at the sharp end, seeing things close-to." He gave a genial, cosmic-view smile. "But this isn't how it's done, is it? I mean, all nationwide experience is against. To be avoided is the fortress condition, as I understand it, at all costs. You've talked to Rockmain? Or call it in Boer terms, the *lager* mentality, if you like – people reasonably safe, yes, huddled behind their circle of defensive wagons, as it were, but at what cost? At what cost, Dave?"

Brade thought it sounded quite a happy notion, to be sealed off at home with a rousing book or two about heroism, a few pieces of well-loved music and a couple or so well-loved girls. But he said: "Sir, there are features in the Dilsom's case that—"

"Again as I understand it, the fortress condition is bad in any number of respects, Dave. First, at what we might call the philosophical level, the sort of level one has to think about in my job and rank – woolly as it may sound to you in the field – but, bear with me – at this general, yes, philosophical level, it hinders easy readjustment for our family and integration. But how? you ask. Why, by underlining their separateness. A miniature ghetto. We have Rockmain, adept in these things, working with all his skills in one direction – that is, assimilation – while we would be pulling quite the other way, giving the Dilsoms a siege outlook." Bullfinch laughed very intelligently for a second. "Or more accurately, Dave, no *out*look at all, only an *in*ward look – upon themselves and their own safety."

"I'm thinking of only a short period, sir. I have to try to read the signs. Possibly there's already someone back on the patch from London waiting to get him. They might not send the same man, and they will certainly change the car make, but they'll be here. Someone will move in and look for a chance. These debts get paid."

"But do they, Dave? You've been reading those Jacobean plays set in Italy. In this country, more ex-grasses survive than not. Far more. There are figures. But you're still inferring from the hit on Glyndwr? I do understand. You have to see the possible worst in what shows, what seems to show. I remain sceptical as to the status of that attack, I'm afraid – which you'll say is easy enough for me up here in an executive suite. From the hospital I hear mildly heartening things, thank God. But no actual substantive change, I believe, Dave?"

"No, sir." Best not to trouble Bullfinch with that quite yet.

"Terrible. To lose our highest ranking black officer would be a tragedy. I mean quite apart from the personal aspect, his family and so on. Fine people."

"They can't be with him all the time, sir, and I can't either."

Bullfinch, though, was on the wing. "Then, you see, Dave, further formalising security for Dilsom is sure to draw attention to those inside the fortress, even help identify them. How do we mount a permanent watch without its being spotted by neighbours? At night, for instance. The nationwide experience is you never do it that way. All right, you'll say put our people in a car and do frequent changes of vehicle. But this is a classy spot, Dave, people with nice posssessions – jewellery, state-of-the-art electronic stuff – even stores of hard cash to defeat the Revenue. Such marina householders are nervy about cars parked with men in them, especially in the dark. Burglars change their recce cars, too, don't they? They've learned from us. This would not be like a surveillance operation, would it, Dave, where, all right, we can sometimes find a spot and keep an eye on a household without anybody noticing? Our people would need to be near enough and ready enough to stop an attack, grab intruders. Otherwise, the thing makes no sense. So, the neighbours start wondering who these men in the cars are. Possibly they ring us and we have to give them a comforting hint that it's OK, this is police. And then they ask themselves, why police? They guess this is protection for somebody. Who? The Dilsoms? Why? You see the hazards, Dave? This is not just my thinking. I hope I'm not as arrogant as that. I'm doing what I'm paid to do and drawing on far-flung experience, as it's formulated for us – a tried wisdom. As I understand."

"It's not just that, sir."

"Sorry, yes, you're right, I'm on a theory trip, rather. Not just what, Dave?"

"An attack on him. I'm afraid of someone bolting from inside."

Bullfinch, seated away from his desk in an easy chair, nodded, unperturbed. "Fair point. Carmel might leave him? Yes, of course, that's bound to be on the cards. I've considered the possibility. She's getting all-round stress, might feel safer, sexually sprucer, away from Dilsom. But do we really care much if she quits, Dave? She's not the target. I doubt whether a vengeance team would go after her. These people are not usually like that, I understand. They have their code. In any case, she could probably disappear very efficiently."

"It's not Carmel I worry about." Brade was in another easy chair, fiercely uneasy about Bullfinch's calm.

"Dilsom himself might flit? You really think so?"

"One of the children," Brade replied.

This got to him. Bullfinch's body tightened and grew hunched, seemed suddenly smaller in the chair, as though he were trying to disappear into the upholstery. The plump, lineless, masterful face looked desperate for a moment, itself like a lost child's. Then he managed a recovery. Abruptly, he stood, walked very briskly and upright to an open wall safe and brought out a file. Now, he went to his desk and sat behind it. Perhaps he felt his casual approach had been abused. Opening the file, he carefully read the top sheet. "We're talking of two children not yet seven, aren't we, Dave?"

"Almost seven."

"Old enough to run from home in a strange city?"

"Not a strange city, sir, so they're told."

Bullfinch hardened his bright, blue, slit eyes. He was in shirt sleeves, a brilliantly white, cotton shirt with small, oblong, thick, gold cufflinks. His hands were slim and long, like a pianist's or couturier's ought to be. He always kept them prominent. They said precision and coolness so couldn't be more useful to such a prime gibberer. "Which child might go, in your view? Or perhaps you think both?" He did not smirk, though, or edge his tone.

"Oh, the boy."

"Because he's a boy?"

"No. Because he's making himself bottle it all up."

"Bottle all what up, Dave?"

"The questions."

"Which questions?"

"About the lies they're being fed, sir."

Bullfinch made some minor, imaginary correction with his pen on the document before him. "That could surely be phrased differently, Dave. Now, really, couldn't it? We've been through this argument before. They have to be helped. It's not a matter of truth or lies. Inappropriate term."

"The girl shows her doubts, and will probably be convinced eventually. Perhaps already. Jeremy swallows it all without any trouble. Seems to."

"Possibly he does."

Brade sat forward, vowing to shake him again. "I think we could get a sudden collapse. He'll break out to find something he can trust. We don't want him loose, lost, do we, sir? Not when we don't know who's about the area." He struck a bit lower. "How would it look, if it really turned bad?"

"Rockmain says this, Dave?"

"I haven't—"

Bullfinch displayed both hands, palms up in front of him, a gesture of more reasonableness, even capitulation. "If Rockmain reported it I would certainly have to take his analysis on board. That's not to suggest I discount your opinion, Dave. How could I, for God's sake? You're there, on the ground, in touch, whereas I – Yes. However, Rockmain, we're told, *is* the expert. The psychologist, for what it's worth. I'm surprised he hasn't come to me himself on a matter like this. I'll have him in, shall I?" Bullfinch reached out towards his intercom switch.

"I haven't discussed it with him, sir," Brade replied.

"Ah." He did not complete the movement.

"From watching the kids, talking to their mother."

Bullfinch yawned, stood again and went at leisurely speed back to his armchair. He sat and stretched out his legs, hands meshed in relaxation behind his head. The crisis had died: there were categories of information and advice: some items would come from an acknowledged, officially backed guru like Rockmain, and these needed to be noted, acted on, possibly panicked over, on pain of CV blots; and then there were items from someone of Brade's standing which, on this kind of occult topic, could be accepted politely and set aside swiftly and safely. If Brade were talking about a pimp-beaten whore, or crack trade at one of the docks clubs, Bullfinch would give attention. "You're certainly entitled to a view and, yes, to extrapolate, Dave. I say again, I'm up here, cut off by bits of paper." He brushed the open file disparagingly with the knuckles of his elegant right hand. "More or less entirely at the mercy of bits of paper. If I don't listen to my lads and lasses at the sharp end whom on earth should I listen to? Oh, absolutely."

"As I see it, sir, a very bright child loses faith in his mother and father, sees them conniving with outsiders to tell obvious – conniving to cocktail fictional and real and call it real: mightn't he break up, lose all bearings, launch out to anywhere, to anywhere but where this is happening to him?"

"Deep water, Dave."

"Plenty of that very near their house."

"But as far I know, there's no instance, nationwide, I mean, of a child in this type of situation made so – so, what shall we say? Disorientated? So disorientated that he/she does a runner. That species of information would surely be circulated. Mind you, I do recognise, naturally, that whatever the received wisdom might be, it is a *general* wisdom only. We are dealing with people, and people are first and foremost individuals."

"I believe so, sir."

"Their cases can be different. Sure. Even with children. But my position has to be, hasn't it, Dave, that I respect the words of my special adviser? I mean, I listen also to you and to anyone else with first-hand observation of these people. Perhaps, though, ultimately, I have to give most weight to what this specialist tells me. Otherwise, why the hell is he here? I could be held remiss, and justifiably, if I ignored him, flouted him, on a sensitive matter like this. And the point is, Dave, I've had no indications at all from Rockmain along the lines you cite. In fact, I hear only good from him about the children's progress, an equal progress, as far as I can judge, as one might expect from twins. Yes, I would be flouting him."

"If Jeremy were to go, sir, or do something similarly desperate, we—"

"I think in that case, if blame required to be apportioned, I would see it falling entirely on Andrew Rockmain. Certainly none on you, Dave. None on anyone in this force. For example, I would regard myself as quite in the clear, oh, quite. We did not ask for this outside aid but we have been told we must make use of him. My view would be that if there were to be tragic slip-ups of any sort, he would be culpable for not having spotted the likelihood and informed me, us. What would that mean, 'something similarly desperate', Dave?"

"Sir, this child—"

"My own feeling, I have to say, Dave, is that Rockmain knows his trade and that the kind of situation you posit is exceptionally unlikely to materialise, without his giving ample early warning. Now, please, I would not have you regard this as in any sense a rebuff, Dave. I take note of your deep commitment to this operation, and to the safety of those in your, our, charge. It is entirely admirable, and only what I would expect from you."

Bullfinch pointed towards the desk. "An incidental matter that occurred to me on rereading the file, Dave: I see we're told by the Yard Dilsom is cock-happy. This could produce some difficult situations. Do we see any evidence of it?"

"Of course, we're watching him for only a small fraction of the day and night, sir—"

"Yes, Dave, I've taken that point."

"Neither Glyndwr nor I has observed anything in that line when we are doing surveillance."

"Of course, he might have spotted you and held back. These London lads, smart. Presumably, if there were a woman, women, we're talking about whores."

"Oh, well, sir, I wouldn't say—"

"He's been here no time, Dave. And under restrictions. He couldn't have built a relationship, even Dilsom."

"I'd have thought he—"

"Whores being dangerous terrain, clearly, Dave. Taken into rough rooms, waste ground, backs of cars. Pimps casting their eye and wondering about him, if he gets to be a regular. He would be laying himself open. You ought to have a word. Oh, of course I see it's awkward – a man's private life. One is hardly likely to – I mean, one would hardly come bearing in, say, on your good self and ask whether you use whores. Or ask anyone, normally. But this man's private life just has to be chartable for a while. Make it clear, no moral point involved at all. Well, plainly. Safety, that's all. We couldn't care less where he's dipping it, could we, Dave, if there weren't these other considerations, I mean, could we, Dave?"

*　　*　　*

105

Luckily, Brade found Boadicia at the beginning of a lunch-time duty tour and scuttled back to the flat with her. It might have been all the talk about whores that made him long for her company. Anything Bullfinch looked down on must be fine. Also, Brade knew himself not to be Captain Oates, and he longed to huddle for a while with comforts and his worries and scars in the igloo, fortress, *lager*, whatever it was called, and however useless it would turn out ultimately as shelter. "Ultimately" had not come, and it was now he needed refuge. Perhaps tonight he would go down to look around the marina and Julie's office building again. No "perhaps": he must.

If she were there late once more, should he wait till Dilsom zipped up and left, then pop in, quote the Venerable Bullfinch, and ask whether she, too, saw herself as a whore? Did it matter? Yes, it mattered. His companion at the moment was a whore and delightful with it, but – Yes, there obviously had to be a "but". Did Brade see Julie like that? Of course not. Just the same, might he have a duty to reclaim her from this one-time villain and full-time shagger-around? "Reclaim" – a term they would use in old tales about fallen women, and the need to save them. And a term he sometimes used about the city and the docks. It seemed such a noble idea, an idea from that other, better age Brade so often dreamed of, an age with clear values, gallantry.

Immediately, then, that recurrent, foul temptation nudged him: should he make Dilsom's destruction easy, so he could no longer taint her? Should he even let them reach Dilsom's family, say his son, because that would probably destroy Dilsom, too, one way or the other? These were questions he wished to discuss fully though informally with Boadicia, or possibly Glyndwr, but only if Glyndwr relapsed into coma. By bloody accident, Glyndwr already knew too much about Brade's emotional life. The kind of discussion he fancied now had to be with someone who would not and could not reply, because, of course, he already knew the proper answers: the questions were not to be asked, were literally unspeakable, or should be, and not gallant at all. Following conversations with Raging Bullfinch, he often felt a need for something more one-sided, his side. With Boadicia or

Glyndwr when unconscious, and only when unconscious, he had control.

He put on the record of *Somewhere Along The Way* and for a while foxtrotted with Boadicia in silence, happily knowing he could start the consoling, opaque chat and so on whenever he liked. First, he needed the familiar and unstroppy to balm him, without talk.

After a time he said: "Sorry, Boadicia, yes, you spotted it, of course you did, yes, I'm a little depressed. Yes, naturally it's Bullfinch. One routed him in the long run, as ever, but these set-tos take it out of one intellectually. You ask if I'm in Mensa? Me? Or I? Never tried. Honestly. Well, no time, I suppose. And isn't joining a bit ostentatious? For a bobby?"

"What is 'bobby'?"

"Exactly. I don't want her cornered, hurt, worse, by some posse, because she happens to have been taken in by that glib piece of fink rot. Oh, yes, we're grateful to him and his kind, live by their disclosures, but finks are finks."

"Finks?"

Someone thumped the door, but it was not Cliffy's "Behold I stand out here on the landing and knock" code.

"Police?" Boadicia said.

"Not at all. Why should it be?"

"How police always come. Like this." With her fists she mimed banging on a door. As usual Brade had placed the Magnum on a side table when he arrived home. He picked up the gun and holster now, but, instead of hiding them again, the fitted the harness, then slipped on his jacket. He opened the door. Although the landing was shadowy, he made out at once a woman police officer in uniform staring at him.

Christ, Boadicia's dark experiences made her right. "Yes?" he said. "A message?"

From out of sight around a corner of the landing came a yell of triumph and Cliffy in full church gear including cap emerged, grotesque with laughter. In his hand he held a long stick with which he had been supporting the inflatable WPC at Brade's doorway. "I just knew Enid would look grand as a constable, Dave," he said. "I blew her up a bit firmer than usual, to give this dear doll real doorstepping presence. May I?" He entered the flat. "Relax, Boadicia. Not a raid. I've always responded to uniforms, especially authority figures. I was having a wardress off and on when I was younger, and the serge she used to turn up in was heavenly. I thought the navy blue tunic and sharp-creased trousers were sure to suit Enid. Don't you think so? Only hired."

He put Enid in a chair and stood before the fireplace, grand, crypt-dark in his cassock, still holding the stick which was something like the crook of the Good Shepherd although Cliffy's.

"I popped down to say there's a bucketful of Christian trouble, Dave. Some creep in the building saw me the other day, you know, when we were going back upstairs from here, Enid and I."

Brade sat down. "Recognised Enid as a blow-up? Saw the two of you come from this flat?"

He raised a hand in a be-at-peace-brother mode. "No, you're all right, Dave. Why should you be implicated? Whoever it was thought I'd been out on the town and had just come in from the street. This is the problem. The slimy sods have been in touch with the cathedral about it – 'bringing the Church into disrepute', 'disco-grooving with a doll'. You can imagine the kind of lurid rubbish. Apparently, the suggestion is I'd taken Enid to a golden oldies session in Queen Street. Only wish I had the nerve. She's far nicer than some of the birds I took to dances. Nicer even than the wardress. Well, hence my feelings for her, obviously."

"Cathedral officials have been at you?"

"Wanting details. Interrogation, Dave. Demanding our itinerary that night. Enid's and mine. Thank heaven they don't burn at the stake nowadays."

"Enid would torch." Brade groaned. "Anyway, what's supposed to be so wrong, for God's sake? You create a fictional person, that's all. In my game we have experts who do nothing else, and on government money – fabricating identities, inducing born-again lives. Cliff, would it be better if you said it was a private thing that night, not a public dance spot – told them you'd been here? Just a soirée?"

Hale-Garning slapped Brade's mantelpiece with his hand, the cassock movement like a wing beat of some tall, black, quite friendly bird. His deeply unholy face went for a moment into a wondrous grin, vibrant with gratitude: "You're a right fucking saint, know that, Dave? You'd alibi Cliffy and Enid? Thank you, thank you. But not good for a senior cop to host doll parties, not good at all." Cliff leaned forward and touched Brade's jacket. "Tooled up like a 'Nam gunship, Enid, yet this lad here is above all a true soul. This is the man who is my neighbour, who lives beneath me, so to speak, and does not pass by on the other side. I look forward to hobnobbing with him when we are both on the Other Side. But I'd never draw you in, Dave. How would you be able to put the frighteners on villains in the interview room if they knew you did foursomes at home with a faded old rev, his latex paramour and a floozy? Haven't the legislators already pissed you about enough by introducing recording machines?"

"Floozy?" Boadacia said. "What is this word also?"

"My cathedral lot would broadcast it, not a doubt. Civilisation depends on you, Dave, and the problems you handle are short-term and very pressing. The Church has eternity." The music still played and, after propping his stick against the fireplace and straightening Enid's peaked cap, Hale-Garning took her out for a dance. Brade watched.

"Dave," Cliff said, over Enid's shoulder, "someone from the cathedral has been instructed to visit the flats, questioning. He'll ask residents about me – general behaviour, nasty habits, that kind of thing – seeking more stuff for an indictment. I think I know the greasy jerk they'll send – Caspar Indicay, probably – bent as a bathhouse, born to do harm and evil, and especially against yours truly. But, Dave, I know they'd pay lavish attention to any testimonial from a totally unblemished, famed, heavyweight dick – incidentally, words to make Caspar swoon. Dave, could I—?"

"Of course. I'll be fulsome."

Hale-Garning sat down, grey-faced, suddenly miserable looking against the drab cloth of the cassock, and folded Enid lovingly on to his lap. There was something disturbing, virtually chaotic, about this tableau: a woman officer on a vicar's knee, even though a rubber officer, even though a vicar like Cliff.

Brade said: "It seems like a harshness to Enid, I know, but

you'd better not go upstairs together this time. I'll lend you a suitcase."

He stayed impassive for a few moments and then nodded sadly. "Yes, thanks." Hale-Garning pulled the plug and Enid subsided slowly, almost noiselessly, in his arms, like the gradual but utter collapse of law and order and sense. At the end, Cliffy seemed to be holding only the clothes, and might have been a priest changing careers. He muttered: "As to this Indicay, he's one of your what's called *caring* priests, Dave – except when he's getting the boot in to me. I tell you this so you can be on guard against his smarms when he calls. Lots of Visiting the Sick, that sort of thing. Well, he's always bleating about your deep sleep lad, Jenkins. Suggests he be included in cathedral prayers."

"It might help."

"You fret about him, do you, Dave?"

"He's unprotected much of the time."

"Oh?"

"Yes, they won't allow full-time guards."

Hale-Garning brightened. "Could I help there, Dave? I owe you so much."

"How, Cliff?"

"I really think I could help there, Dave."

"But how?" Brade asked.

"It would be a privilege," Hale-Garning replied.

Chapter 17

This was quite a hospital. It excited Rick Cole. Of course, he knew the name of it from when Uncle Bart was ringing up asking condition and putting on the black accent. He knew the ward number, as well. Well, he would not have travelled without information. Information was the most crucial factor in any task. Someone who was longtime unconscious would be in a separate room, probably, but as long as you knew the ward you could soon find which. He had the Ruger in the pocket of his long black topcoat. Len Everdon could have sold him a holster, but Len said holsters, waist or shoulder, always gave a bulge, it did not matter how well they were made, and you did not want that if you were going into some area where there might be really sharp security. You would have thought this was just a general remark from Len, but, of course, the smart bugger knew all right that Rick Cole *would* be going into an area where there might be sharp security. No might, would. What Len had in his head was what was known as a scenario. He could be so clever. He saw it all and said not very much that anyone could nail on him. This was why he stayed working and free, and why he had a girl like that one in the bikini, who probably stayed fairly faithful despite the adam's apple and clothes.

This hospital had some great corridors, almost tunnels, underneath the main building and spreading all ways. Rick Cole had been hoping for this. He knew hospitals. When he was eighteen and thinking about a career, he worked for nearly a year as a hospital porter. Of course, Uncle Bart said what kind of slob job was that for someone in his family, but now a situation like this came up and showed how useful this time was – more good information. When Uncle Bart and Rick's father said it was not necessary to go for the black cop now, they were saying it because they could not think how to get someone in a hospital in a private room, not really because they thought the black cop did not matter. Fear. Rick Cole was young, but he had the experience that made this part of the outing seem very nice and possible. He knew he had to keep on and on, telling himself he could be right and Uncle Bart could be wrong, because within him always lived the fear that usually it was Uncle Bart who had it right.

This was what a lot of modern hospitals were like. They had these corridors underneath to send the dirty bedclothes or contaminated stuff down to by freight lifts in big skips on wheels. Then the sheets could be wheeled away to the laundry, and the others to the incinerator. Of course, bodies came down this way, too, on their way to the morgue, so visitors did not meet them in the usual lifts. Also, a lot of the building's pipes and wiring would be boarded into the ceiling of these tunnels, so electricians and engineers could get at it all easily, for repairs. It all meant that there were usually some people in the tunnels, but not too many, and nobody knew who was supposed to be there, anyway. You could have a good saunter, getting the layout of the place, knowing he was up there, a couple of floors above you, and knowing there were lifts and stairs that could get you down here fast after it was done, so you did not have to go out through Reception, where the alarms would undoubtedly be banging. What it made Rick feel like, moving through these tunnels, remembering the routes and exits, was like some animal, even a rat. He did not mind that. Many animals were clever, especially rats. They had learned how to find all sorts of secret ways for getting to places and escaping. Uncle Bart would be lost down here, lost and scared and useless. That was definite. There was a terrific humming all the time from all the machinery in the hospital and the energy going along the wires and pipes, and Rick felt he was a part of that, too – not just like a bright and hard animal, but someone with power. He put his hand into his pocket and gripped the Ruger for a minute as he walked.

Just exits. That's what he wanted to know about, and did know about now. He would go in properly through Reception, because you could draw attention coming out of a freight lift on to the ward, or using the special, staff staircase. On the way out, of course, he would have to risk all that. What he could not let happen now was for someone to notice him and stop him before the job was done. That would be just the sort of thing Uncle Bart would expect to happen to him. He left the tunnels and entered through the main doors with some other afternoon visitors. He saw the direction signs to the wards and went up by the stairs. None of the other visitors did that. People in a lift could be very close together and they noticed one another, and could remember one another's faces and clothes. He just wanted to appear at the top of the stairs and sort of drift into that ward solo. He had the brown hat on today because he thought it made him look more ordinary than the other one, which was too racy.

What he realised, of course, was there could be people sitting with this cop. There might be guards, there might be family, his bird, there might be friends. This was the thing about people who comatosed – all sorts wanted to get close, all sorts wanted to be the one who brought him out of it, by talk or touch or even a kiss, like Sleeping Beauty. Rick had seen a lot of that in the other hospital, and it was understandable. It was crazy, because the brain would only come out it when it wanted to, if it ever did – yes, crazy, but understandable. He never told anyone in the other hospital they were stupid to wait. Here, now, people in the room could be a problem, obviously. He did not want to hurt any of them. The black cop had not spoken, so they knew nothing and there was no reason to get them out of the way, too. But, of course, they would want to protect this sleeper. If there was a guard, he would be *paid* to protect this sleeper, and he would be carrying something to protect him with. What it came down to was, the black cop might not be the only one who was hurt. Rick Cole had realised this from the start. What he had done was what was known as "taken it on board". He wanted to finish the black cop and get out. This was not even the main job, after all. It should be kept limited and simple. But, if it could not be like that, he would have to play it how it went.

He stepped into the ward. This was just how he remembered things from the other place. He was right, he was right. He could do it, he could do it. But he had started to shake a bit.

He never shook on the night he did the black cop. Things had moved too fast. The same when taking the Peugeot. Here, it was drawn out. Maybe he had spent too long feeling great in those fucking tunnels. If he pulled the trigger here, was he ever really going to get back to them?

What you had was the private rooms on both sides first, and then the ward beyond. That was great, wasn't it? He need not walk among the beds looking lost. Two of the rooms had their doors open and he could see women lying there. He did not put his hand into his coat pocket yet. That would make him look like some crude heavy. He was not that. He had come to avenge a brother, a fine assignment, and the road to it began here.

The door of one of the other rooms opened suddenly and a middle-aged black woman came out, closed the door and then stood a little way in front of it, head bent forward and obviously weeping. She was muttering something, perhaps "Never. It won't ever change. Never." Rick Cole would have ignored her. In hospitals you expected weeping. He was grateful to the woman, that was all. This would be the room. He turned towards it, still shaking, but not so anyone would notice, and now he did put his hand in his pocket. The Ruger would give him solidity again, wouldn't it?

And then from somewhere, Rick Cole did not see from where, a fucking priest or vicar in full dark clobber and hat came forward and stood in front of the door, and put his arm around the woman. In his other hand, he held a clipboard. "You, sir, for instance," he said to Rick Cole. "Your name is all we need."

Cole, unnerved, stopped, and the shaking increased. Jesus, Uncle Bart was right, *was right*. Uncle Bart was always right, this killing could not be done – or not done by Rick Cole, a kid whose only training was in a slob job. Police dressed as priests?

"I ask for your name, and so give you mine first. Hale-Garning. Rev. What I'm doing is gathering names for what would, in other contexts, be called a petition, I suppose."

Rick Cole should have shoved him and the woman to the side. But it seemed too late. That power he had thought was part of him in the tunnels had left. The rat-like push and ruthlessness were abruptly gone.

"To try to persuade the cathedral authorities to mount special prayers for our friend in here, Glyndwr Jenkins. They dither, if you'll pardon the coarseness. A list might exercise some influence. You'll know the circumstances of the case, I'm sure, sir. Yes? This is his dear mother, I think. Can you so help, sir? Your name on this piece of paper."

"I'm in the wrong ward," Rick Cole said. He turned and left.

Chapter 18

There was a time then, a long-lasting, foul time, when Rick Cole thought, Forget it and go home. As he galloped from that ward, and galloped from the hospital, he tried none of the so brilliant exit ploys he had taken half the afternoon preparing. Freight lifts, staff stairs, the lovely, helpful tunnel network – he never thought of them. All he wanted was to reach the 605 and drive, clear out of this place – not just *this* place, the hospital, but the town, the area, the whole assignment. He wanted to be in a place he knew. He wanted to be where there was support. Christ, the terrible loneliness, stepping into that ward, seeing that mock-up priest in the full, fucking, hellish gear, even a tassle on the hat. That priest would be on his hand radio now, with the description. That priest could be behind him, bringing out something big-calibre and final from under the robes. Rick Cole took half a glance back as he ran, and listened hard for shouts. What warning would the bastard call out if any: "Stop, armed priest"?

Rick Cole hurtled down the ordinary visitors stairs and was sill rushing when he passed Reception. People here were going to remember him. He had to get ahead of that radio call, though. Where were the rest of them? Jesus, he wanted Uncle Bart here, Uncle Bart and his father if possible, but especially Uncle Bart. He could read a situation, even when disaster came. He would see the way. He would give the right orders. That's what Rick Cole needed – orders. What a fool to try this solo. A petition for prayers! That mad fucking tale. Were they just playing about with him, laughing at him? And asking his name! Cold cheek. *Tell us who you are, sonny boy, so we'll know what to write on the charge sheet.* He used to think out-of-town police had no idea. Something else he had wrong.

He was at the car. As he climbed in, he took a more thorough look behind, but saw nothing to scare him. He stared around ahead of him, too. They might be working some subtle ploy here, letting him get out, so he could lead to the rest of the team. They might not believe someone so young in a brown hat and squatter's overcoat could handle all this on his own. But everything seemed clear. He drove up towards the M4 entrance, still watching hard – in the mirror and everywhere. What he had to think was, once he reached the motorway and they saw he had finished here, they might stop him. He'd be the bird in hand then. If Uncle Bart was here he would probably have his fine radio with him that picked up all the police talk. Rick Cole could have done with that, but he knew that what he heard on it might turn him more scared and helpless. He saw how it was with him, how it always was. He could handle three quarters of a big job, manage it with true smoothness and perfect system. And then would come this last quarter, the important one. This was where he was always left behind. This was where he turned out to be a kid, just the way Uncle Bart said. It had happened today. It had happened when he knocked the black cop, against all orders. It was to do with youth, that was all. When he was as old as Uncle Bart he would be as good as Uncle Bart. You could not hurry experience. He had tried to hurry it. God, so he knew a bit about pushing hospital trolleys. Did that make him a mastermind? Fool.

On the motorway, he let the Peugeot build some speed, but nothing mad, nothing to send signals. It was late in the afternoon now and getting dark fast. Soon, it would be hard to know whether he had a tail. Headlights in the mirror all looked the same to him. Some could read the difference. That was the kind of experience he needed now, not the kind he gained as a sodding dogsbody in a hospital. At the first exit, with some Welsh name on it, he drove off and did about a mile into a housing estate. If anything came with him or suddenly appeared in front he would know they had him marked. He stopped, with the engine running. Nothing showed. He gave it twenty minutes and still nothing. Then he had a bit of a smile, the first for a quite a time, and pushed the hat back on his head. He was sweating up there. Staring in the mirror off and on, he caught a view of himself in this hat and thought it made him look sharp at that angle, even though brown. He thought he looked the sort who would have the money to buy a big, top of the range Peugeot like this. Or maybe a BMW or even Porsche would be more right for someone of his style. He slipped over into the passenger seat and folded down the sun visor there so he could take a proper gaze at himself in the mirror fixed behind it. What he thought he looked like was some businessman who had made it fast, but who did not let the worries of the firm turn him dull or miserable. That face under the hat said there was rich fun in him, and real guts. This was a lad who would meet a few troubles, maybe – well, didn't everyone in a roar-ahead business? – meet troubles, yes, but troubles he would deal with, and deal with with a happy, unbeaten grin, too. This was a poky street where he had parked. This was the wrong sort of street for a car like this to be in, and the wrong sort of street for Rick Cole to be in, lurking, waiting, hiding. He pushed the visor back up, got behind the wheel again and moved off, turning towards the M4 again.

That had been a mistake at the hospital, no question, but, when you really thought about it, not such a big mistake after all. The point was, he had not been caught. This was the same kind of situation as when he had hit the black cop. Sometimes, you did things because you had to, if you wanted to be around to handle other matters later, possibly more important. When he gave the black cop that knock with the wrench, it was so he could get back to Dad and Uncle Bart and bring them a gifted report. When he left that ward today, it was so he did not get snared by that cop/priest and identified. If that had happened, where was the rest of the job? Or maybe the priest was a real priest after all. He did not seem to have come after Rick or called up aid. But, even so, he . . . even so he would have spoiled that task for anyone, not just for Rick Cole – getting in the way like that, and the spooky uniform, and asking a name. Uncle Bart would have shit himself if that priest had come in front of him like that, just when a task was starting. Rick Cole had been damn bright not to try to exit through a freight lift or the staff stairs, because that would have shown he had been at the hospital on some rough mission and needed

118

a secret way out. It would have screamed "villain". He had not thought out bit by bit about how to escape at the time, but it was instinct, or what was also known as flair. If you had that, it did not matter how young you were. This was a supreme gift.

When he reached the motorway Rick Cole turned back towards Cardiff. There was one thing Uncle Bart might be right about – maybe the only thing. It was that this black cop could never be the real job, and it was a waste of time stalking him. Probably he would never come round, anyway, but just dwindle away and never speak. Rick had seen cases like that in the other hospital. Those wrench blows had been good ones. Don't forget the whole assignment, but forget the hospital. The main part of the duty was still there to be tackled. When you really thought about it, he had done well at the hospital today. He had seen what the situation was very fast and had seen what to do about it, also very fast. He was free and ready again. It would have been so feeble to hurry home. Childish. There was no need for it. He took a hand off the wheel for a couple of moments and half pulled the Ruger from his pocket, enjoying its weight.

When Rick Cole was at the marina again, Dilsom's car was outside the house and, sitting in the 605, Rick watched from Schooner Way. He pulled the brown trilby down over part of his face now, but not enough to show the haircut. You had to adapt. This was the kind of subtlety Uncle Bart kept on about and which came natural to some, although Uncle Bart would never believe that, only that it was true about himself, naturally. Rick had to think Dilsom was home now, and he had to hope Dilsom would go out later, where he could be seen to, still before Uncle Bart and Dad arrived. What a giggle – they turn up, and Dilsom is already only a memory. This would shut Uncle Bart up for ever. If so, it might not be necessary to do anything savage to him, he being a relation after all, and with definite good points intermittently.

It shook Rick to find he thought of Dilsom only as Dilsom, not Hector Vale. It was like giving in to the whole dirty hideaway scheme, and he was ashamed. But Rick had forced the new name into his head originally in case he needed to ask a milkman or postman where the family lived. Mind,

119

that would have been only if he was desperate, because people remembered this kind of question and could later turn up at identity parades full of the fucking noble urge to citizen. Just as fall-back, though, he had taught himself to think of Hector Vale as Geoffrey Dilsom, and had repeated the name to himself a dozen times that day and often since. Names did not matter much, but it would definitely be good old Hector Vale he killed, for what good old Hector Vale did, not Geoffrey Dilsom. Hector might like to think he was born again as Geoffrey Dilsom. Well, see if Geoffrey Dilsom could be born again again, when Geoffrey Dilsom was full of 9 mm metal from a Ruger and from Brydon Maurice Cole via Rick.

It was dark, with a good, heavy mist. Now and then he could hear a foghorn sounding off in that bit of sea whatever-it-was which they had here, though definitely genuine, being important for a marina. He could just about see Dilsom's car. That was all right. If it was hard to see it was hard to be seen, and this would probably be a sweet night for Dilsom to slip out unobserved later in search of extra. People must feel very maritime lying in bed here, listening to the foghorn bleats, and thinking of fine ships from all round the world progressing slowly towards their haven through the mighty, eternal, rolling sewage. One day he might get a place on a marina himself. Water and boating folk he reckoned he could take to. Think of Sir Edward Heath and his complexion.

He had the windows up to keep the muck out, but no music on, because he wanted to listen. More subtlety, more wisdom, and after a while he thought he heard running footsteps from somewhere in the fog towards Dilsom's house, very light, frequent footsteps, possibly a child's. It was late for that, but when he lowered the window an inch or two he was sure. Immediately then he saw a boy of about six or seven coming towards the car out of the fog, yes, running, perhaps sobbing. Once he glanced back, as though expecting pursuit. He staggered, then straightened again. Rick sank a bit in the seat, pushed his hat down harder. Dilsom had children, didn't he? Twins? About this age. The boy was round-faced, with dark hair, not like Dilsom. He tried to remember Dilsom's Angie, or whoever she was now. Wasn't she dark, and a round, very pretty face? Of course very pretty, or Dilsom would not have picked her. If Uncle Bart was here he would know right off from looking if this kid was a Dilsom kid, even through fog, or he would say he did.

This was a cold evening in January, but the boy was not dressed for it. What it looked like to Rick was, this boy had come from a house in a rush, no time to get proper clothes, and the boy still did not know if anyone in the house had heard him go, which was why he looked back. He was doing a runner. What it looked like was that nobody in the house *did* know, because they would have instantly come after him, no question, in this weather, wearing only some dungaree trousers and a T-shirt from what could be some Cardiff sports team. It would not keep out the cold and fog. His mother and father definitely would not want him out like this in the dark and fog with all this water around, but nobody was chasing him and there was no shouting from back in the fog. What was the matter with him? Maybe too much stress in all this moving and changing names. Now he was close, Rick could see he looked bad, yes, sobbing, and like he was lost and maybe sick, say with some fever, his eyes full of wildness and, well, agony, yes. If he *had* a mother and father. You never knew with small kids these days. This might not be a Dilsom kid, but from some other house where he was not looked after properly or even abused – there was a lot of that about now people stayed home so much through satellite TV. That could be why there was agony in his eyes, the kind of things that could happen. Families could be great, but they could also be a pain in the arse. Yes.

This kid, six or seven, it was probably the first time he was ever out by himself, and now, here he was, a dark evening and in a fog. If it was Dilsom's boy, he might not even know this area at all, coming here from London and the family lying low. This lad did not know where he was going, this was obvious. He ran across Schooner Way without looking and in a fog like this any car could have had him. Where he was running was down towards that bit of the old dock which was now a sort of lake, to give the special seaport touch to the marina. The boy might not even know about this water. This was where Rick had seen the other cop rushing up on the last visit, carting that weapon, nearly falling over the barrel of it. That old dock would still be deep although a lake, and this child was galloping towards it like a hare from a whippet. He did not even glance at Rick in the 605, just went right past.

The thing was, obviously, pick up this kid now and this was a way to Dilsom, if it was Dilsom's kid, which it would be, for almost sure. Take him somewhere, then get on the phone to Dilsom if the kid knew the number, because he would be ex-directory, naturally, or a letter if not, and saying to Dilsom he could come and collect his son at some useful spot, but if he told police this was the end for the kid. Dilsom would come, he would have to, his wife would make sure of that, and this would be to a place where it would be easy to give him some of the Ruger, not like climbing in through the window of his house with the best alarms, or getting into some girl's place where he was giving it to her. Even hitting him in one of these streets could be tricky. You never knew who was about, and police would have some sort of off and on lookout here. But some field or a wood, which there must be some of fairly close . . . this would make it really straightforward. It would not need subtlety then, because all the subtlety would have come first, by getting the kid, then getting Dilsom to this useful spot. Following this death, what to do with the kid would be tricky, no question, because this kid would have seen a lot and could help police, although only six.

Rick left the 605 and ran down towards the water after the boy. Luckily, he had trainers on, so no noise. The fog was thicker near the lake. There were smart lights all round, but you could only see the ones closest to you, and they did not do much. He reached the edge of the lake but could not see the lad, or hear his footsteps. It was deserted here. The thing was, the boy could go right or left along the edge of this lake, and Rick did not know which. He stood still and listened for a while. He listened for footsteps, he listened for the sound of someone in the water. It would be a waste, this boy drowning, no use at all. Rick would not be able to help him. He could not swim. He looked around for a life belt to throw if he was in there, but, of course, nothing. This is how it would be at a place like this, of fucking course. They would look after all the pretty stuff, the smart lights and vistas, but what if a six-year-old kid fell in the dock in the fog one night? They never gave a thought to that with their architecture.

Well, he turned right and started to walk. If Uncle Bart was here he would say why not turn left? He would talk like nobody-before-ever-heard of left: like soccer teams had two right wings, but thank God he had just discovered left, the way Isaac Newton discovered the apple. Rick would not have minded asking his Dad or even Uncle Bart now what he would do about this kid if he did find him. Experience did matter sometimes or why did the old exist? The thing was, if he phoned that house later he would not know if the police were listening on it. This was a house they gave Dilsom and they might want to discover who had talked to him and who he had talked to, too. If you said come and collect your boy somewhere you might get the whole flak jacket and beret lot there, marksmanshipping and jumpy. Police did not like people who took kids, even a Dilsom kid. The police could feel like guardians of the innocent when they were looking for a taken kid, and this warmed their souls and thawed out trigger fingers.

Of course, it could be a mistake coming after this kid at all. The thing was, if none of them knew the boy was out Dilsom might leave the house on his gratification search while Rick Cole was down here walking the lakeside and be gone by the time Rick returned. Maybe he had made the same sort of mistake as Uncle Bart said he made last time. Last time, Uncle Bart said Rick forgot who was the target and hit the black cop. Uncle Bart said that even if the way he was hit had had subtlety, which it did not, he said, it would still have been the wrong one to hit. This time, maybe Rick had forgotten who was the target again, and was following this child instead. What he had to think was, maybe deep down he had come after this child because he was worried about him out in this kind of weather at night, and near the water, like he was this child's big brother. But he ought to worry about his own big brother, inside for ever because of this kid's father's bought mouth.

Of course, maybe it would really work – pick up the boy and pull Dilsom out to that useful spot alone to find him and get the job done once and for all. But was this a way of going all round the job, instead of going straight and getting Dilsom

123

now, bullets in the teeth, not all the messing about? That's what the P-85 in his pocket was for. Mess about too long and what could happen is Dad and Uncle Bart might come down and see to Dilsom, so when Rick was ringing up or sending letters about the boy there would be nobody left to answer or come out to a useful spot, and he would be left with the boy and that was all, and having to tell him about his father wasted. Then Dad and Uncle Bart might hear about this, his complete cock-up, because it was the kind of thing the police would broadcast, seeking information, if there was a voice or letters trying to get to Dilsom after he was dead. And then Rick would look a right turd and they would never finish telling him.

Rick leaned against a rail and had a good stare into the fog on the water and around the edge, plus another good listen. All he got was those far off, helpful grunts of the foghorn. So, maybe turn back to the 605 fast and do what he was supposed to be doing and wait for Dilsom to leave on the pussy run. In fact, he had half turned to go when the child came up from the right without Rick seeing him and put his hand into Rick's. Rick did not even jump. He held the boy's hand. It seemed just right. All he could think at first was he had been fucking right to go right at the edge of the lake, and Uncle Bart could go stuff himself about left, even if he did get to kill Dilsom first. "Hello," Rick said. He could feel the child shivering. He could see the T-shirt was for an ice hockey team. The boy's hand was freezing.

The child said: "In your car it's warm. I saw you in your car. With that hat on."

"Do you want to go in my car?"

"Is it warm?"

"I can make it warm."

"Well, but my mother said, Don't go in men's cars. Ever."

"What's your mother's name?"

"But if your car is warm I'll go in your car."

"I don't even know your name."

"Jeremy."

"Jeremy what, then?"

"This is the night and it's dark but I can still find your car, I

124

think." He tugged at Rick's hand, drawing him back towards the 605.

"And fog," Rick replied. "I don't know what a small boy like you is doing out. Does your mother know you've come out? I wonder what her name is."

"I think you were looking for me."

They walked hand in hand by the side of the lake and then up the slope. Rick said: "Why were you running away from your house? Who lives there with you? Your mother and who else? I think you're Jeremy Dilsom, that's who I think you are, and your mother is Mrs Dilsom and your father's Mr Dilsom."

The boy stopped and pulled his hand from Rick's. His voice went hard and scared. "Do you know Andy? Are you one of his friends?"

"Who's Andy?"

"Are you the one who will be coming to see us and talk to us with Andy?"

Rick reached for the boy's hand again, but he wouldn't take it. "Come on. Let's get to the car. You're really shaking. You'll be ill, you know."

"No, my mother said, Don't go in men's cars. Ever."

"For a warm."

"No. Do you know Andy? Is that why you were waiting, in the car and by the water, because you help Andy Rockmain?"

"Who's he?"

"Who are you? You don't talk like here."

"Just out for a walk."

"Why do you know my name? Do you know Andy? Does he keep telling you my name?"

"Is that your name then, Jeremy Dilsom?"

"Tell me where the circus was," the boy replied. He sounded like he might start crying.

"Circus?"

"Tell me where it was."

The child almost shouted that, his face fierce. Rick had the feeling this boy might run again, anywhere, any minute. Something had gone wrong. He wanted to grip the child's hand to hold him, but he was standing away from Rick and kept his hands behind him. Rick said: "Did you used to be Jeremy Vale? I don't think you like the name Jeremy Dilsom."

When Rick spoke the name Vale he saw the boy bring one hand suddenly from behind his back and put it over his mouth, as if he had spoken the name himself, and as if it was bad to speak it, like swearing. Rick said: "I used to know people in London, near New Cross, whose name was Mr and Mrs Vale, and they had some children. I thought you might be one of the children."

The boy dropped his hand to his side. "Andy never says that name. He would never say that name. Don't you know that name is gone?"

"Is it? Doesn't Andy know you used to be called Jeremy Vale? Who is he, then? Doesn't he know you very well?"

"How do you know I used to be called Jeremy Vale?"

"Did you?"

"If you know about Jeremy Vale do you know it was not Cheald Meadows?"

"What?"

"You know – clowns, horses, elephants, all that."

"The circus?"

"Not Cheald Meadows."

"Where's that?"

"Don't you know that? Are you just saying it? People just say things sometimes. Andy just says some things in Mrs Canter-Williams's house."

"There was a good circus used to come to Lewisham," Rick replied. "In London. Yes, clowns, horses, elephants, everything."

"Dogs doing tricks?"

"Of course. Did you see them?"

He thought about this. "Yes, I saw some clever dogs, and some clowns, all of it."

"When you were in London, with your mum and dad, Mr and Mrs Vale?"

"I don't think it was in Cheald Meadows."

"Where's that?"

"By the ice skating."

"Here? In Cardiff?"

"At first my sister didn't think the circus was in Cheald Meadows but I think she does now."

"What's her name?"

126

"Anita. We call her Nita sometimes."

"Nita what?"

"Well, the same as me, of course."

"Nita Vale?"

"Andy would be really cross with you. He doesn't shout, but I can tell when he's cross." The boy took Rick's hand again and they walked to the Peugeot. Rick put the heater on max and drove away.

Chapter 19

Rick motored slowly with the boy for a few miles around the docks until the car was warm and Jeremy stopped shivering. This kid was rabbiting about this circus and this Andy singing songs the kid hated in some old woman's house, not the boy's own, and Rick let him rabbit, he was only a messed-up kid which had to be sad in its way, and you never knew what he might say which could be useful in all this circus shit and Andy and old woman shit. Letting him rabbit and listening to him was clearly another thing that would come in the category of subtlety. He did not have to think a lot about planning this subtlety because it was in him, he had it natural, this was the point, the same as getting out of that hospital in time this afternoon. He could not understand, now, why he had thought he messed that up – could not understand why he had wanted to hurry home to Uncle Bart. Uncle bloody Bart! This subtlety Rick Cole had was bringing all kinds of information. For example, this old woman's house could be a discovery, a useful thing, if the kid's father also went there. This was also where he could be seen to. Would Dad and Uncle Bart ever find out about this old woman's house? Never. How could they? They were far, far back, where they deserved to be.

After a while, Rick returned to exactly where the 605 had been parked before, stopped and switched off the engine. The boy did not realise what was happening until they were back on the marina. Then, suddenly you could see him get all tiny angry and upset because he started to recognise the big hotel and some apartment blocks through the fog, and he shouted: "Mister, I don't want to come home. Why did we come back?" He made it sound like he had been sold, which was too fucking rosy coming from a kid of Hector Vale.

Well, Rick was not quite sure about that, why he had driven

back, but pretty sure. He did not want to be tied up with a kid. He did not know what he would do with a kid if things went wrong, or even if they went right. That was far outside what he was used to. You had to do what you knew about, and only change a small bit at a time. This would not be small. Kill a grass or even kill a black cop, if it had worked, was different from kill a kid and he knew he would never be able to do that, unless it was really essential, and maybe not even then. This kid did not seem too bad like some kids, just full of misery and lost, and who was going to put a gun to his head? Not Rick Cole, not unless there was no other way, and at this moment there *was* another way.

"You better go home now, Jeremy," he said.

The boy began to cry, crouched down against the front passenger door, as far from Rick as he could get, face against the window. This was a pain, a kid crying.

"I'm not going to tell anybody about this, so don't you tell anyone either," Rick said. "If I meet that Andy, I won't tell him you came out and were talking about him that way, about the songs you rubbished."

"Will you meet him?" He asked it full of hate and fear again, like he realised all along Rick knew this Andy and would be telling him things and helping him.

"If I bumped into him," Rick replied.

"Where?"

"Anywhere."

"You mean Mrs Canter-Williams's house?"

"You never know who you'll meet. It's a small world."

"No it's not. There's Africa, Russia, many islands."

"It's a saying. Where is that house, the old lady's house?"

"I expect he's your friend."

"Andy? I told you, I don't know him," Rick said.

"Why do you call him Andy, then? Why don't you call him Mr Rockmain, if he's not your friend?"

"It's what *you* call him, that's all. Who is he? How do I know who's talking to you about a circus and singing?"

"How would you meet him, then? How would you know it was him?"

"I said 'if'. In a pub, on a bus, that sort of thing. This happens to men. They start talking and say their names."

"Are you going to meet him in a pub?"

"No. Just if. Tell me about the old lady's house."

"He's got a car, you've got this car, so you won't be on a bus."

"Can you get back into your house, without them knowing?" Rick replied. "What about alarms? Are there alarms? I expect so in such a nice house."

"How do you know it's a nice house? I switched them off when I came out or they would go off, through opening the back door. I know how to do it."

"Oh?"

"The key for it is always under the table lamp, with the back door key." He brought them both from the pocket of his dungarees and showed them to Rick.

Rick said: "Shall I have them?"

"Why?"

"In case they find them in your pocket, which would be bad trouble for you, wouldn't it?"

"I wouldn't be able to get in if I didn't have the back door key, would I, silly? I can put the alarm key back."

"Yes. Will you switch on the alarm again?"

"Yes. Why? Well, I'd better, or someone might notice. I must. Sometimes I think my Dad's afraid of things here."

"No, I don't expect so, Jeremy. You should go now. Run so you don't get cold again."

The boy spoke ahead, out through the windscreen, not looking at Rick, a little, tired voice. "I still don't want to. You're the only one who knows I'm Jeremy Vale. You're the only one who knows the circus wasn't in Cheald Meadows."

"No, not the only one. You know it as well."

"Yes, but – if you know who I am I want to stay with you. When I'm with you I'm really me. If I'm not with you – well, I don't know." He sat up straighter in the seat and turned towards Rick. "If I ask Andy or that other one, any of them, they say 'Jeremy Dilsom'. They say, 'Jeremy Dilsom, of course, of course.'" He tried for a big, grown-up voice. "And my own Mum and Dad say that. My mother says. 'I am Mrs Dilsom, and this is Anita Dilsom and Jeremy Dilsom.'"

"As long as me and you know."

"But I want to be with you so you can tell me all the time. If you don't tell me, well – well, sometimes I don't really know, that's all. And Nita, well she doesn't—" His face went longer, and he was going to cry again.

"I'll come back," Rick said. "I'll park here. You'll know this car, and my brown hat. And when you come I'll shout out of the window, 'Hello, Jeremy Vale.' Never Jeremy Dilsom, I promise. So you'll know you're still you."

"Will you? This is honest? What name will I shout out to you?"

"Honest."

"Don't shout it too loud, because of the others. They wouldn't like it. When?"

"Tomorrow. Not so late. Just after tea."

"If I can come out."

"Yes."

"You see, I'm not Jeremy Dilsom."

"I know."

"What name will I shout out to you?"

"So, run now. Don't shut the door. I'll do it." The boy went from the car and was gone, rushing up the street towards Dilsom's place, the two keys in his hand. He looked back once before the fog swallowed him, stopped and waved, then galloped on. Rick lowered the window and waved back. He leaned across and noiselessly pulled the door to. He knew what Uncle Bart would say, letting those keys go, and even his father would say it. So, he was supposed to tear them from the hand of a kid of six in hopeless clothes for January nights who trusted him like some kind of saviour? If Rick had taken those keys, the kid would have put two and two together, he was bright, and he would tumble right away that Rick might not be a saviour after all but peril. Perhaps he would even tell his mum and dad, although having to say he had been out. Then where would Rick be? In the middle of a call-out of police is where, including some with guns.

He decided this spot for the car was not too clever. If Dilsom came out he would notice, and he would notice it was occupied. Dilsom would be living on edge every minute these days, expecting visitors, noticing everything. If police passed on security patrol they would notice, too, and come and discuss why he was waiting, or ask the computer about the reg if the Peugeot was empty. It did not need any big subtlety to know this, only ordinary sense, only doing a job, as long as you had some ordinary sense to start with, which Uncle Bart would say Rick did not, no question. This showed Uncle Bart could be an arsehole though once brilliant, admitted, and a relation.

He drove the Peugeot into the car park of an old warehouse that had been polished up into an apartment block to suit the marina style. From here he could still watch and about half an hour later, saw Hector Vale who was Dilsom come down the main street, walking towards the marina exit and the road outside. Rick let him go about thirty yards until he was almost out of sight, then left the car, locked it and went after him, pretty silent in the trainers. This was how he had planned it from the start. This was a plan working out so exactly right. You planned, you waited.

Chapter 20

Mid-evening, Brade and Boadicia left bed and Brade made up a meal for them. Soon now it would be time for his night prowl of the marina and around Julie's office building. He washed the dishes while Boadicia made herself tidy, checked his Magnum and they left. He would have liked to pop up to Cliffy's place and give him another word of assurance, but did not feel he had the time: he wanted to make a detour for a brief look at Glyndwr in the hospital. In any case, he thought he had heard Hale-Garning go out during the afternoon. Brade could call on him tomorrow and minister unto his various concerns. Cliff was a real cause for worry and had to be helped a hundred per cent. Somehow, standing in his gear on the stairs today, clasping his stick, and with Enid in the suitcase, Cliff had looked like a refugee in those old news photographs you saw from the last war, beaten and desperate, not too sure there was a promised land after all. The back of his neck under the biretta seemed skinny, aged. It must be foul to put yourself in the power of the Church, worse than joining the police. Brade hoped Cliffy had in fact been able to get out and break up the day for himself a bit.

Boadicia was going home and he put her down near her flat, then went to the hospital. He called first at the ward office, where they knew him by now. "What sort of inquiries come in about Glyndwr?" he asked the staff nurse.

"Sort?"

"Who are they?"

"Look, am I supposed to tell you this? Is it a police matter? Didn't you ask before? The hospital secretary handles all that."

"Glyndwr's a friend of mine, not just the force."

"Well, yes, all right. And you probably know already,

anyway. There's an uncle who usually rings up in the evening."

"Which uncle is that?"

"Just an uncle."

"From?"

"Who knows? Not local, I wouldn't think. He never talks about coming in to see him. Just his condition. If you're a friend, didn't he ever mention his uncle?"

"A lot of uncles. I expect he wants to know if Glyndwr's talking yet, does he?"

She slammed down her Biro on the desk. "Now, listen, this *is* just for the police."

"Does he ask about that?"

"Perhaps. Sometimes," she admitted grudgingly.

"Relieved when you say he hasn't spoken?"

"I couldn't say."

"Accent?"

"Again, not local. A bit of cockney? Could be. Plus, could be West Indian. Or not. Overdoing it maybe? I don't know. Now, I'm busy. I'll be damn glad to go off tonight. You. Plus some damn, prowling, crazy priest."

"Priest?"

"He's still probably here."

"Where?"

"Outside Glyndwr's room, of course."

Brade went there urgently. Someone dressed as a priest? He found Hale-Garning in heavy conversation with a stoutish, middle-aged nurse in an alcove near Glywndr's room. Cliff broke off immediately he saw Brade and approached like the start of a church procession. "Dave," he said. "I'm glad." He nodded towards the nurse, back in the general ward now. "What do you think of that one then? A smell of desire there, above all the hospital pong. I think she could wean me even from Enid. Yes."

"What are you here for, in that outfit?"

"Sick visiting. Caspar Indicay can move over. I do catch a real burn of interest in that gal, Dave. Didn't I tell you I'd come? Helping you out. Reciprocity. I think I may have saved his life."

"Yes?"

134

"Someone here. Youthful, London accent, white, possible ridge haircut under a trilby."

Brade looked anxiously about. "Where is he? I know this lad."

"I think I scared him off," Hale-Garning said, beaming.

"But where to?"

"Ah. I'm only a priest, Dave. I could hardly give chase. One side of his overcoat seemed weighted down to me. I didn't want to find out with what. Suddenly, Dave, I long to live." He glanced back towards the nurse and trilled again. "Long to live. Did I fail you?"

"You did brilliantly, Cliff."

This late, there should be no other visitors and Brade might not have to listen to Glyndwr's girlfriend from the Tourist Board declare the clear importance of the Welsh language to the new Europe. For Brade, she used to talk in English, of course, though he would not have minded not. Probably her terrible bilingual fluency was what used to turn Glyndwr on, and Brade never tried to shut her up in case she suddenly reached him again. Brade had heard what a mystery sex could be.

Glyndwr looked as if he might have relapsed. "I think you can forget the bait ploy," Brade said. "It seems the call has already been made and not followed through."

Glyndwr did not respond.

"And is there a far-flung uncle?" Brade went close and checked Glyndwr's breathing, then sat down. "How nice to have London relatives fretting over you every day." Yes, Glyndwr seemed to look as always – as always before the recovery: serene, far, far distant, flat on his back, eyes shut but not clenched, head still bandaged in brilliant white. What was he seeing behind those lids, what pictures kept him so damn equable? His breathing was hardly audible but certainly there.

"Well, I thought you'd ask that, Glyndwr. You heard all the stuff from Julie, didn't you, sod? No, I haven't levelled with Bullfinch on my divided motives. Can't, can I? Well, can I – a police officer, for God's sake? Yes, you're right – the result, as you say, is he's on one tack, me on another. Usual state of affairs, really. I want to make sure Julie doesn't catch any

135

of the killing stuff that will be thrown at Dilsom very soon, I fear. This lad here today – almost certainly the start. OK, OK, OK, yes: at the same time I might – might – want to make sure Dilsom *does* catch some of it, all of it. Wouldn't you? This is some crook getting it away with – no, you're probably too noble. You *are* too noble. You'll be a loss if you go, Glyndwr. You're already a loss, you malingering fucker. Speak! You're all right, remember? You've talked. Are you acting the part, even for me? You realise I'm carrying this whole sodding situation because you can't keep your head neat? But you mustn't think of me as totally evil. I'm on at Bullfinch to get extra protection down there for Dilsom, which plainly means I'm trying to look after him. Duty still calls. It's automatic. If we had more police around the area it might frighten any vengeance party right out of the city – away from Dilsom, away from Julie. So, you see? And, yes, sure, it might also make it impossible for Dilsom to get out on the quiet to be with her. I'm talking at Bullfinch in one way and thinking another, and he's preaching to me the merits of integration, freedom of movement, the need for inconspicuousness. All desirable, nobody denies it."

There seemed to be a small movement of Glyndwr's lips. It looked laboured, miniscule. Perhaps he was truly under again, but struggling. This was often the kind of impact Brade had: he made people who did not want to talk, talk. Bloody medics. He, Brade, had done it all, alone. So, should he let them know, call them? But was this bastard genuine? And then Brade thought about Glyndwr's considerate, phone-prone uncle. He stood and went close to the bed, bending low. "Say again, Glyndwr," he whispered. "Between you and me only again, yes?"

The eyes remained shut, breathing virtually silent, although Brade had his head down almost to bed level. Glyndwr's lips did move again, as if striving, searching for their old way of forming words, maybe a way he had forgotten once more. Jesus.

"It's Dave, Glyndwr. We've all been waiting for you."

He seemed to have slipped back into that awful impassiveness again. Perhaps this kind of stirring of the lips was commonplace, something the staff often saw, just a twitch.

"Everybody turns up, your girl, your mum and dad. They live their lives around you, you posturing layabout. Well, as you know. Knew. It's just that it's night now. They have to sleep, so no one here but me. There's a priest outside, in case you'd like last rites." Brade stayed standing at the head of the bed, but straightened up. The moment had gone? He felt a kind of guilt, as if he should have been able to secure that instant – lassoo it, drag Glyndwr for keeps into the paddock of the with-it. Yes, perhaps he ought to have gone for help. "If you could tell us what happened, you dozy bastard. But in your own time, obviously, Glyn. Absolutely. Who we're dealing with."

And then the lips struggled and stretched and contracted again. Brade crouched forward once more. "Good lad, Glyndwr," he said. "The sweet brains's still ticking there, the memory whole?"

Speech was forming, Brade felt sure of it. The bloody great butt of the Magnum, jutting in its holster from under his coat, stopped him getting right down to Glyndwr's mouth, and with one hand he pushed the gun back flat against his chest. His left ear brushed Glyndwr's lips like a butterfly on a flower. There was a sound that could have been a death rattle from Glyndwr's throat and, suddenly terrified, Brade let go of the gun and with a jumpy finger felt for a pulse on his neck. It was there, steady enough. The noise had been only Glyndwr dredging for utterance. Brade pushed the Magnum back again. "Yes, Glyn? Good lad."

"My next career move will be . . ." Glyndwr said. It was almost at normal voice. There was marvellous passion in the statement, like some star actor in a heated play on telly, say *Hamlet*. Glyndwr's eyes remained shut.

"Right," Brade replied. "I got that. Will be what? Talk to me about it, Glyndwr. Talk about any bloody thing."

Brade waited another hour, but there was no more. Leaving, he said to the nurse: "Tell uncle, very unchanged."

"As a matter of fact, we think Glyndwr's doing well."

Christ, doing well! He goes blotto for weeks, wakes up, goes back, lurks like a beggar at the door of death, and all the time, in and out of the deep well of isolation, he dreams of nothing but his bloody job prospects.

Chapter 21

Dilsom felt nervy, unsure what was behind him, yet walking down Bute Street towards Mount Stuart Square and Julie's office block, he did manage a bit of a smile. He kept very alert, but, yes, a grin. It was about his identities. Christ, what a game. At times he found it easy to think of himself as Geoffrey Dilsom, marina resident, businessman, even if Brade and the brass running him still had not fixed what kind of business. In fact, Dilsom often enjoyed being Dilsom: money kept coming, a lot sweeter than the giro, and the house was fine: a box but a chic box, and plenty of light and briny environment. Although Brade lied like a cop or a villain, he could be human now and then, and even the thinking Rockmain might really want to do good. This sort of life, you were bound to see another side to the police. You could see without believing. They waved their caring at you, like semaphore. It was better than pistols.

And then came other days when Dilsom knew he was not Dilsom at all, and Hector Vale returned to him, in him, as full of ploys and bounce and hardness as ever. No, not as ever. As full of ploys and bounce and hardness as he was before they led him, funnelled him, pressured him and bought him into – well, into doing what eventually got him born again as the gorgeous nobody, Geoffrey Dilsom.

Tonight, of course, it was the Ruger that made him certain he would be for ever Hector Vale. He wore a padded, red and blue check blouson, which had a deep, zippable inside pocket capable of taking the automatic very nicely, with no obvious bulge. This naff garment produced the smile. It was absolutely Geoffrey Dilsom: the sort of flashy leisure thing a businessman might pick to show he was not all pinstripe. Never would Hector Vale go for anything so rampant. If it came to the worst, Hector Vale would prefer even one of Len Everdon's dud suits. However, Hector Vale did appreciate the blouson's large, sealable pocket. Because of these quiet footsteps somewhere behind in the fog he had the zip unfastened now, but he would close it when he got to Julie's place. You did not want a gun sliding from your discarded coat in front of a fine girl like Julie. Clearly, an unexpected, loaded piece might jinx a love meeting with any woman executive.

Meeting Len again had done quite a lot to roll aside the stone and bring old Hector back from the dead, naturally. How many people would Len motor that distance for, eat in a service station for? When he agreed to come, it was the grandeur of the past speaking, and that comradely, profitable past was Hector Vale, not Geoffrey Dilsom. Yes, this had been the start. Then, tonight, actually to feel the P-85 tucked in against his tit, paid for and heavy with shells, did a still better job of reviving those rough, *conquistadore* days, also supposed to be dead.

It might have made more sense to drive to Julie's office, but he needed his car outside the house, a signal to any guardian police that he was home. And he had told Carmel he wanted a stroll along the foreshore after his trip. She might believe it, and he always observed the formalities. Why be deliberately hurtful? As he was leaving the marina, and once or twice now, he had the impression of someone tailing him and he cursed the fog. Someone talented and probably in rubber-soled shoes and trainers. Of course, he had Len's half hint of a warning to think of. For a couple of minutes he waited in the doorway of a steel-shuttered shop half way along Bute Street, to see who caught up, his hand on the butt of the pistol. He felt totally steady, totally Hector, lumberjack jacketed or not. No one came and he continued walking. Either he had been wrong or the shadow was smart. Sure, there were very gifted tails in South London, among the injured families. A routine skill. Or could it be Brade, doing a combined surveillance/protection turn? Was Brade smart? Probably he had his moments, even working this kind of town. But basically he and all the rest here were in fairyland. Because Brade gave him an order against guns did Brade believe there would be no gun? Did this hick woodentop realise what it was like, trying to manage Hector Vale? Did he even realise gems like Len Everdon existed back home – yes, the true, London home – and would always honour bond to a one-time contact, regardless?

Julie had asked him not to come in through the office main door any more, although it was still open when he arrived in the Square. She had taken against the reception lad, Danny, for some reason. Perhaps she found he talked. In that big job she would not like gossip around the building about her: it damaged status. In the doorman sort a belt across the chops and the threat of more usually guaranteed silence, but he knew Julie would not want him hurt. It would have been better if they could go to her flat in Penarth. Somehow, he sensed she was not keen on that, and he did not push it, not yet. Julie offered hardly any information on her life away from the office, so perhaps she had difficulties at home, though she said she lived alone now. He did not know what that meant, either – the "now". If he kept seeing her, he must do some digging. Naturally, he had already done a bit of that, and located that picture of her and Brade in the desk. This certainly provided a worry or two. And so did the fact she never mentioned it. Of course, he did not tell her much – not much that was true – about himself. He couldn't, could he? He had orders. With her he was Dilsom, he was make-believe, maybe more in fairyland than the police here.

She would leave a fire door open for him at the rear of the office block. He could pull that to after himself, though not shut it properly because the door had to be slammed, and the noise might alert Danny. They would shove it shut properly when they left, by which time the building should have closed and Danny gone off duty. There had been times not long ago when he would have paid a good price for this kind of information about a place stuffed with pricey media equipment, but he must not think like that. As Hector Vale, he nipped over the back wall into a small yard and made for the fire door. Before he went through it, he pulled the zip shut over the Ruger and summoned charming Geoffrey Dilsom back to duty.

Chapter 22

Brade drove on to the marina and did his usual night tour, covering most of the streets at least a couple of times. Dilsom's car was outside the house, and the house itself looked peaceful. Three lights burned inside, two down, one up, and the security lamp above the front door was on. Apart from a little taxi activity at the Celtic Bay Hotel he saw no movement anywhere. The fog hung grubby and possessive in the streets still, and the long, then short, horn blasts from Flat Holm were doing what they could, but sounding frail, outgunned, like police in a shady world getting shadier. *Fuck off Brade, you self-pitying jerk.* Now and then the fog siren of a ship would answer in a blurted conversation of the fretful. This marina reeked of authenticity.

On these trips, Brade never knew what he was supposed to be looking for: probably whatever Glyndwr had seen down here – whatever caused him to leave the car and back into an ambush. Had he actually spotted a move against Dilsom? Someone casing, someone trying the house, or hanging about for Dilsom to come out on one of his merry cock saunters? Were they much more than a safety-first tic, these random police patrols? After what he must have seen, Glyndwr might say yes, they were. That is, if only he could think of anything for long enough now and say anything worthwhile – think anything beyond the endless, sunken, egomaniac reverie where he was Britain's first bilingual black Chief Constable at thirty-one.

And another tic: Brade suddenly realised that on this little expedition he was searching for what he saw the night Glyndwr was attacked. Among the parked cars, he sought an Escort. Among the few people entering and leaving the hotel he tried to pick out a youngish, fair haired man with a freak coiffure, like one from that great pack of mugs sent by the Yard. And maybe like the lad so cleverly stopped by Cliff at the hospital today. Brade knew where these dim tactics came from: police wisdom said villains rarely broke a pattern. So, if one of them liked Escorts he liked Escorts and never used anything else. If one of them failed on a job he would have to come back and try again. It was pathetic, but this comforting lampoon of the crook mind did keep its timeless grip. And, in any case, there was that hospital invader, who might be something bad – probably was. Maybe he proved police wisdom was right. Brade scanned the car parks at the hotel and at all the apartment blocks but saw nothing that looked like hazard. Or, if they were trying something new, *all* of them looked like hazard.

He parked his own car at what was once a vast warehouse, now born again as flats, and did what he always did on one of these visits, walked swiftly to Dilsom's street and past the house. Everything seemed intact. The three interior lights and the security lamp still burned, the security lamp nine tenths strangled by fog. He went on. In a few minutes, he would turn and go back, and this time move more slowly and slip in close again to make a real examination of the house. A house was a castle, but if someone unwelcome got in it could be a death pit. So what, then? Didn't he want Dilsom done? Did he? Of course. And, also of course, he had a responsibility for Dilsom, and responsibilities always lay niggly and fat and inescapable on Brade, like carrying your mother down the fire escape. There were times when Brade suspected he was split as much as Vale–Dilsom. Perhaps everyone was. In any case, he certainly did not want the children hurt. At least, not hurt more than Rockmain could manage in a splendid cause.

On his return, Brade was taking a look at the rear door of the house when Carmel pulled it hard open and said: "Dave, quick, we've got trouble here."

He grabbed at the Magnum under his jacket. "What trouble? Who's here? Is Geoff all right?"

"Come in. Bad trouble. It's happened." But she took his gun wrist and drew his hand gently down. "You won't need that. Other trouble." She had on an old, plum and gold tracksuit, too big for her, probably Dilsom's. There was a tasty smell of sweat, and he hoped it was hers, not his. In the darkness,

Carmel's face seemed beautiful, full of suffering, as aggressive as ever, yet sexless for now: any woman was entitled to an evening off, unless she took fees, which was what made girls like Boadicia so reliable.

It was understood, and actually spelled out by Bullfinch, that Brade would never call on the Dilsoms, because he was recognised all over the docks, even on this smart new enclave. If he were seen visiting, someone would want to know why. And among the someones would be Bullfinch.

"Please," she said, pulling the door open a bit more.

But he would not be seen, not at this time of night and in this grand, filthy fog. He went in and she immediately closed the door. "Is Geoffrey here?" he asked. "He's OK?"

"I expect so."

"Not here?"

"He needed fresh air, so he's strolling the foreshore in that murk. The tale."

"It can be impressive, bracing, even moving, gazing out to sea this kind of night."

"Gazing out and seeing nothing," she replied.

"But not a good idea for him to be there alone."

"If he is."

"What?"

"There. Or alone. Take your pick."

"Where else?"

"You tell me, Dave."

Yes, perhaps he could do that. Jesus, two sex-rejected people, statuesque by an Aga, their pain so nicely interlinked, though she must not be allowed to know that.

"What trouble?" he replied. The kitchen was spacious and gleaming, the cleanliness a lesson. Brade's flat could have done with some of this spending.

"Come through," she said.

They went into the sitting room: a couple of long, light coloured, pricey settees; pale, boaty watercolours with the mud done a flattering yellow-gold; tall greenery in stout red pots; mild décor. Bullfinch must have got them a Laura Ashley stylist. "It's Jeremy," she said.

"Yes?"

"Jeremy Vale," she replied.

143

"What?" Brade yelled as she mentioned the unmentionable. "What's that mean, you throw-back bitch?"

She glanced up towards the bedrooms. "What he says he is."

Quietening and getting his recovery in fast, he said: "Well, Carmel, this is a snag, but we mustn't—"

"Dave, it's happened. He's come apart. I want you to see him. But go easy."

"What, now? The middle of the night?"

"He's awake. They're both awake. He woke up Nita to tell her. I think he's been out."

"Tell her?"

"That he's Jeremy Vale, and she's Anita Vale. She said he kept on and on, made her cry. I heard the sobbing. That's how I discovered."

Did he want to be pulled into this? Brade was at his best talking to those who made no reply, not to a rioting, self-saving, brazenly smartarse child. "How could he have been out?"

"His clothes are damp from the fog."

"Without your knowledge?"

"Of course."

"In and out of the house, unseen. Your alarms?"

"He knows how to manage them, naturally. Sneaks back upstairs."

"Out in the dark, you mean? Where? We're talking about a child of six, yes?"

"As though he's talked to someone, Dave. As though someone tells him he's Jeremy Vale, tells him and tells him and tells him. The way Rockmain does it, but round the other way." She spoke fast, a mixture of bitterness and fright. "There's this certainty, this clinging to the name, the repetition, as though he's scared he'll lose it again. You know how the dying clutch at bedclothes, so as not to slip away."

"Is that certainty?"

"OK, may be not. But it is a certainty that he's not going to give in again – not fold up and become Jeremy Dilsom."

Brade sat down on the lime green and white settee, hoping to put off seeing the kid, perhaps for good. "Are you saying he met someone in the street who—?"

"Tells him he's Jeremy Vale? I don't know. Is that impossible? Why? If we've got someone stalking us, he'd know the family history, wouldn't he, the family name, real name? That's why he'd be here."

"Nobody's here."

"So why are we on your beat?"

"Because—"

"Bollocks, Dave. Why was your black friend around the place? You both know we might get hit, and thanks for trying to stop it. But is it so stupid to think Jeremy might bump into—"

"Bump into a hitman who lets him go so he can run home and alert you? Come on, Carmel." He gave the full, old-pro disdain, a helping of scorn from the sharp end. Did she have it right, the intuitive cow? No wonder this difficult kid was so bright. In both of them, mother and boy, the podge face lulled: had made Brade hope for amenable, slow wits he could help govern, subdue and save.

Carmel frowned, tugged at something in the weave of the tracksuit. "OK, again. It doesn't quite add up. Perhaps he hasn't seen anyone. But something *has* happened, Dave. I do want you to talk to him." Her head slumped forward. She whispered the plea, though without trying to charm him into agreement. At least, not that got through to him.

"To say what?" he asked.

"Whatever you think best. See if you can sort out where the change comes from. He'll tell me nothing, nothing except his name is Jeremy Vale and his sister is Anita Vale."

"And you?" he asked.

"He doesn't seem to care what I'm called." She lifted her face and gazed at him, a miniature, phoney smile hard at work, making out she was not desolated. At least the handed down hate of police did not glint there, for now.

Brade went formal here. "You'll understand, I know, that this is entirely beyond me. Not my domain. I must send for Andy Rockmain."

"I won't have him in the house."

"Carmel, it's his —"

"And don't call me that."

"Carmel? But what else? Christ, don't *you* start. We've got to stick to things. No, they mustn't come apart. Suicide. We're building something good and necessary here. Rockmain—"

"Necessary, maybe . . . but I won't have Andy Rockmain in the house."

"But why? I thought – look, as a matter of fact, he believes you're – he believes mothers in this situation often fall for—"

"The prick."

"Well, yes, that, but a more all-round dependence, too."

"The stupid prick."

Brade thought he heard some muttering from upstairs through the ceiling. "This thing, it's like a science, Carmel. A mystery. Andy knows how it all works, people's psychologies, memories. He's got the expertise and the sensitivity. Me, I'm only one up from directing traffic. The mind is such a delicate area. I don't want to go barging in, especially the kids. Like a doctor with another's case, except I'm not even a doctor. If I get on the direct phone he can be here right away. The operators will reach him, wherever. It's part of his job, to be on call. As I say, like a doctor. Believe me, he's the genuine article, and full of caring although he's police."

"Shall we go and see them then?" She spoke as if his arguments were nothing, or a routine only. She had not sat down and moved now towards the door into the hall.

"I should try to find Geoffrey." Yes. There were twenty reasons, even if it had not been Julie. "I don't say he's in danger, but this is a needless risk, walking alone, somewhere so remote in this weather."

"You really think he's there?"

"I have to go on what you say."

"No you don't."

"What else?"

"Don't tell me you still don't know what he's like. Don't tell me the Yard haven't sent you a profile. They know how to spell shag-happy. Come on. He gets back from a trip and feels entitled."

"What trip?"

"Search me, Dave."

"But for what?"

"I'm telling you, I don't know."

"Meeting someone? Business?"

"Could be. Some little triumph. He seemed pleased."

"Did he bring anything back with him?"

"Like what? Weaponry?"

"I've told him he's not to go for armament."

"Which would send him looking for something out of the area? It's possible. Likely. I don't ask him. Anyway, forget him for a minute, will you? Talk to my children, Dave. Help me. Nobody else will, can." Her eyes shone with something, possibly tears, possibly will, possibly both.

"Not true."

"Please, come." She left the room and he heard her climb the stairs. He had the plan of the house in his head and could visualise her making for the children's double bedroom at the back along the neat, little landing. In a while, he followed. Not to would be inhuman and he always worked on seeming human. It seemed proper. Ten minutes, maximum. After that, get to Julie, which would probably mean Dilsom, too. But above all get to Julie.

In bunk beds, both children lay on their backs wearing pyjamas, eyes open, Jeremy above. The bedroom light was on. Thick, ornamental bars protected the windows here and throughout the house, though he could not see them in this room because the curtains were drawn. The fire people disliked the bars and the tough glass and could not be told why they were crucial. The girl had stopped crying, but looked appallingly miserable and defeated. When Jeremy saw Brade he at once turned his head towards the wall and Brade heard the boy's breathing accelerate.

Carmel said: "That's so rude, Jeremy."

"I expect he's tired," Brade said. "Another time?" He made half a step back towards the door.

"You or Andy, it's all the same," Jeremy replied over his shoulder.

"I heard you were upset," Brade said.

"No."

"Not upset, just nasty," Anita said.

"What's it about, Jeremy?" Brade asked. He leaned against a *Hobbit* wall poster. Carmel, too, remained standing, but nearer the beds, perhaps meaning them to feel her influence from close by.

"Why did you bring him up here, Mum?" Jeremy replied.

"Did you send for him? Oh, why did you send for him? You know what they're like."

"No, I called in," Brade said.

"Why?"

"To see you're all right. The bad weather."

"You never call in," Jeremy replied.

"No," Anita said.

"Dad told us it's security," Jeremy said, still talking to the wall. "Why we go to that other house."

"Your mum mentioned you've been wondering about your name," Brade replied.

"Not wondering. I know my name," Jeremy said. "Of course I do. Well, every boy knows his own name, doesn't he?"

"Good," Brade replied. "I'd say so."

Jeremy turned back to look at Brade, his round face steady. "My name's Jeremy Dilsom."

Carmel hissed: "Jeremy, you—"

"Jeremy Dilsom," the boy said. "This is well known."

"That's not what you said just now," Carmel replied.

"Jeremy Dilsom."

"No, it's not what you told me," Anita said. "And I'm Anita Dilsom, am I? Not what – not that other name? Am I, Jeremy?" Her voice was raw with confusion and the need for hope. She stuck her head out from the bed and looked up to his bunk, pleading.

On his back still, the boy spoke now to the ceiling. "Well, of course you are, silly. If I'm Jeremy Dilsom and you're my sister who else can you be, the Queen or somebody?"

"You're saying this because I'm here?" Brade asked.

"Playing one of your damn, cold games, Jeremy," Carmel said.

"Well, I talked to Anita. She told me I was Jeremy Dilsom and she was Anita Dilsom. Sometimes I forget. But now I remember. She helped me. Didn't you, Nita?"

"I said Dilsom," she replied, "but he said—"

"Playing a game, Jeremy," Carmel said.

"Jeremy Dilsom, Jeremy Dilsom, Jeremy Dilsom." He intoned the names.

"Have you been out, Jeremy?" Brade asked.

"In the street? Tonight?"

"Yes," Brade said.

"It's too late, too foggy, Dave," Jeremy replied, laughing aloud. "Well, Mum and Dad would not like that and this house has alarms, you know. Nobody could go out and in, only with the right keys."

"You met someone out there, Jeremy, didn't you, didn't you?" Carmel screamed at him.

"Who?" he asked. "How could I, Mum? I didn't go out."

Brade was reminded of a Brando movie he had watched part of on television, where two children kept contact with a dead couple while well-meaning adults were shut out. But if Jeremy had met someone it would be no spook. Brade said, "This could be quite important, Jeremy. It might be a man who doesn't like your dad, perhaps looking for him. You know – there are stupid people about."

"No. Why are they looking for him?"

"Just listen to what Dave says," Carmel replied. "Don't ask so many damn questions."

"I don't know if he went out," Anita said. "I was asleep. Then he woke me up."

"A man not as old as your dad?" Brade asked. "Perhaps where he could watch the house, without being seen. Maybe in a car. An Escort? Do you know car makes, Jeremy?"

"Escort is a Ford. Everyone knows that."

"Right," Brade said. "Someone in an Escort, possibly a white Escort."

"He knows all cars," Anita said.

"Or in any other make," Brade asked.

"He's brickwalling again," Carmel said. "He won't let you near, Dave." She put out her hand, as though about to grip the boy's shoulder, shake him, perhaps, but did not go through with it. "You're wrong, Dave's not the same as Andy Rockmain, Jeremy. You don't have to pretend with him. You don't have to kid him that he's forever emperor of your mind."

"Pretend?" Jeremy replied. "No. I'm Jeremy Dilsom. I don't want to pretend, Mum, not ever. No need."

Chapter 23

Waiting in her office for Geoffrey Dilsom, Julie realised suddenly that she was afraid. Her breathing had become shallow and fast, there was an ache in her chest and her throat seemed awkwardly constricted, her spit thick and hot. Usually, to stay late in the building gave her real pleasure, and it had been like that long before she met Geoffrey. A career thing. This was her domain. To work into the night now and then was part of the job, part of the wished-for load, an accompaniment to juicy status. When the building was more or less empty she would grow comfortably aware of her central role in the company. As they said, it could be lonely at the top. Never before tonight had the solitariness unnerved her. Now, this horrifying free fall into panic.

It was the worst kind of fear, the kind you woke up with sometimes, or that dogged you as a child: the kind you could not explain, could see no clear cause for, but which would not let go. Struggling to account for it, she would have liked to put the blame on the dull shroud of dense weather outside and the chilling, far-off blare of foghorns. Yes, sometimes winter did get her down. But never this much. In any case, it was not a matter of depression. Terror had taken over.

Her habit when something might weaken her was to ignore it, move to something else before the damage spread, and she did not try to analyse what undermined her now. But what she did know without having to think about it very much was that the fear began with Geoffrey. Tonight, she intended telling him it was over between them. For a few days she had been picking the words – reasonable, regretful, definite words. She was good on words: also part of the job. He might disagree with these words, but would undoubtedly recognise her right to call it to an end. He would not turn difficult. Although she had known him only a short while, Julie thought she had a fair idea of what he was like. Well, naturally. Would she have wanted him as a lover otherwise, for God's sake? Would she have brought him into her eyrie here? True, for some reason she had always drawn the line at taking him home. Another mystery, that. He had rough sides, yet surely was basically decent, sensible, considerate? Well, he had been all those things to her, at any rate. This was what mattered. She had had her worries about him, yes, but worries based only on those vague, self-interested, poisonous warnings from Dave. Her decision to finish it was certainly not the cause of her fears. Geoffrey had never shown violence. All the same, somehow he was mixed in with those fears.

Julie thought she could hear him coming up the uncarpeted rear stairs from the fire exit now and she stood behind her desk. It was important to get a touch of formality and distance from the start, otherwise she would not trust herself to go through with it. Geoff could talk damn well, a bit of a chat-up merchant, no disputing that. That was why she had to be determined. She would say her piece, keep things wholly amicable, bring out the utterly logical, soothing sentences, and eventually he would accept their message. This was how it had been with Dave, after all, when they finished. True, at first, Geoffrey might not believe her reasons, might not even understand them. How could he when she did not believe them or understand them properly herself? What was it, really, that convinced her she must get free of him? Yes, what? Had it really been those warnings from Dave? Was it also Dave who had planted this contemptible, undefined sense of dread? He would be good at that. He saw threat everywhere, like all his tribe, lived on it, sponsored it.

Geoff did not appear. She was certain she had heard something, someone on this floor, and decided that if he had not arrived in a couple of minutes she would go to the emergency stairs and look. It troubled her that the fire exit should be open. Anyone prowling the yard could spot it and get in, and there was plenty of late night prowling here. Perhaps, then, this explained her anxiety: simply a basic security worry, only natural to an executive, not the least occult or catastrophic. Was that it? No, it was not. She knew with total certainty her fear came from nothing so glibly definable, nothing so manageable. She sat down again, wanting to get a bit of strength together, in case she did have to go to investigate the emergency stairs. Should she give Danny on Reception a ring and ask him to take a look? But she did not really want him around up here: not when he had that link with Dave.

And then through the glass walls of her room she saw Geoff appear in the outer office doorway looking damp from the fog but otherwise fine and in that marvellous lumberjack-style blouson which suited him so well. He had the blunt, handsome features, solid shoulders and general physique for it, yet somehow dodged looking like a day off, middle class macho trip. For a couple of seconds, she was so relieved she forgot the way this meeting was supposed to go, and gave him her fullest grin of welcome as he shut the door. She forgot, too, that she had meant to be standing and radiating goodbye. Dave used to complain he continually saw goodbye in her smile: and, yes, she always liked to feel she had a right of exit. Geoff grinned back, and, coming swiftly forward, entered her room and bent to kiss her on the mouth. And, Christ, she sensed herself start to respond. Her arm went up around the back of his neck, and she pulled him down hard to her. Clinging? Her?

She realised it might be symbolic: she wanted to tug him, drag him, right into her realm. About Geoff there was always something unreachable. She would say she knew him, yet was never really sure. That slice of mystery made him intriguing, of course, but ultimately troubled her. She liked her life ordered and neat, even her love life. The suspicion that she would never get Geoff nicely regularised could be one reason she wanted out. Riddles were fine and exciting for a time, but at her age and in her position you were eventually looking for the reliable, the consistent. God, how pissily bourgeois. God, how true. So, why *had* she broken with Dave? Wasn't he reliable, insistnt? Too much.

"Your hair's soaking," she said. "Cold."

"It's rough out there, kid," he replied, in a mock Bronx accent.

"How do you mean?"

"Weather wise."

"All right down below?"

He put his hand on his crotch. "Think so. Why?"

"Idiot, not that. I meant the fire door. Getting over the wall."

"You worry about these old limbs? They still work OK." He sat down in one of her easy chairs, undid the blouson, but did not take it off. "As a matter of fact, I *am* a bit shattered. Had to drive back in this stuff from a business do near London."

"Successful?"

"Oh, not bad. You know how these things are, Julie. They might produce in the long run. Nurturing relationships. Do they call it 'casting bread upon the waters'?"

"What kind of business, Geoff?"

"Oh, as ever – property. That's what I mean, long-term. Clearly, it's not the time for big ploys right now. Got any drink?"

She went to her cabinet and produced the Scotch. She poured a couple of trebles and handed him his. He stroked her wrist. "You're looking great," he said. "*Also* as ever."

"Geoff—"

"Well, I think I'm thawing and could take this off now," he said and, standing, removed the blouson. He set it on another chair and seemed careful to keep it within reach. "You're looking great, Julie, yes, but also a bit solemn." He sat down again.

"I've been thinking about you and me." She went and stood behind the desk.

"That sounds nice. I often do that, too."

"No, not nice, Geoff."

He was drinking and kept his eyes on the whisky. "Oh?" Behind the glass, his face seemed to tighten for a second, become a face she only half recognised: bleak, hostile, even savage, his jaw line rigid. Shaken, she tried to recall all those comfortable terms about him she had listed only minutes ago. What had they been? Decent? Sensible? Yes, and considerate. Wasn't that Geoff, behind the bluffness? But she could not find any of these on show in his features now. Her fears piled up. Perhaps, after all, she had realised without really knowing it that he might not take his dismissal easily. Possibly, after all, those hidden doubts about him explained very well the inexplicable fear.

"Geoff," she said, getting back to her script, "it's been lovely, every minute of it."

"Of course it has. Of course it *is*." He put the glass down on the carpet and grinned at her again. And suddenly he was back to the man she felt happily familiar with, and thought she knew, his face friendly and warm again, his voice warm, too, and free from that appalling enmity. The switch bemused her. Whereas he had seemed so frightening then, now she was anxious once more that she might hurt him. "I've never known anyone like you, Julie," he said. "And I—"

She pushed on with her statement. "Geoff, I don't think we can go on like this. I have to think of—"

His hand moved suddenly towards the blouson, lifted it quickly on to his lap. He turned his head sharply towards the office entrance.

"What, Geoff?"

"Talk on," he whispered. "Talk normally. Just talk normally." Yes, a whisper, but a fierce whisper. "Sod it, I wondered about a tail." He was unzipping the inside pocket of his blouson.

"Heard something? Tail?" she asked, also whispering. She felt no fear now, only a mixture of anger and embarrassment. Christ, was this Danny again, or even Danny and Dave, snooping, voyeuring, they hoped? She, too, stared towards the door.

At normal voice level, Geoff chatted: "Yes, really dense on the Severn Bridge and in Wiltshire."

When she looked back at him, he had a black automatic in his hand, and had stood up. But Jesus, a shining new-looking *automatic*? Who was he? The blouson fell from his lap to the floor and he kicked it to the side, so it would not hinder his movement.

Also at normal voice she said: "Geoff, where the hell did you—? What are you doing? This could be a man I used to live with, that's all, Geoff, that's absolutely all."

He ignored it and took a couple of steps out of her room into the general office and towards the door, the gun ready, pointed waist high in front of him. With his free hand he waved at Julie, telling her to get down behind the desk. "Christ, who *are* you? What is this?" she said, but whispering again.

154

And then she thought she might have caught a faint sound from the other side of the door herself – a very careful, wary movement, as if by someone not knowing what to expect in here, and as if by someone who wanted to view secretly whatever was going on, without stopping it. The Peeping Tom operation again, Dave or Danny or both. They'd get nothing tonight. Or they'd get something else. Christ, Geoff might fire! Was it real, that gun? Everything about the situation screamed yes – his hunting crouch, the obvious trust in the weapon, the way he and it seemed to fuse. How could that gun look so right for him? How the hell could he look so right for it? But, my God, he might kill Dave! She moved from behind the desk and ran, actually ran, across her carpet and into the outer room, a hand stretched out, wanting to pull that stiff gun arm down, ruin his stalking pose, bring him back. As she ran she yelled: "Don't come in. Dave, don't come in. He's armed."

Geoff kept the gun arm out in front, kept his eyes towards the door, but swung his left, free hand at her in a fist, catching her on the side of the head with a sweeping blow, so that she slewed away, hit the wall hard and tumbled to the floor. Was that what he wanted – to make her get down out of the firing line? Or was it just rage with her interference, self-preservation? She hung on to consciousness, and lay crumpled and helpless under the big, framed, aerial photograph of Cardiff Bay. She saw the office door shoved hard open from the other side and a man there holding what seemed to her an identical black automatic. He was young, about twenty-five, in a brown trilby that seemed all wrong, another era. The gun, his age, the hat – the only points she noticed at first. She was hurt, dazed, and had a momentary thought that this must be why the guns looked the same and why the hat seemed stupid. She did not know this man, she was certain of that.

Then, as she stared at him, she saw his gun was aimed direct at her. It must have been the noise she made falling. He had heard this when the door was closed and came in expecting any trouble to start from that spot. "Geoff," she screamed, "stop him! He'll kill me. Stop the bugger!"

And Geoff stopped him. She heard what seemed to be two very rapid shots, but found afterwards it was three. The man in the hat had tried to spin and face Geoff on the other side of the room, and tried to swing his gun arm around from her to him, too. Fast, but nowhere near fast enough, he had seen his error. Briefly in his face then appeared an almost infantile look of hopelessness and defeat, a pathetic little smile showing good teeth, as though – she thought – as though he had known before he came here he would muck it up, maybe, go for the wrong target. His body suddenly jackknifed over the gun, and his hat fell off and rolled towards her: under it he was blonde, with a very pricey, very modish Mohican haircut. Why cover this with a crazy hat? Then he pitched forward, on to his hands and knees first but they would not hold him and he went flat a few yards from Julie, face digging into the floor, arms spread like a pavement chalk outline of the victim in TV murders. The gun had dropped and skidded a few yards over the tiles towards her, finishing near the trilby. He made some sort of noise, but not for long: a composite of sucking, gargling, mewing sounds, sounds like a child in hopeless difficulty and pain. She saw blood spread from under him on the tiles, edging out slowly in an almost symmetrical half circle, nearly as far as the hat and gun and the carpet. Geoff came and stood over him for a second, the automatic pointing at his head, as if he would fire again: his face with that virtually unknown look on it once more, feet wide apart, avoiding the blood. She said nothing. The harsh odour of whatever it was reached her – cordite, gunpowder? Geoff watched the man die, then turned to her, put the gun into his left hand and giving a small, worried smile, offered her his right to pull her to her feet. "Good girl," he said.

She tried to stand without aid, but felt too shaky. Putting a hand under her armpit, he lifted her. "Who is he?" she said.

"Some fool kid."

"But thieving? What? The guns look the same."

"Yes, I noticed."

"The guns – look, are you police, too, Geoff?"

"Too?"

"Are you?"

"Not police."

"What? I mean, carrying a gun."

He was closing the office doors. "I think we should put the lights out, in case the lad on Reception heard."

"What do you mean?" She was appalled by what he said.

"Then clean up. Get rid of him."

"What do you mean?"

"What do you mean, 'Are you police too'?" He locked the doors and switched off. "The noise might not carry down so many floors. And there can't be many other people about."

"For Christ's sake, Geoff," she said, "we've got to report this." She made a move in the dark towards the telephone in her room.

"No, hold on, love. It can't be like that." He took her arm, though gently. Their eyes grew used to the darkness and she saw him pick up the blouson and put his automatic back into the pocket.

"Not like what?"

"People would want to know why I have a gun."

"Yes?"

"It would be tricky for me. 'Dave'?" he said. "You shouted 'Dave'. This is your ex?"

"I was afraid it—"

He held up a hand, signalling for silence. Briefly, she made out through the dark that same look of total ferocity and remoteness in his face again. Julie heard a lift moving, but recognised the sound as downward. It would probably be the last of the people from another office, on their way home before Danny finally left and closed up. She felt a frantic envy.

"It was self-defence, him or you, that's all," she said. "There'd surely be no dispute, Geoff. When we report it." She tried to speak as she always spoke in these surroundings: calmly, precisely, like someone in command, of others, and of herself. She deliberately said "when" we report it, not "if" – shaping the outcome, as she would in a business negotiation.

"Don't be so fucking stupid, Julie," he replied, his voice loving but educational. He put his jacket on.

She wanted to run from him, from here, just get out and away to anywhere, but knew she couldn't. For one thing, she saw he would not allow it. In any case, executives did not run, not from their own terrain, damn it. Searching for a reply, she found only a dowager cliché: "You can't speak to me like that," she squawked.

"Of course I can't," he said. Once more his face had softened. "Sorry. But I don't think you're seeing things straight, that's all. You're off your perch, Julie. Understandable, entirely. From when you fell." There was to be no explanation of the blow? He knelt and began to go methodically but very swiftly through the dead man's pockets. "We shouldn't hang about."

She hated the "we", as though their involvement was equal. It was he who was shaping things. "You know this man?" she asked.

"People with a grievance. It tears them, won't ever leave them alone. And so—"

"What grievance?"

"From another time." He was making a heap of the man's possessions, well clear of the body and the arc of blood. "Multi-model car keys," he said, putting them with the wallet and other items. "There'll be a stolen vehicle somewhere. Well, clearly. Maybe near my place, if he dogged me."

There had been the rumours about a vengeance party, perhaps a London vengeance party, looking for someone on the marina when Dave's black colleague was attacked. So, in that other time Geoff really *had* been someone else?

"You expected him?" she asked.

"They get like there's no choice – obsessed," he said, not turning, speaking down towards the floor and the corpse. It felt to her like having a conversation with a mechanic under a bonnet. Geoff had to lift the body's head and face a little to reach his inner pockets. There was a sudden weak groan from him and she could not prevent a tiny scream. "It's all right, Julie. Doesn't signify. Just trapped air. He's got three rounds in him where they count. Nobody could make a mistake at that range."

She had an idea that most people could. "But about what? Obsessed about what?"

"This is from another time. *I* understand him."

"Understand someone trying to kill you?"

He laughed. "Understand it, don't *like* it."

"Is this, well, vengeance for something?"

158

"They can't let it go. I do see that." It was as if there were some kind of vile alliance between him and the dead man. She felt excluded.

"Have you hurt someone, Geoff – to start all this?"

"They think they run a special kind of law. They're beyond the normal one, Julie."

"And he's so young."

"A kid who thinks he's big. Thought. The others probably don't even know the dull sod gave himself this mission."

"Which others?" She felt glad that Dilsom, working there, almost obscured the body. It was best not to look at it, even blurred by the darkness, and even though the face was down: perhaps that doomed smile and the fine teeth would still be in view otherwise. She bent and examined the hat and the gun instead. "How could this be the same as yours?"

"The pistol? Probably not really the same. A lot of these automatics are very similar. All built to do the same job, aren't they?"

She crouched lower, trying to read the name on the barrel and butt: "'Ruger'?"

"Yes, I think there *is* one called a Ruger."

"Is yours?"

"Very common."

"I never realised you knew guns. As if you lived with guns."

They were standing near the main room doors, listening. He said: "If we can get some water and brushes, the tiles will make cleaning easy. And then something to wrap him in. Something strong. Waterproof if possible, so no staining in the car. Sure, it's going to be a tricky one. But we can cope."

He stood up, gathered the possessions and put them all into his pockets. "Get him into deep water somewhere, weighted. I might strip him, too. It will slow identification, in case he ever comes up. If he's found anywhere around here – more grievances, never ending trouble. Clearly. Like I said, bread upon the waters, liable to return after many days or less." He leaned forward and she thought he wanted to kiss her. She recoiled, almost stumbled again.

"It's all right," he said. "I'm only looking at where I hit you." At last. "Bruising, but not too bad. Sorry, lovely. Just

159

the quickest way to get you out of the firing line. Seemed."
He laughed again. "And then he's aiming direct at you. My
mistake. Almost. Thank God, only almost." He faced her,
smiling right across his face. "I thought it was great, that shout,
to kill him. No messing. For you to see the situation so stark
like that, so right. Grand."

She gasped. "No," she sobbed, "no. Never."

"You don't even remember? Natural enough. This was big
stress for you, Jule. But you still came good."

She would not be sucked into this. Her words were clear
in her mind. Verbal recall was another of her valuable career
skills. "Not kill him. I said *he'd* kill *me*."

He imitated her: "'Stop him!' How else? This is a mad boy
with a Ruger P-85, fifteen rounds."

"'Stop him' is not 'Shoot him', for God's sake."

"All I could think was I had to help you, Julie."

"He wasn't even aiming at me then."

"He'd have done us both. These people. He's travelled a
distance. He's not going to leave risks. That's basic, even for
a kid like this."

Not long ago she had read of some famous trial after the
war when a man was convicted and hanged because the
prosecution said he urged an accomplice to shoot a policeman.
Derek Bentley? Was she equally involved after all? Had she
already been sucked in? God, if she could only talk to Dave.
That was forever impossible.

"Your car's handy?" he asked. "I'll open up the yard. You
can come down the lane and drive right in." He unlocked the
office doors now and stood listening for anything elsewhere in
the building. "We're all right. Your ex-partner calls on you
here, in the middle of the night?"

"Sometimes. Not what you think. Not like you and me."

"Is he police? Some of the things you said."

"What things?"

"Police 'too'. And then 'Dave'. 'Don't come in, Dave.'
There's a cop called Dave Brade here, isn't there?"

"Would I know all the police?"

"You lived with Dave Brade?"

He spoke almost casually, as though he were aware of it
already. But she stayed careful: "You know him, this Brade?"

Quietly, he began to croon:

"I wonder if she ever tells him of me,
I wonder who's kissing her now."

Nothing seemed able to shake him for long. He turned and
pushed the man's arms and legs closer to the body, making him
parcellable. "No wonder this lad could get to me, then. He's
useful to Dave, isn't he?" He toed the body. "Christ, though
– Brade's supposed to be looking after me but would like me
out of the way? He still loves you? I can understand that, too."
Again he spoke as if he had considered this possibility before.

"Well, *I* don't understand *you*. 'Let this man get to you'?
What the hell are you saying?"

"I expect you know," he replied. "Somewhere there'll be
cleaners' gear, won't there, Julie? Any idea? A bucket, water,
mop, scrubbing brush?"

She went out on to the landing, down one flight and opened a
cupboard. She collected the equipment and returned. He took
the bucket into a washroom and filled it. He switched on one
light, a desk lamp, then began to swab the tiles. The bleeding
seemed to have stopped.

"There's a big canvas sheet in the cupboard, used for
protecting office machines when they're moved."

"Good girl," he said. "Could you bring it?" She went back
down to the cupboard and began pulling the sheet up the
stairs. He heard her struggling and came out to help. They
had a corner each, tugging. It was a very joint operation.

"This will be fine," he said. "Where would I be without you,
Julie?"

He would be somewhere else, and so would the dead man,
if the dead man had been stalking him. She would have settled
for that.

Geoff spread the canvas near the body, then lifted him
carefully on to it, first head, then feet. He left the face
down. He folded the sheet over him. "Is there some heavy
string? Flex? I'll forget about undressing him." She found
herself looking for exit wounds in his back, but no.

She brought Geoff an extension lead and he tied the bundle
tightly around the middle. She thought of Vietnam body bags.

161

He pushed it to one side and worked again with the mop and water. "That's all right," he said eventually. She gathered up the cleaning equipment and returned them to the cupboard.

"I'm going to need some help with him, I'm afraid, Julie."

"We can risk the lift in a little while. After midnight. Danny will have gone off and locked up."

They sat on the floor hardly talking for a quarter of an hour, the swathed body between them. Then, with her at the feet end of the roll and Geoff with the head, they carried him to the lift. Julie closed and locked the office. At the ground floor, they took him to the fire exit and Geoff opened the lane doors while she went for her Senator. She backed in and they loaded the body into the back. Then she drove into the lane and Geoff pushed the fire doors to and bolted the lane doors from inside before climbing the wall and joining her.

"Where can I drop him?" he asked.

"The dock?"

"You mean the lake on the marina?" He sounded horrified.

"No, a real dock. Some depth." She saw she had become entirely a part of it now, and her mind operated in the practical way it would in meeting any problem.

"Good girl," he said.

She drove on to the dock. He wanted a weight for the body and with some spare on the extension lead lashed her jack and spare wheel to the canvas cover, first deflating the tyre. "I'll get you replacements," he said.

"Might mine be traceable?"

"Never. How many Vauxhall Senators are there in the world?"

"Maybe."

"He's not going to be found." They pushed the roll off the side of the almost empty dock so that it hit the black water lengthwise with a fat, noisy splash. They had feared the body might slide out from the cover if they slanted it in, and float free of the canvas and weights. The water closed over the bundle at once. They waited a couple of seconds until the bubbles ceased. Nothing surfaced.

"We're all right," he said. "That ship moored there is mothballed. Nobody aboard."

"I'll drive you to near your house," she said.

"No. Police are around there a lot, off and on."

"Why?"

"Prosperous neighbourhood. Your car could be familiar, couldn't it? Can you drop me at a club in the middle of town?"

"Alibi?"

"Yes."

"Done this before?"

"Plus I could do with some fun, couldn't I? Feel like coming in?"

"No."

"No. I'll get a cab back."

She drove him to St Mary Street. There might be still time for him to sneak into a club, buy some drinks, talk, get noticed.

"You've been great, Julie," he said. "So great. I'll give you a ring."

"No, don't," she replied, "ever," and did not wait to see what happened to his face this time.

Chapter 24

Brade talked with the Dilsom children for far longer than the ten minutes he had promised himself. It seemed necessary. The duty towards Carmel and the twins still pressed him, in that worthy, burdensome way duties always pressed Brade. And he decided he would be wrong, selfish, to abandon them now to go and check on Julie's safety. After all, did she fret about him, the drifting, grubby-soled wretch, bare arsed on status carpet late at night? The Dilsoms were his job. Julie was not. She was simply part of his past, and wanted to be that only.

Short of sleep, the children looked blank-eyed and battered by tension. Carmel was just a villain's lady, yes, and from a long breed of villain's ladies, but some were great mothers and worried over their kids. She might be right to sense catastrophe close. Brade sensed it himself. Probably the boy was lying wholesale, yet these kids deserved gentle consideration. From Rockmain they would not get quite that: expert treatment, yes, but this was what it would be – well-intentioned, coercive *treatment*. At the moment, they might need something different.

Even when Brade and Carmel said good night to the children and went back downstairs, he did not leave immediately. She was still twitchy. If these bad moments were not handled right, Brade feared the whole operation could drop through the hatch. That sort of failure would stick to him: Bullfinch would make sure of it, in his polished style. Carmel had to be talked back into compliance, tonight, now. Later, she might be irrecoverable. She made some tea and they sat for a while in the winsome living room.

"Did you believe him?" she asked

"Oh, yes."

"No you bloody didn't. He doesn't think so, either. I could see that. He's a nice kid – assumes everyone is at least as clever as himself."

Not bare arsed, Carmel was sitting on the yellow-beige check carpet, her back against one of the smart settees, legs folded tight under her. Even in the old tracksuit, she looked pretty sound, and Brade could understand why Rockmain would yearn to think she fancied him. How could someone trained in psychology get this so wrong, even someone with clothes like Andy's? But perhaps psychologists were the same as everyone, and sometimes believed what they longed to: sex hacked its own paths, and one whiff of fine pussy kicked learning dead. Poignant really: Rockmain convinced he must fend her off, she thinking him offal. As for Brade, he had always liked knees and hers were directed conversationally towards him under the plum material, because of the way she sat. Her position made her body seem relaxed, youthful, lithe, yet her face remained full of anxiety and perhaps a sort of dangerous, mounting impatience with her predicament. Christ, how Brade loathed contact with women's agonies, almost always so damn genuine and multi-stage.

She pulled hard at the tea then leaned a little towards him. "Look, Dave, couldn't Rockmain ease off for a while. Say, catch up on his self-abuse? Just until the kids—"

"We get him on charter for a set time. Then he's wanted elsewhere, so he works to a schedule."

"Slow it down?"

"I see the point, but I'm not in charge of this job, Carmel."

"My name's Angie."

"No, it bloody well isn't," he bellowed.

"I'll come back to being Carmel, fear not. But we're talking important things, Dave. I'd like to feel it's me talking them." Her tone said he would understand this and not really object. She had the poise of a beautiful woman, and there must have been times, and times not so long ago, when her breeziness would have done the trick with any man she tried it on. To lose control of Dilsom had probably amazed her, half devastated her, poor bird.

"What does Geoff call you?" he asked.

"We stick to the programme, I promise. Yes – Geoff,

165

Carmel. It wouldn't matter much to me what he called me. Nor vice versa, I shouldn't think. We don't talk too straight to each other. What's there to talk about? I mean, he'll be out fucking something now, you realise that? Naturally you do."

"You shouldn't say so, Carmel," he replied. No, not such brutal exactitude. "You shouldn't say that, Angie."

"Thanks."

"For tonight, only. God, in your house and calling you Angie. It's indiscipline. I'd get flayed."

"Pull Rockmain back, Dave," she replied. "Your word would count. You know the situation better than anyone."

"Not better than Rockmain."

"Yes, of course better. That one's text-booking, career-mongering. You see things."

"Anyway, that's not how a police force works. People at the top make all the big decisions, not the people who know how things are."

"My whole family hate police, you know. Like a faith."

He tried to work out where that had come from. "Yes, I heard."

"And here I am putting my kids in their hands. Your hands."

"I like them."

She smiled in a genial, grateful style. "Obviously, you don't give a monkey's about them, Dave."

"That's not true, Car – Angie."

"You'll do what you can for them, because they're on your manor. You wouldn't see any kid hurt, I know. But they're nothing to you as persons. How could they be? They're a crook's kids who've been dumped here. How can they matter if you're trying to change them into somebody else?"

"I have to get around the area a bit now, Carmel," he replied, standing. "If Geoff's down the foreshore, I should try to find him. It's not too wise."

She stood, too. "Carmel. OK. You won't call Rockmain off – just for a while, so they can recover a bit?"

"I'll talk to him. He might agree himself, if he thinks it's becoming too much. He's very aware."

"No, he won't agree. It would be like admitting he was a cold, smart, devious sod."

166

"It's all in a good cause."

"Who's been coaching you, Dave?"

By the time he reached Julie's building, it was approaching 1 a.m. The main doors were closed and Danny had gone off. From the front he saw no lights anywhere. Brade had an idea a security firm did random calls throughout the rest of the night. He left his car and walked around the building, mainly so he could look from different points at the fifth floor where Julie had her office, and see if he could pick out any light or movement. No. He checked the doors front and rear and found them secure. Perhaps Dilsom really had gone to the foreshore. If so, stuff him. Let the bugger commune with Neptune and the effluent. Driving back up Bute Street he watched for him making his way home on foot from Julie's office but, although the fog had thinned, saw nobody.

At the flat, he fixed himself a big gin, took off his jacket and gun harness and sat down for half an hour with Captain Scott, restricting himself to the early, hopeful part of the story: he needed a dose of thumbs-up which the gin might not be able to provide on its own.

Just before 2 a.m. when the *Terra Nova* was so gamely leaving New Zealand, Bullfinch telephoned. "Apologies, Dave. Were you bedding seamily with one of your gals? We have an incident. Not a matter for an open line. Could you pick me up from home soonest?"

In the car, Bullfinch said: "I'm informed automatically on anything affecting Dilsom. These born-again jobs have to be the direct responsibility of a staff rank. Well, as you know. It's not unreasonable since the implications are extremely large-scale. And so, a call at 01.40. Only par for the course. What I always say is, if one wants a night's sleep and a KCMG one should have joined the Treasury instead."

"What do you mean, sir, you're informed when Dilsom is involved? How many of our people know about him then? I thought it was restricted."

"So it certainly is. But I must have some extra eyes, Dave, mustn't I? It's crucial I know about an unfortunate event like this tonight. Surely?"

Brade was enraged, and fearful. "Is he all right?"

"I think so. More or less. Four Horsemen Club, city centre."

Brade pulled in some distance from it and waited. He would follow the security rigmarole, despite what he had just heard from Bullfinch, and they must have no public contact with Dilsom, especially in this sort of place. There would be many here who could recognise both Bullfinch and himself. A couple of police cars and a paddy wagon stood near the club doors and uniformed officers were bringing people out and escorting them to the wagon, manhandling some. There seemed to be injuries, police and civilian. Brade did not see Dilsom among the men arrested.

"He shouldn't really be in this sort of dump, Dave, at this sort of time."

"He's been told, sir. But he can't be supervised nonstop, especially now Glyndwr—"

"Let's hope Dilsom comes out alone for a cab. We can pick him up then. Yes, news on Glyndwr? Speaking yet?"

"Nothing."

The police vehicles drew away. Shortly afterwards, Dilsom appeared and looked about. He seemed undamaged. Brade let him walk a few yards from the club, then followed and pulled in. Bullfinch lowered the window and said: "Taxi, sir?"

Dilsom saw who they were and climbed into the back. Brade drove down St Mary Street towards Bute Street and the marina.

"I expect I've been naughty, have I?" Dilsom asked.

"Have you?" Brade said.

"I get so I'm desperate for an outing now and then. Stir crazy?"

"The Met kept you *out* of stir this time," Brade said. "Remember?"

"I heard the Horsemen was a nice, respectable place and, of course, the night I go there's the fight of fights."

"These spots are much of a muchness, Geoffrey," Bullfinch replied. "You should make them out of bounds, really."

Brade said: "You didn't start the fracas, did you, Geoff?"

"What's that mean?" Bullfinch asked.

"Oh, alibi tactics."

"Alibi for what?" Dilsom replied, guffawing. "Word from another era. Those evil days, gone for ever, thank God."

"You might guess we'd hear you were there, Geoff, especially if police come to a disturbance," Brade said. "Been in the Horsemen all night? Of course you have."

"Here and there. Pubs, clubs. Just unwinding."

"Alone?"

"How I always unwind."

"Not what we heard," Brade replied.

"But we would like you to be more careful, Geoff," Bullfinch said.

"Yes, it was stupid. I can see that," Dilsom replied.

"Things are coming along so beautifully," Bullfinch said. "Madness to put it in jeopardy. Rockmain tells me he needs only a little while longer and our main difficulty – that's the children, naturally – this main difficulty will be resolved. It's a remarkable piece of work. He's a remarkable man. He deserves cooperation, Geoff. I'm afraid tonight is not exactly that."

Brade stopped not far from the marina entrance. "Think your virginity will be safe if you walk from here?" he asked. He got out from behind the wheel and, bowing slightly, opened the rear door for Dilsom, as a taxi driver might have done, thirty years ago. Brade managed to brush a couple of fingers against Dilsom's great-outdoors blouson as he left the car, and decided the bulge he had noticed in the breast pocket was probably an automatic pistol, about Ruger size.

"Don't loiter," Bullfinch said. "We worry about you. We made you, you see. You're ours."

Dilsom waved and walked.

On the way back to Bullfinch's place in Lisvane, he said: "Alibi? You're suggesting what, Dave?"

"Just my try-on, sir. But it's standard – start a fight, to get noticed."

"A try-on based on what, though?"

"Just my try-on."

Bullfinch sighed. "Dave, Dave, part of the work on Dilsom entails treating him as we would like him to be. What we would like him to be is a respectable part of a decent community. Does it help to talk to him as if he's still a villain? Going to a nightclub is unwise, not illegal. Slurring him as you did, Dave, lets him see what we – or what you, at any rate – still really think of him. You're looking for the old self, the Hector Vale self, as if it can never be dispelled, whatever effort is made. "Can the leopard change his spots?" and so on. Don't you see that to regard him like this is itself a means of producing that very condition? He's liable to say, If they think I'm still the same old villain, that's what I'll fucking well be." Bullfinch went louder, more affable. "Do I sound naive, Dave? Your experience tells you he might slip back? And I have to say mine does, too. Shit's undeniably shit. But, Dave, we must close our minds to those normal police reactions. We are engaged in a wonderfully worthwhile salvage task. We *have* to believe in it, have to believe that once in a while good can beat evil, or where are we in our job? I certainly don't hold it against you that you should be sceptical. I know I sit up there, lording it on the management floor, in a sense remote from the detailed problems of this operation. But, please take it from me, Dave, remoteness can sometimes be an advantage. It does furnish the overview. It does make possible a kind of creative impetus. That's a bit corny? But you know what I mean."

And the altitude ensured that when he was into fluttering panic and strewing blame about it hit with a real smack and got a good scatter. "I think he was impressed, genuinely chastened, sir, that you, you personally, I mean, should have turned out at such an hour. That was in his voice. in his eyes."

"Occasionally, Dave, it's what rank is for. Occasionally, all that damned insignia earns its keep."

Chapter 25

Walking the few hundred yards to his house from Brade's car, Dilsom unzipped the gun pocket. He felt jubilant, full of victory, high on blood. He was Hector Vale. Didn't a brilliantly rigid, beige parcel in the dock prove it? Poor old Rick Cole. He had recognised him straight off. Forget those clever, dirty, pressurising police schemers who had worked the alchemy on him. Thought they had. Could Geoffrey Dilsom produce a triumph like this evening's? Could Geoffrey Dilsom cluster three bullets so sweetly in a lad's chest at that speed? Julie was bound to turn nice again when she did some real thinking about these events. Clearly in her office tonight and then at the dockside that girl had suffered more than customary executive stress.

It was very late and he saw nobody in the streets. What he had to think, though, was that this area had definitely been located. It had looked like it when that black cop was hammered. Tonight made it certain. Rick Cole must have known, and maybe more than Rick Cole. Hector Vale – yes, Hector Vale, Hector Vale, Hector Vale, not sodding Dilsom – Hector Vale brought the Ruger out of his pocket and held it pointing down to the ground. He made sure it was hidden from the road by his leg, in case Brade and the other one decided to drive past and check he had made it home. Clearly Brade knew about the weapon, and had done that quick, nearly undetectable fondle to check when he opened the car door. But knowing and seeing were different, and if they caught him with the Ruger in his hand they would have to act: at least take the gun away – leave him open – and possibly worse. They might *want* to leave him open. That Brade was all-round smart. He needed watching. Was he smart enough, and hard enough and sick enough to make a path for Rick Cole? With police you never knew how far they might go. They felt so entitled, such eternal winners, and they muddled things to fit.

Well, hard luck, Brade. It came unstuck. The clever bugger had had the Four Horsemen situation almost right, too. Although Dilsom did not start the fight there – how in hell could you start carnage like that and not get hurt? – no, he did not start it but was creating on alibi for himself in another club nearby, heard what was happening and rushed over to be present and noticeable before the riot squad arrived with the dogs, staves and notebooks.

The night was icy. Long fingers of cold fog still lurked, yet he glowed with a sense of decent work nicely brought off. The Ruger was a gorgeous friend: its shape neat, the fifteen rounds in the magazine so weighty and irresistible. Those could dispose of a deal of opposition, if more opposition showed, which had to be likely. Naturally, he had taken Rick Cole's unfired Ruger for himself, wiped his own and put it in Rick's pocket before committing him to the reasonably deep. This would give the police a puzzle, if the body ever came up, which also had to be likely. He had said the boat in the dock was mothballed, but he could not be sure, and the splash might have been seen or heard. The dock gate office had seemed unmanned when they went on and off, but you could not be sure of that either. There had been a light burning. Someone might have wondered and watched. Or would some huge propeller disturb the bottom one day and spin ex-Rick slowly to the top trailing bubbles, like Esther Williams in an old movie on TV, but only a bit like?

Of course, by then Rick might not be identifiable, not even with that haircut. Shot with his own gun? Suicide? But how did the Ruger get into his pocket then, and how did the body get into its canvas envelope, adorned with Vauxhall sinkers? Let the police try to sort it out. Julie would not feel like helping them, even if she was once Dave Brade's, as certainly did seem: Julie was part of the action – had yelled for the kill, found the shroud, donated the weights, supplied the hearse, been a solemn bearer, helped him give Rick to the dark water. He did not think he had ever shared a girl with a cop before, but she had real kindness and vim. That jokey bastard, Len, though, kitting both with the same fire power! So straight and fair. Len had this gentlemanly streak under all the rough crust

172

and must have wanted to make sure two clients blasted each other in conditions of pure equality.

Near the house, Dilson became even more wary – not scared, just on guard. He and the virgin Ruger could cope. Clearly what he must consider was that Rick Cole might not have travelled down alone to find him. His father or bloody uncle Bart could be around, waiting. Would they trust the boy to manage something like this on his own? Trust Rick? Rick Cole? It was a mighty surprise to see him come through that door solo. Just finding South Wales must have been tough for his brain, never mind the rest of it. And, even if he had done the trip unsupported and in secret, others of the family might follow as soon as they discovered he was missing, afraid he would foul up and spoil the scene, perhaps get hurt or taken. Get killed.

Dilsom walked past the house first, and on the opposite pavement. He saw nothing to worry him, but kept going a good stretch, listening, occasionally glancing back over his shoulder. Then he crossed the street and began to return faster, the Ruger still in his hand and on the traffic side now. Some risks you had to accept. He upped his speed even more.

Derwent and Barty would feel a real duty to help Rick. From far back in his career, Dilsom knew him as a kid who always fouled up. Always they had kept him right at the edge of jobs, ten per cent cut max: sentry, messenger, run a little diversion, something like that, or preferably nothing. Probably it was Rick who got it all so stupidly wrong with the black cop. A black officer hurt always produced busy police activity – a chance to act out big the politically correct stuff – and also brought them extra public sympathy, except from black villains, of course, who felt special joy when a sell-out brother suffered. Rick certainly did it all wrong tonight, though the actual way he passed away showed more than due tone, despite that noisy wind rush. It could happen to anyone shot. Now and then something was bound to come right for him, even if only death.

Dilsom looked about with appetite as he reached the house and exulted again that he had changed his Ruger for Rick's. Moving into the little front garden, he raised the automatic to hip height. Come on, then, laddies. Derwent Cole and Barty Linacre were a lot different from the boy. They would be angry, but not foaming angry, not angry beyond. They would stay very capable, meaning to survive and write "paid" in the ledger against Hector Vale's debt to Brydon and the clan. In the circumstances, fifteen rounds were so much cheerier than twelve, the circumstances being the foggy darkness and Derwent Cole and Uncle Bart. So come on then, laddies.

But he met nobody and went in and closed up. He did a swift tour of downstairs and found everything all right. Before going to bed he looked in on the children to make sure they were all right, too. Jeremy must have heard him and sat up suddenly in his top bunk, brown eyes open and staring, but maybe not focused. He seemed more than half unconscious. Anita slept on.

"All right, Jeremy?" he whispered. "Dad's home." He liked to say this in a thick, warm voice, as if it meant everything would be great and safe now. Because he never felt certain this was true, he said it often.

"My name is Jeremy Dilsom."

"Well, of course. I know that."

"I told him."

"Who?"

"The one who came."

"Which one?"

"I said, 'Jeremy Dilsom', not the other. Over and over I said that. I went to a circus in Cheald Meadows. In Cheald Meadows – clowns, horses, elephants, acrobats . . . Oh, what were the others? I can't remember the others." He began to shriek in terror at his failure. Dilsom closed the door, to contain the noise. Anita stirred. "I can't," Jeremy moaned.

"That doesn't matter a bit." Dilsom thought he should not help him. Jeremy had to do it himself, find himself, or find Jeremy Dilsom, anyway.

"But the others. Please, please. Clowns, horse, elephants, acrobats . . ."

"Lions and dogs, performing dogs."

The boy nodded and frowned over the defeat. Perhaps it had been a mistake to give assistance, after all. But Dilsom could not bear to see him tortured. "Yes, lions and dogs," Jeremy muttered. "Good. It was better to say 'Jeremy Dilsom' to him, wasn't it?" Now he gave a mighty smile, though he never looked at Dilsom but straight ahead, towards the foot of his bed, perhaps seeing nothing. "I knew he would be cross if I said the other, so just 'Jeremy Dilsom', nothing else."

"Who did you say it to, Jeremy?"

"The one who came here, not the other one."

"Which one came here?"

"From the house."

"Which house?"

"Oh, you know. That house. The born-again house."

"Mrs Canter-Williams's house? Why do you say the born-again house?"

"Books there."

"Yes, that's right, her husband was a preacher. Lots of books."

"One day when we were waiting she read a book to us, 'Ye must be born again.'"

"Yes, I've heard of that. But who came here from the house?"

"He's there sometimes."

"Andy? Andy came here when I was out?"

The child shook his head. "Not Andy, the other one. Not the other one who was in the Peugeot 605. The other *other* one, at the house."

"Dave?"

"Yes. I think Mum told him I said the other name, so he came up to see me and Nita, but when he came I said 'Jeremy Dilsom'. They were so surprised! And Nita." He smiled again and seemed about to sink back and go the rest of the little distance into full sleep.

"And then the Peugeot. Which one in the Peugeot, Jeremy?"

"Wearing a brown hat."

"Ah."

"That's the one."

"What did he say?"

"He said 'Jeremy Vale'. This is the one in the Peugeot 605, not the one who came here, you see. I said 'Jeremy Vale', too, but only when I was with him. That's the one in the Peugeot 605. When the other one came I said 'Jeremy Dilsom'. It was easy."

"That's best, I think. What colour was the Peugeot?"

"Well, a black Peugeot 605."

"Did you have a ride in it?"

"My Mummy says never go in a car with a man."

"Right. How did you talk to him so much, then?"

"How did he know 'Jeremy *Vale*'?"

"A mystery. Where is the car?"

"This car was—" But Jeremy sank down now and closed his eyes.

In the morning, Dilsom did a walk around the marina and found a black 605 Peugeot in the car park of an apartment block. On the back seat, there was a trilby like the one Rick Cole had been wearing, though navy not brown. The other one had gone down with Rick, also stuffed into a pocket, with the used gun. Rick liked a change of hats as well as underpants when he went out of town? Dilsom returned at around tea time and saw the car was still there in the same position. Bad for it to be on the marina, so near his house. The Peugeot had probably been stolen from somewhere handy for Rick in South- East London and might give Brade a link to him, if the body did reappear. And if it was not stolen it could tell an awkward tale to Derwent and Barty.

Using Rick's all-purpose keys he opened up, put on the trilby and drove in to Schooner Way. As he turned towards the marina exit he looked in the mirror and saw Jeremy on the corner of their street staring after the car and waving desperately with one hand. In the other he held a packed duffle bag from the house, as if he were going on a journey, and as if he was expecting to meet the driver of this car. Dilsom kept moving towards the exit and when he glanced in the mirror again saw that Jeremy had begun to run after the car, the duffle bag banging against his legs. He was weeping and seemed to be shouting something. Dilsom did not wait to hear what but accelerated away.

He would have liked to stop. The boy should not be out alone. Where the hell did he think he was going with the bag? But it would not do to be recognised by Jeremy when driving this car. It set up all sorts of connections, and the child spent so much of his time talking to police, being tricked and led on by them. Dilsom turned out of the marina and lost sight of Jeremy. The boy would soon give up and not go far.

Chapter 26

Brade slipped in for a talk to Glyndwr. There had been no news from the hospital, so presumably he was still in relapse, or still acting relapse: still hoping to solidify his career by catching solo and unarmed whoever came to finish him. Nobody would come. Hale-Garning had seen to that. Cliffy did not seem to be doing his sentry term any longer.

Around tea time as well as late at night there was a fair chance of being alone with Glyndwr: day visitors had generally gone for a meal and the evening contingent not yet arrived. There would come moments when Brade urgently needed another of these happy, fruitful conversations, preferably one-way. They were as bracing as renewed contacts with Captain Scott. By now the nurses realised Brade liked things *tête-à-tête*, even if one of the *têtes* was *blotto profundo*. They kept clear. Living alone, Brade had lost the notion of clean bed linen. It was a treat to gaze undisturbed on Glyndwr's. "Look, I feel I must give Julie the full story on Dilsom," B.rade said. "Now. Everything. His identity, his lech CV Yes, yes, I know, as you say, it's 'a flagrant breach of security' – Christ, where did you find language like that? – yes, a flagrant breach of security, but Julie has to learn what she might be drawn into. Well, has already been drawn into and should get out of prontoest. Why the rush, you ask? What's changed? Plenty. How do you expect to keep up to date dozing here? Or mock dozing. First, Carmel Dilsom suspects her son slipped out of the house and met someone, someone he won't talk about. It could be true. Bright, intuitive bird, not just a pair of openable knees. Think, Glyn: was it someone watching their place, ready to follow Dilsom and do him? Dilsom goes to Julie. These people blast off at anything in range. Get the full, frightening picture? I knew you would.

Coming back to what I just said: you don't miss much, you somnolent sod."

Under the brilliant head bandage, Glyndwr's closed eyelids began to flicker, very feebly, but unmistakeable, small, jerky movements, like a new chick breaking the shell. Then his lips trembled, twisted, seemed to be so bravely seeking words, as they had on that other occasion. "Oh, Christ, we're in for another clarion pronouncement on your future?" Brade said. "Just listen, will you?"

Glyndwr's hard brown eyes opened and rested on Brade, almost as if they saw him again. That had not happened last time, but had the time before. "Yes, tell Julie, Dave," Glyndwr remarked. "She's a fine girl, with a degree in Japanese. This could be the same bugger who skulled me, obviously."

"Obviously," Brade replied. "So, suddenly, you're feeling more with it again?"

"Obviously."

"Tired of the cabbage rôle at last?"

"Only you here, Dave?"

"The others come, devotedly looking for signs and dekinking your pee tube."

"They're a decent lot. I always knew it. A man's parents and his woman can be definite assets, on balance, Dave. But do you find that yourself?"

"Have you been hearing and understanding the whole time?"

"Which whole time?"

"Weeks."

"Weeks? You've been here before, then?"

"Don't give me that. We had a plan. You playing bait."

"Bait? I, Dave?"

"It hasn't worked. You can allow yourself a rapid improvement. Which bugger who skulled you?"

"Shit-head haircut. You know, Mohican. Fair. Boy-who-would-be-man sort. Twenty-five?"

"You saw him when he attacked you?" Brade said.

"Not when he attacked me or I'd have stopped him, wouldn't I, cunt? *Before* he attacked me."

"Why didn't you see him when he attacked you, then?"

"What's the other reason?" Glyndwr replied.

"For what?"

"Telling Julie."

"I find Bullfinch broadcasts about Dilsom, upping the gossip risk to infinity. It's one reason I prefer people in your state, Glyn – your recent alleged state."

"Bad. Just like Bullfinch: 'a flagrant breach of security'."

"Christ, where did you find language like that?"

"Dave, inform her right away she's banging an illuminated target."

"Won't it be a flagrant breach of security?"

"Christ, where did you find language like that?" Glyndwr replied.

"Then, as to security, if the medics learn you're talking, they'll inform telephone inquirers. You've a devoted uncle eager for bulletins. Once he finds you can speak again they might try something mad, before you're fully restored."

"That would be good, wouldn't it? Bait again. Some potential *gloire* for me, Dave. Anyway, you never know: I think I might slip back. As previously. These spells could be remissions only." His eyes closed. "Now and then in that state I get stupendous visions." He gently smacked his lips.

"Of career moves?"

"Religious."

"Your career dreams *are* a religion."

"Fair point, Dave."

From the hospital vestibule Brade telephoned Julie at the office and the Penarth flat but failed to reach her.

Chapter 27

In the late afternoon Julie gave up trying to work. She must see Geoff Dilsom again. Over the last couple of hours, the idea of permament separation had grown unbearable – had come to seem lunatic. God, why had she spoken those terrible words of dismissal? The unexpected power of the longing shoved her off-balance now, and her head was in tumult, her thoughts a jumble. Geoff had meant, had he, that from jealousy Dave had allowed the gunman a free run? Dave? Dave would do that? It was flattering, it was nauseating. Wouldn't Dave ever recognise things were over between them?

But, God, how could she have left Geoff in the middle of the night at a club where he might meet—? Well, who knew what he might meet at those places, what he might pick up for consolation, after her fanged goodbye? She blamed this bloody job: the big desk, smart room, nice salary – they had gone to her brain and made her think she could stand alone. He was worth more than all this rubbish. He had brought core and genuineness. Ludicrously, she had spurned them – had not even acknowledged them until now.

Announcing she had clients to call on, Julie left the building and drove. She had no means of reaching Geoff. Always, he was the one who made contact. She hated that, could not imagine how she had ever accepted it – Christ, this was the behaviour of a big-wheel executive? – but *had* accepted. That was how badly she had wanted him. Geoff was married, of course: she knew this and had from the start. It had caused her regret and shame, but not enough to stop. Because of his situation, he said she could not telephone him or even write. She had no home number or address for him, anyway, and he was not in the telephone book. Apparently, he worked from home, meaning no office number, either. Frequently he had promised there would be changes and that they would arrange a system. It did not happen. About him there existed a kind of manic secrecy, though she was coming to see the point now. Secrecy had its fascinating side, of course, its silly, grubby glamour, like adultery.

She made her way to the marina. The only geography he had ever given her was that he lived here. She had to assume this was true and hope to see him going to a shop or the pub, anywhere, on foot – a tiny chance, she realised, but how else? If she failed, he might never again get in touch and the thought ravaged her.

Driving in slowly past the Celtic Bay Hotel and beflagged apartment blocks, eyes skinned, she toured the smaller streets and found nothing. It was almost dark and many of the houses had lights on. As she passed, she tried to glance inside some of them but did not spot Geoff. It would have helped to know what his wife and children looked like. Had he ever told her even the children's sex? She could not say. Perhaps she had not wanted to keep his family details in her head. The human memory was kindly sometimes, let one forget.

If he was what she had come to believe, a hideaway grass, would they have a police guard at the house? Should she look for a sentry? Probably not: if that told her where he lived it would tell others. Persistence and luck were what she needed. She had no idea what car he owned, so could not identify the house that way either: he used to walk to her office, and if they went out would use hers or taxis. In any case, even if she located his house, was she going to knock the door and hope he answered? No, but she could lurk somewhere near, wait for him to emerge and apologise – implore him to pardon what she had said and take her back. Forget it, forget it, please. But what a miserable collapse after her show of steel last night! She was ashamed, found her state incomprehensible, and went on searching.

As she drove down towards The Wharf pub, she wondered whether she should object to being the lover of a grass – that outcast breed, loathed by their former crooked mates, and despised by the officers they helped. As a species they offended her, too, but Geoff was Geoff, not a species. She did not care what others thought of him. One

181

thing about the job: she had grown used to making her own decisions.

She was coming to the end of her first circuit, still crawling, still window peeping. In the headlights now she saw a woman walking urgently up one of the little streets towards the main marina road. As Julie watched, the walk increased to a run for twenty or thirty yards. The woman had on what looked like a plum coloured tracksuit a couple of sizes too big and training shoes. Late thirties? Over the track suit top she wore a large, multicoloured shawl to counter the evening chill, and in her right hand carried a long, silver coloured flashlight, though she was not using it. She glanced about constantly, agitatedly it seemed to Julie, and, hearing the car approach from behind, turned to gaze at it, stared at her behind the wheel, then looked away and resumed examining the houses and front gardens as she passed. She and the car reached the junction with Schooner Way at about the same time and Julie saw her cross the road and go down by the side of an apartment block towards what seemed to be a dock or ornamental lake. She was running again now, and had switched on the flashlight.

Julie turned right and prepared to do another criss-cross survey. She had seen nobody who looked anything like Geoff. Had he lied about living here – another element in that thick pattern of secrecy? And also, of course, he might have simply packed his bags – perhaps the family bags, too – and left, gone to ground elsewhere. Might Dave know that? Could Dave be asked? Did the arrival of the man with the Ruger last night mean Geoff had been pinpointed? Might more enemies follow? It could be suddenly too dangerous to stay. Had she cut him adrift at just the time he needed her support?

But he would not do a retreat like that, would he? Everything about last night said he had guts and did not crack. She loved this in him. Dave probably had those qualities, too, but she had never seen them violently tested, nor seen them so triumphant. There had been a noisy exuberance to Geoff as they drove from the dock after losing the body, as if he had won a fight, which of course he had, but also as if he had expected to, and expected to win any others that came. In her dismal, negative way she had tried to puncture his loneliness and he had ignored her. Naturally. What the hell did she mean by shunning him? Serves her right if he replied by cutting her off now. Possibly he suspected she would turn to Dave, talk to Dave – perhaps suspected she had never altogether turned from him or altogether stopped talking to him. And, yes, last night, in her confusion, she had wanted to call on Dave for help. She had not actually said so in Geoff's hearing, had she, God, had she? It had been a sadly childish impulse only, and it was past. Oh, Jesus, don't let Geoff have gone and don't let him shut her out.

As she turned into Schooner Way again, she saw the woman in the tracksuit, far ahead, apparently making now for a field on the other side of The Wharf pub. Even at this distance and seen from behind, she looked acutely troubled. Her head swung from side to side, as if she were still searching, and, although she did not run any more, she walked very fast. Once, she turned around to stare at the car again. Julie turned off and, keeping her speed at twenty, tried to sort out why she had changed so much towards Geoff in these last few hours. Part of it must be the knowledge that she lacked any means of finding him. That brought a crippling sense of desolation.

That desolation might have come if she had simply finished it last night, as she intended, without the events that followed. On top, though, was their total complicity in the death and the disposal. This more than anything must hold them together. In the brutal farewell she gave at the club she had tried to deny this alliance, or destroy it. Idiotic. They were linked. What amazed her now was to find how gladly she recognised this. It seemed to make her stronger, more secure. They shared something. It was something terrible, yes, but also something that bound them by its gravity, its risk, its excitement. It encompassed only the two of them, was gloriously and frighteningly private. There had been no voyeurism this time, no Danny or Dave. Crazily, she even felt a kind of sympathy for the two of them, at being no part of that terrible sequence. And there was some contempt for Dave, too. Had he really cashed in on Glyndwr's absence from duty to make an easy path to Geoff for this murderer? Thank God, that came unstuck, and now she was bonded to a man who had acted to protect herself and had acted with marvellous efficacy, and ready courage. He had not sought to kill anyone, but had unavoidably retaliated, to save her and himself. He must be right when he said he was only answering her yell of fear. To be tied to him was a privilege. This was a man who, if the rumours were true, had helped police and must now be wholly on the side of good. It might even have been a good action to shoot that man last night. The world was one killer less.

Near Foudroyant apartment block, Julie spotted the woman in the tracksuit, this time walking towards the car. Again she stared. The headlights showed she looked haggard with anxiety, yet was still beautiful, in a dark, heavy-faced, flinty style. Then, as they were about to pass, she suddenly stepped into the road in front of the Senator, shining her flashlight direct at Julie through the windscreen and holding her other hand up, like a policeman stopping traffic. Julie braked and rolled down the window. The woman moved swiftly around to her and shone the beam into the car, front and back, then front and back again, as if desperately looking for something. "So who the hell are you?" she asked Julie. The accent was harsh, not local, possibly London.

"What? Who the hell are *you*?" Julie replied. "What goes on?"

"Stop it, stop it. Tell me, sod it. Snailpacing around here time and again. What are you looking for? What's it's about?"

"About?"

"What are you doing?" She suddenly stepped away from the window and went to the rear of the car. Julie turned and saw the boot lid rise. Was this to do with last night? Jesus, this woman was police? The lid went down and the woman came back to the window.

"Bloody cheek. What are you looking for?" Julie said.

"Why are you trawling? Who are you with, smart cow in the big car?"

"With?"

"So why?"

"If it's your business, I might buy here," Julie said. "I'm interested in the houses."

"You look at houses in the dark?"

"I can come back, can't I, if I like the general layout? What's it to you, anyway?"

"I don't believe you."

"I don't give a shit what you believe."

The woman stood up straight, alongside the car, weeping.

When she spoke now, her voice was weak and Julie could only just make out the words. "I've lost my son, haven't I?" She began jerking her head about like a bird, staring all ways, as though suddenly aware she had been wasting her time here.

"But how?" Julie glanced back towards the boot. "You thought I had your son?"

"Somebody has."

"Oh, but how do you know that? Look, if I could help—"

She crouched down to the driver's window again. Most of the hostility had gone. "This is a boy of six. Perhaps carrying a duffle bag."

"I haven't seen anyone like that."

"You've been all round?"

"Yes, looking at property."

"You say."

"Have you informed the—"

"Plus there's a lot of deep water here."

"He goes out to play alone? In the dark?"

"He's upset."

"And your husband – his father? Is he searching, too?"

"What?"

"Your husband."

"Not here."

"But you must inform—"

"I've had a good look at that bloody, barmy lake."

"Well, I'm sure he'll turn up. I'll definitely keep an eye. If I should see him—"

"He's called Jeremy."

"Right."

"Jeremy Dilsom."

"Right."

She hesitated. "Look, he might say he's Jeremy Vale. Could be either."

"Oh?"

"He's upset, that's all. He doesn't know what he's doing, saying. A sort of game."

"And where do I bring him, if I find him?"

"Where the Orion is." She pointed. "The house with the lovely ornamental bars on the windows. They don't keep trouble out."

185

Chapter 28

God, what a grand tangle, though! Who the hell was he?
Dilsom, under Rick Cole's hat and driving Rick Cole's car, felt
even more like Hector Vale than he had last night. Glorious.
The car, the hat, were more symbols of victory, a victory
only Vale could have won, never Dilsom. Dilsom was just a
tough-guy jacket. He did not have it on now, not even for that
handy gun pocket. Instead, he carried the Ruger at his waist,
using a Wild West holster of Jeremy's. Oh, boy.

This mad trilby and the stately car – they were not trophies
he would be hanging on to for long, but they did give a little
glow and giggle. See how your identity could move, except it
never moved if you anchored it in something good. What he
would have loved was to meet Derwent Cole and Bart Linacre
motoring down in the other direction, supposing they knew
about the hats and the Peugeot, which you could not definitely
suppose. But if they did, the sight of him behind the wheel,
grinning in their lights under the navy brim, would heliograph
in one perfect flash that Rick had made another supreme
balls- up and would not be coming home with a prize. Dilsom
might have liked to tell them also that Rick would probably
have killed twice if he had not himself been knocked over, but
communications about the death of kin should be kept short,
especially to someone like Barty. Grins that passed in the night
were enough.

Dilsom thought he would ditch the car and hat in one of
the mid-town multistoreys, then walk home or take a bus.
Eventually or sooner the Peugeot would be noticed but there
would be no connection with the marina and probably by then
not with much else either. It would be just a London vehicle
stolen by someone wanting a comfy trip back to the land of
his fathers. And although it was not the land of Rick's fathers,

Rick's father might do a trip here any day to see what had happened to his little, ungifted lad.

On the way to the parking, Dilsom found himself driving past the spot in St Mary St where Julie had put him down last night, and where she had spat the get lost message. Twice she had told him *finito*: once before Rick, once after. Dilsom stopped grinning. The recollection pained him, and angered him. Or it pained Dilsom. It angered Vale. It might have flattened Dilsom. It made Vale wonder about a response. Also, it frightened Vale a bit, and all at once he decided that he should not lose the car yet. He drove on past the multistorey. Suddenly, he had realised the Peugeot could be an asset. By ingenuity and cheek, Vale had often lifted a plus out of what looked at first like loss or lumber, was famed for it. This car might lead back to Rick Cole. Or, if it had been stolen, would almost certainly lead back to Rick Cole's region, South East London. It certainly could not lead to Dilsom. This car had beautiful confusion fitted as an extra.

What he had to consider about Julie was she might grow into a hazard, and something would have to be done, and done soon, before she had time to open her mouth. He had learned a lot about her this last day or so, and most of it he did not like. That girl had too much neck, some of it on account of her brilliant bloody job and education, some of it for other reasons. She was still a great and sweet girl, but she was a great and sweet girl who probably used to have something deep going with a cop, and might still. This had to be grave. He could not get over her shouting like that last night – calling "Dave" when she heard Rick Cole outside the door. "Dave" made a habit of visiting her there? "Dave" was Dave Brade? It looked like that. It looked very much like that to Hector Vale, who never grew complacent, and was generally spot on and hence still alive, free. So, Julie chatted to "Dave"? They did not need to be sleeping together, though it could be that, too. Some people stayed friends when love affairs ended. It was civilised. There had even been a couple of seconds during last night's journey when he thought he sensed in her a yearning to cry out for help to Dave Brade. She had not done it, and he could be wrong, but the notion had been powerful.

Although she was implicated, it might not stop her talking

to Brade, one-to-one, in confidence. Police made all sorts of special rules for themselves and those they fancied, and she would know it. How could a girl with a nice background who saw a man killed and sunk keep quiet about it to a cop who was a friend or more? The only way she could keep quiet about it was to be lovingly and fully bound to the one who did the killing and dumping, and she had made sure she put an end to that, twice.

Brade would not use such information to bring a charge. He would not drag for Rick. Love and sex were thicker than dock water, and thicker than law and order, and he was not going to push Julie into a messy court situation. No, but Brade might somehow flight a word to Derwent and uncle Barny about the death of Rick. It would be easy, routine: police adored that kind of ploy when they wanted someone awkward dealt with off the record. They got the forces of villainy to handle it, meaning by forces of villainy not police forces, although they were that, of course, but the target's roughhouse *confrères*, as was. When Derwent and Bart heard how the boy went they would really frothy and mobilise. God knew how big it would get. Kill somebody's son and was your own son safe? For a moment then, Dilsom had a recollection of Jeremy in the car mirror this evening, out alone, unprotected in the dark on what could be very harsh territory. Tonight, he would have abandoned the chase and returned home safely. But was he going to stay safe? Putting three rounds into Rick was not the same as helping get his brother jailed. To Derwent, Barny, Len and all the others, grassing was vile, yes, but this had been mightily worse: execution, and a disrespectful way with the body. Dilsom had smiled just now at the idea of driving past Derwent and Bart in this car and this hat, sending the jolly message. But it was only that – a cheery idea, a fancy. It would not happen. If Julie opened her mouth and Brade opened his, the retaliation *would* happen, not at all a fancy. And perhaps more than Derwent and Bart would come stalking.

All right, he still had the Ruger and he also still had the confidence and taste for a fight. He might be able to cope. He might be able to look after himself and the family. The point was, though, as he suddenly saw it now, he probably did not need to face this danger, and Vale hated useless risk. It was sloppy. The Peugeot, employed with some skill, could wipe out most of the menace. It was crucial to do the best with what you had. That was Hector Vale. If the Queen gave honours for such flair he would spend half his life getting dubbed, etcetera.

He kept returning to the fact that Julie was a woman who had brushed him off twice, despite him saving her life. He had been really fond of her, but, Christ, ultimately she had turned savage, distant, and what it came down to is Julie might have to go. She had humiliated him, and she could make life so rough for him and his. Very regrettably, the case against her now looked strong. This was the kind of unsparing logic Vale had always been known for.

What he had to consider was, if she should be retrieved from this car, wouldn't all the signs point away from Cardiff and up the M4, possibly even to Rick Cole himself or one of his clan? Maybe it was Derwent's car, lent for the mission, or Uncle Bart's. This Peugeot, with her found in it, could really end all sorts of problems and lead to a tidy future for him and the family. Once she was dead, and by what must look like a South London hand, Brade would be right off his back. Then, if Rick did float up one day and they found Ruger rounds in him, the same as Julie, they were bound to make the link. Obviously, they would know the bullets in her did not come from the gun on Rick, because the tests would prove it, and the three rounds from the Ruger in his pocket would be in him, supposing he still had pockets and there was enough of him left to have bullets in. But police would find it was the same mark of Ruger for both, which signalled the same supplier and the same culture, a South London culture. The hunt would turn that way. Everything seemed to say that if Julie had better go she had better go now.

Or everything seemed to say so to Hector Vale. He knew that someone like Geoff Dilsom would probably back off from such a solution. This was a lovely, loveable, very bright girl, who could not help it, for God's sake, if part of her past had been spent with a policeman. After all, she had broken from him, and broken from him a long time before Dilsom arrived. There was no evidence that she would talk to Brade, no real evidence that she ever saw him these days. So, she shouted "Dave". Who said it was Dave Brade? Who said a cry like that in a crisis was not just an instinctive rush back to a time when this Dave – maybe Brade, maybe not – did look after her? Plus, she might have already spoken somewhere about what she had witnessed. Wouldn't killing be a pointless cruelty then?

On the other hand, Hector Vale saw all that as shit.

Chapter 29

Brade drove from the hospital to Julie's office, tortured now by the need to give her everything on Dilsom – and give her the perils in lights. He felt terrified for her. On the phone, her assistant had said she was out, which might be a brush off: perhaps Julie no longer wanted to talk to him. He did not want her to talk to him, he wanted her to listen. Of course, she would see only another try to make her break with Dilsom. It *was* another try to make her break with Dilsom, but not from jealousy. Not *just* from jealousy. She was right in the field of fire and did not know it. God, why should he still fret about her skin? He could not say. He did fret, though. Yes, yes, yes, of course, he could say; she was Julie, and that was enough.

Danny at Reception said she had left late in the afternoon. From Danny's desk, Brade tried another call to her flat in Marine Parade and to her car phone, with no success, and he went home in despair. He would wait an hour, then try her numbers again, perhaps revisit the office. He cooked a mackerel and to soothe himself caught up on a videoed episode of his most loved TV show, *Prisoner: Cell Block H*, while he ate. There was a knock at the door, very mild, very apologetic, and he wondered if Hale-Garning was pulling another jape and had Enid done up as a timid nun now. Brade considered not answering. He had to be free to make his calls, and free to leave at once if necessary. The knock was repeated and Brade, afraid it might be Cliffy feeling low, did open up.

He found a clergyman there, though not Cliffy. "Mr Brade, I wonder if I might beg a quick word. My name is Caspar Indicay. I'm on the Archbishop's staff. It's to do with a dear colleague of mine, a neighbour here, I think." He was looking past Brade towards the screen, his nose flaring to the fish aftermath. "Don't you adore *Prisoner: Cell Block H*? Such genuine face lines and the tension. My!"

"I've not much time."

"To do with the Reverend Clifford Hale-Garning."

Brade brought him in, switched off the set and poured two beers. They sat opposite each other near the record player. Indicay was tall, big shouldered, fair, very bright-eyed, saucy and at ease. To Brade he looked like someone you might trust with your soul, but not with your arsehole. "Cliff?" Brade said. "One of the very best. Such a credit to the Church. Frankly, would there were more."

"We're all immensely fond of him, of course."

"Rare," Brade replied. He downed his beer. "Mr Indicay, I'm afraid I—"

"It's a matter of – there have been some reports, Mr Brade. I won't say disquieting exactly. Untoward? Yes, untoward."

"Reports? About what? Where from?"

"Ah, you're a police officer, I believe. Plainly, if I may say. I expect very much used to getting down to the, as it were, nitty-gritty. Status of the sources, and so on. Absolutely understood. Some speak less affectionately than they might about the police, I fear, but I always feel we are in very capable hands. Oh, yes." He nodded and gave a large, contented sigh, then drank a mouthful. ,

"Look, I really must—"

"It's recognised at every level that Clifford might be under spiritual stress leading to utterly uncharacteristic behaviour, Mr Brade, which is one reason I am making these entirely confidential and I hope entirely sympathetic inquiries, but it concerns his apparent—"

"I don't want to hear this," Brade replied. "Spiritual stress is not my corner at all. This sounds like a matter private to Cliff. You know, Mr Indicay, I object to snooping." He stood. "I have to go."

Indicay had a pleasant chuckle. "Pots and kettles? Mr Brade, I understood you *are* a snoop. I mean, as it were."

"In a good cause."

"This, this too, is in a good cause. Oh, absolutely. This is to do with the mental well-being of a salaried servant of God, and to do with the very reputation of the Church."

"I've seen nothing to make me doubt Cliff's mental state. Never. That all? Something very urgent on. Something nitty-gritty."

"On no occasion have you noticed anything, I won't say *outré* – far too judgemental, which is not at all the purpose? Anything, yes, let us call it quaint in his behaviour?"

Brade said: "As a matter of fact, by remarkable acumen and courage he saved someone."

"Saved? A soul?"

"A life. Someone utterly helpless."

"Where?"

"The hospital. A patient."

"The hospital? Hale-Garning never goes to the hospital sick visiting. Indolence."

"Yes, saved," Brade said.

Indicay thought a while. "Someone utterly helpess? Do you mean saved your unconscious colleague somehow?"

"Not somehow. By acumen and courage."

"I've sought prayers for this man."

"Cliffy did better than that." There was a ferocious knock at the door and when Brade opened it, Hale-Garning rushed past him. He wore purple slippers, no dog collar and was in shirt-sleeves and blue bracers.

"I heard heavy talk. I knew it would be this one. One of the voices sort of sacerdotally sliming up through your ceiling, Dave."

"You had your ear to the floorboards, Clifford?" Indicay asked.

"I have to leave, Cliff," Brade said. "Now. Julie could be in danger. It's an involved story."

"Stuff her, I'd say," Hale-Garning replied. "As you know, Dave. The cow. How she's behaved to you. But what's this jerk asked you?"

Indicay now stood, also, the beer tankard in his hand. "Clifford, this—"

"Are you threatening me, you sleazy cleric?" Hale-Garning bawled. "Going to pull a bit of glassing? Come on then." He went into a wrestler's crouch, arms hanging loose. His breathing had become fast and hoarse and he kept his eyes hard on the beer glass.

193

Indicay turned, smiling, in appeal to Brade. "And this is our saviour, yes?" Cliffy saw Indicay's attention move and immediately flung himself at him, knocking the tankard from his grip and trying repeatedly to butt him in the face, crack his nose. Indicay brought his elbow down fiercely twice on the back of Cliffy's neck. After a half minute grappling they both fell heavily to the floor and fought there, punching and kicking.

Brade had left the door open when Hale-Garning burst past him. Now, he stepped over them and hurried to shut it and confine the din. As he did, Carmel Dilsom emerged on to the landing from the lift. She still wore the old tracksuit, with a shawl around her shoulders. She looked agonised. "I found you in the phone book, Dave. But not something to say on a clear line. Oh God, Jeremy's disappeared. Really gone. He took a bag."

"I'll come right away."

He brought her into the flat and she stood watching Cliffy and Indicay tear at each other on the mat in the beer pool.

"It's good and evil warring, as ever," Brade said.

"Jeremy could have been taken, Dave," she replied.

"Do you want me to get a proper search going? I'll ring now." He stepped towards the telephone. "I must."

"Police?"

"Of course, police."

"Not yet," she said. "But you – you come. Help me."

Brade bent down and pulled Cliffy and Indicay to their feet, then shoved them out of the flat and shut the door. He strapped on the Magnum under his jacket. "Where's Geoff?"

"Who knows?" she said.

"We need more people. What can I do unsupported? And I've got others to look after."

"Who?"

"Geoff, obviously."

"And?"

"We need a full, systematic—" He had been going to say trawl but stopped. "Street by street job."

"He wouldn't like it. Mobs of police."

"Who?"

"Hector. Geoff."

194

Stuff Hector/Geoff, too. "Well, if we can't find the boy in an hour, I'll—"

"You're scared of blame? Follow me, will you? All sorts around there. He'd been with somebody, I told you. Then some woman cruising and cruising. What's happening?"

"Which woman?"

"Smartarse. In a big Senator. I got the number."

She passed him a piece of paper but he did not bother even to glance at it.

"Oh, Christ, Dave, get him back and then get me and the kids out of it all, will you? I mean out of it all for keeps. Far, far away. Please."

"Hold on a minute. Sod, I should have done this before." He did move to the telephone now and called Julie. The office had gone over to answer-phone and and there was no reply from her flat or the car.

"Oh, please, hurry," Carmel said, pulling the door open.

Indicay and Cliff were still loitering on the landing when Brade left with her. The fighting seemed to be finished, but they did not speak to each other. Cliff wanted to go back into Brade's flat to pick up a lost slipper.

"Isn't he the chicest Cinderella you ever saw, though?" Indicay asked. Brade waited for Cliff to recover it, then locked up.

"Yes, make some speed, Carmel," he said.

Chapter 30

So, that was Geoff's wife. Julie drove around the marina a couple of times more. She no longer expected to see Geoff, but knew she should put up a show: if she retreated at once, it would look suspect, make her seem guilty. Perhaps she *ought* to seem – and be and feel – guilty. After all, wasn't she seeking the woman's husband to say she still wanted him, on any terms he liked, and never mind what she had seen him do, and never mind how much the style of what she had seen him do proved she had no idea what he really was? The absolute nature of the need thrilled her. All the dignity stuff, the status stuff, the thinking stuff was out of the window. The basics could still take over, thank God.

The woman had winced when Julie called her Mrs Dilsom, and the boy might want to be called Jeremy Vale. What was that about, for God's sake? Geoff and his family used to be Vale in a previous time? Should she know the name, Vale? If she read the London papers' crime pages would she have known it? Did it matter? The past could go forget itself, could go fuck itself. Not much at all mattered, except to find Geoff and patch up a future for them by flushing last night's evil farewells from his mind. Sometimes the memory could be managed and she was a smart manager: otherwise, would she be driving a new Senator, or have an office carpet thick enough for love?

Mrs Dilsom was certainly beautiful. A round-faced kind of beautiful but that was not impossible. Clara Bow had been round-faced and there must be one or two others since. Did Mrs Dilsom look sullen? Maybe more than that. The bite of her voice and the jut of her jaw seemed to signal not just the anxieties of the moment, but a deeper, more settled anguish. This woman habitually had trouble. Was there something horribly askew in the family, something that had reached even a boy of six? Julie looked out for this runaway child with his sad duffle bag now, this Geoff kid from far outside her realm and time, but did not spot either. As she drove towards the marina exit, she thought she did glimpse Mrs Dilsom still walking urgently and alone from one of the turnings off Schooner Way. As a mother she seemed no-end committed.

Something urged Julie to drive to the dock. It was not that she expected to find Geoff there. He would never be so crass. Folklore said people went back to the scene of a crime, but Geoff would not be one of them. No question, last night she had been with what Dave and his cop mates would call a complete tradesman. From Geoff there would be no daft twitches, no revisits of the scene. But as for her, she needed to be assured nothing had burst the surface over there in the dock – no long, intimate, pale envelope – that was all. It would be a lift to look at the stretch of black, featureless water with its powerful tale to tell, but not telling it. Not yet, at any rate. She did turn the car towards the dock gates, then almost immediately corrected. She must not be so stupid, either. They were a pair. Stay in synch. She had to be worth his while, behave like a complete tradesman – woman – herself.

She drove back to the office. If Geoff wanted to get in touch with her this was where he would come or ring. And, surely, he would want to get in touch. Jesus, surely. He must realise her attempts to ditch him last night were only mad spasms and would forget them. He distrusted car phones, and although there had been calls on hers while she drove, she left them unanswered, knowing they could not be Geoff. So, she must just sit at her executive desk in her executive suite and nervously wait, like eternal, waiting Woman. Yes, at such times, the lustrous career, too, could go fuck itself.

Danny said Dave Brade had been there and left a message asking her to get in touch. She could not be bothered with Dave tonight. He would be simply scheming to resurrect old feelings in her – trying yet again. The feelings had certainly once been real and strong and so lovely but they wasted away as feelings sometimes did, and would not come back. His persistence was nice, and a pest, and one day he would finally cotton on. Even now, after what had happened last night, it would offend her to hear Dave smear her new personal life with his sly, bullying, standard-issue police chat. There was a message from him on the answer machine, his voice taut and untrustworthy, and she ignored that, too. Best leave the phone on automatic: she could listen to any call and respond only if it was Geoff.

Realising he would certainly not want to come in past Danny, she went down the emergency stairs again and unfastened the fire doors. Then she returned and made a pretence at work. After a couple of minutes she raised her head and gazed about, smiling. A killing had taken place just outside this room last night. The recollection did not chill or frighten her or seem unbelievable or a long way off in time, as unusual events often did afterwards. No, she saw those events as more or less part of now, a yesterday that ran into today, and that drew her even harder towards Geoff: together they had seen this place become totally unlike itself, and then, also together, had made it ship-shape and innocent again after unique moments of vivid, grim violence. Vital to think of them as grim and not merely thrilling, or one might slip into moral chaos. It was also vital to think of them as defensive, or Geoff became an intolerable figure. But of course, of course they had been defensive. Above all, he had protected her and would always protect her. He reminded her of Gatsby: the crooked roughneck, the gallant knight. And, God, what a swinishly ungrateful response she had given to his gallantry. Oh, forgive me, Geoff, and forget it, please! Forget it, but never forget me!

She put out most of the lights, leaving only her desk lamp – their customary signal that she was here alone. More lights meant some of the staff were working late, and he should wait in the street. She tried to hound from her own memory now every one of those grotesquely self-destructive moments when she stood stiff behind this desk and addressed her brilliantly modulated, insane, sod-off words at him. The sickening gall. But what counted was the bright alliance they had in the later things, and this was bound to endure, just bound to, wasn't it?

Her telephone rang and the answer apparatus did its thing. She waited damp with anxiety to hear who would give a message and ready to break cover as soon as she heard him speak, but nobody did. Christ, Geoff might be unwilling to put his voice on a tape after last night. He would not know the situation here, not know whether she had opened her mouth somewhere, somewhere being Dave. She grabbed at the receiver. Whoever it was had rung off by then, though.

After another half hour she grew impossibly restless. She left her desk lamp burning and put a note under it: "Back in fifteen minutes." Geoff would wait. And if anyone else saw the message it gave nothing away. She drove again to the marina and did several more slow tours, passing the barred house twice, but still without seeing him and without seeing Mrs Dilsom this time. About to make her fourth circuit, she grew suddenly, joyfully convinced that he would be waiting for her at the office. It was the way things always went: you let your patience crack and immediately afterwards what you had been waiting for would happen – as if contrived by Fate to expose you as weak and panicky. She did not mind looking weak and panicky. At once, she turned around in one of the enclaves off Celerity Drive, to make her way back to the marina exit. As she did, the swing of her headlights caught for a moment a khaki bag of some sort on the pavement near the low front wall of one of the houses. Well, not of some sort – it was a duffle bag, no doubt of that. She stopped and sat in the car for a few minutes, her body half turned in the driving seat so she could look at the bag through the rear window.

She wanted to get out and walk back – would have to in a minute – but felt scared of what she might find nearby. Nothing moved in the street. The bag sat there like some small and partly dead mongrel. Eventually, she did grow ashamed of herself and left the car. She walked slowly towards the duffle bag and was bending to look more closely, perhaps to pick it up, when she became aware of the sound of gentle breathing. On the other side of the little front garden wall and tucked in against it lay a dark haired boy asleep, one arm folded to form a pillow for himself on the patch of grass, his legs in jeans huddled up towards his middle, perhaps in an effort to keep warm. He was about six or seven. She leaned down and shook him very gently. "Jeremy," she said. "Your mother's searching everywhere for you."

He took a while to wake up properly. At first, he glanced around, dazed still, and obviously uncertain where he was or how he had got there. Then he partly sat up, looked about him urgently and put out a hand in the darkness as though feeling for something.

"It's all right," Julie said. "Your duffle bag is here."

"Because I'll need that."

"Yes?"

"I brought a lot of things. Did I just put it there while I had a little sit down?"

"And you fell asleep, so tired. Your mother is worried."

"I expect so. How do you know? Who are you?"

"I met her."

"How did you know it was my mother?"

"She told me her little boy was missing."

"But how did you know it was my mother?"

"I didn't when I first met her. But when she said – then when I saw you there I thought you must be the little boy."

"Do you know her?"

"I met her in the street when she was looking for you."

"Do you know what her name is?"

"We should go back. This is someone's front garden."

He stood up and climbed over the bit of wall on to the pavement. Picking up the duffle bag, he opened the top to check thoroughly that everything was present. "Do you know her name?"

"Mrs Dilsom," Julie replied.

"Do you know my name?"

"Jeremy Dilsom." He looked like his mother: same colouring, the round face, similar surly intelligence in his dark eyes now he had woken up properly.

"That's right," he said. But he sounded disappointed. "Once, I met somebody else with a car, a man with a hat, and he knew who I was. He really knew."

"Which man was that?"

"This man really knew. I was going to meet him. He said he'd be there."

"You must be cold. If you get in the car I'll drive you to the top of your street and you must go home. I won't come all the way with you. I have to be somewhere."

"I don't want to go home, you see. This is why I brought these things." He gave a little shake to the duffle bag.

"But you must. Everyone so worried."

"Well, yes. Do you know my father as well?"

"I told you, I met your mother in the street, by accident, that's all."

"Do you know my father as well?"

"How could I?"

"Yes. I don't think you could. I don't think he's home. He wasn't home. He went somewhere."

"Your mother told me he wasn't home."

They went to the car, and he climbed in, holding the duffle bag. "A Senator," he said. "Quite often my father is not home."

"Oh?"

"It's what's called business. Like going to work, but more important?"

"I see."

"Do you know about business? I mean, with a big car, K-reg, although a lady."

"A little. I know a little about business."

"You might meet my dad then. He's called Mr Dilsom. Well, you know that I expect."

"Yes."

She started the engine but did not move off yet.

"Please don't take me home." He said it almost off-handedly, like someone directing a taxi driver. "Not now. I will go home later. Honest. Even though I brought the things in the duffle bag to stay away, such as bread rolls with Marmite and a sweater, I will go home. I think you could help me."

"How?"

"Because I think you know the way around this town, well, city, having a cathedral, you see. Being in business and having this car. And you talk like people who live here, so you know Cardiff, not a stranger."

"Yes."

"We're strangers – us. Where I want to go first, before I go home, is a place in this city. I know it's here."

"I have to be somewhere in rather a hurry, Jeremy."

"I'd like to go to a place called Cheald Meadows."

"I know Cheald Meadows, of course. In the centre."

"You see, they tell me lies about Cheald Meadows. I know it." He still spoke in that casual, definite way.

"Who?"

"This is people who are trying to help us." He stared at her, obviously wondering how much she could be told. He must have liked what he saw. "Well, I think they're trying to help us. They are not bad people. But to help us they have to tell lies." He fell into a whisper and glanced about. "Shall I tell you what I think? Shall I? I think they could be police, but they don't say they are police. Not police in uniform or I would know. Anyone would know that. But in ordinary clothes, like detectives on television. One called Andy. He wants to be our friend, that's my sister and me, taking us to Cardiff Devils, which is ice hockey, and singing. We have autographs. So, you see, I need to see Cheald Meadows. Did they have a circus there?"

"Sometimes they do."

"Did the circus have clowns and horses and elephants and acrobats and lions and dogs doing tricks."

"I should think so. That's what circuses are like."

"Yes, I thought so. I think all circuses are like that."

"What a circus is."

"I went to the circus, but I don't think I went to that circus. They took me to see Cheald Meadows and I don't think it was the same field where I saw the circus, but they kept saying it was and after they kept saying it I didn't know then."

"Who kept saying?"

"Andy, and Mum and Dad. Then Anita said it was."

"Your mother and father said so? I should think they'd have it right, wouldn't you, even if Andy is wrong? I shouldn't think your mother and father would tell you lies. Why should they? Perhaps you've forgotten where."

"That's what they keep on telling me. Really often."

He sounded desolated by what she had just said.

"Why do they keep saying that? Is it so important?" she asked.

"Elephants remember a lot you know. They never forget."

"I heard that."

"But even if you're not an elephant you can remember."

She switched off the engine. "And you remember all the things you saw there, so very clearly. Not just the elephants."

"That's easy. Andy told us how to remember."

"Did he?"

"If you say Cheald, you see – well, if you can spell that word Cheald, I know my letters, you see, and Anita, so then it's 'c' for clown and then 'h' for horses, 'e' for elephants, and all like that, you see?"

"Yes, I do."

"And so I would like to see this Cheald Meadows, and when we are there you wouldn't say all the time this is where I saw the circus, would you, because you don't know where I saw that circus at all, do you?"

"Of course not."

"And if you don't know my mum and dad, if you only met my mum in the street and did not know her, and if you don't know my dad at all, well, they could not tell you you must tell me Cheald Meadows, and keep on telling me Cheald Meadows, could they, until I said all right it was Cheald Meadows so we could go home?"

"No. But it's dark, you know."

"I know, but it will be all right. I will be able to see it enough. I will know if I really know it."

"All right," Julie said, and started the Senator. When they passed the end of the Dilsoms' street she glanced down towards the barred house and saw another car standing outside, perhaps a Granada, though it was only a glimpse in the dark and she could not be sure. Dave and some of his colleagues generally used unmarked Granadas. Perhaps Mrs Dilsom had reported the boy as lost.

Jeremy said very little at Cheald Meadows. She parked near and just let him walk part way around the perimeter, gazing in. There was no circus or any other visible activity there tonight and to her it looked simply like a dark field, with the shadow of its long pavilion building in the distance, and then the city lights beyond that. He was silent as they drove back. She hurried. It was worrying to drive on to the marina again, knowing a search might be under way. She pulled into the car park of the Celtic Bay Hotel.

"I don't want to come any nearer," she said.

"Why?"

"It will be a nice surprise for your mum if you just arrive by yourself. And if she asked where we had been I might have to say Cheald Meadows. You wouldn't want that would you?"

He shook his head. "You were kind. They do tell lies, that Andy and Dave, and my mother and father."

"Dave?"

"He's one who helps some times, not denim like Andy. Older and not pretending to be young at all like Andy. Dave came to my house. I told him I was Jeremy Dilsom."

"But you are, aren't you?"

"I've got to say that to him or he'd be so cross. He thought I would say – he thought I would say something else, but what I said was 'Jeremy Dilsom'."

"But you are Jeremy Dilsom, aren't you?"

"Sometimes." He leaned across and kissed her on the cheek. "Goodbye."

"Promise me, now, you'll go home."

"Oh, yes. Because you took me there, you see."

When she reached the office again, it was as she had left it. She checked for any sign that Geoff had come back and gone again because she was away so long, but could see nothing. The note was still in place. The things on the desk looked exactly as before. Nothing had been added on the telephone tape. She sat at the desk and began to cry, holding her chin cupped in her hands.

After a time she recovered control and her brain unfroze. She wondered whether Danny might have done one of his rare security tours of the building and fastened the fire doors. She cleaned herself up in the cloakroom and then went down the emergency stairs again to check. The doors were ajar still, and her sense of despair rushed back. She went into the yard and looked about but saw nobody. She drew back the bolt on the lane door to make things as easy as possible. When she returned to her room, Dave Brade was there, standing near her desk. "I've been trying to get you all night," he said.

"I've been really busy. I would have called back tomorrow."

"I meant to look in earlier, but some bother at home and then a small boy missing on the marina."

"Oh, dear."

"It's all right. He's back now."

"Thank goodness. All that open water."

"We've no idea where he's been. Child of six, but like a clam. Julie, this lad – it's connected, really, to what I must talk to you about."

"What now?" She had to get him out of here, fast. "Sorry about the gloom." She switched on more lights.

"This boy's called Jeremy Dilsom."

"Yes?"

Dave sat down. Julie went behind her desk and remained on her feet, like last night. Things must not get relaxed here. "Julie, you see someone called Geoffrey Dilsom. I know that. The point about him—"

"Dave, I don't want to discuss this."

He held up a hand. "Please. This is not – This is a police matter."

"When you came before with those vague tales of menace it was a police matter."

"Yes, it was. Things have moved on. It's worse."

She looked at her watch. "Danny will be locking up, Dave. I'm going now."

"I can say what there is to say in—"

"I've told you, I don't want to hear it. This is unfair of you. Can't you see this taints the memory of the very good times we had." She started to yell. "Dave, you're becoming obsessive, vindictive. It's bad. Please, leave now, would you?"

"Dilsom has a difficult—"

"Dave, stop it. Stop it, stop it. It's poisonous."

He went silent, gazing at her from his chair. Then he said: "All right. But can we talk about it later? Tomorrow?"

"Perhaps. I don't know what there is to say."

He stood and they moved towards the office door.

"Shall I switch off?" he asked.

"No, leave them. The security people like some sign of life."

They went down in the lift. Danny was about to close the main doors.

"Can I call you then, in the morning?" Dave asked.

"Not too early."

She went to her car and, sure he would watch, drove out

into James Street, as if on her way home. She turned off before Clarence Bridge, though, and waited for a time outside the Conservative Club in Burt Street. Then she went back to her office parking spot. Dave seemed to have left. Of course, there was not really any request from the security firm to leave lights on and Danny must have gone up and switched off. The whole building was dark. To check that the emergency entrance remained open she went in by the lane and fire doors rather than through the front with her key. And, then, mounting the stairs in the dark she suddenly had the impression that someone was ahead of her, a floor or two higher. She stopped and listened. There was a tiny sound, like someone very practised at moving quietly slowly ascending the stairs. Instantly she felt jubilant. "Geoff," she called in a big whisper. "Oh, Geoff, is that you?"

"Of course."

She could not see him but now heard footsteps begin to come down the stairs towards her, any attempt at silence abandoned.

"Darling," she said, "thank God. I knew you'd come back."

In a few seconds, he was with her and she clung to him in the darkness. He hugged her and they kissed and kissed again.

"But where have you been?" he said.

"Looking for you – on the marina. Driving around and around and around."

"Poor Julie."

She did not know why, but she kept quiet about meeting his wife and the boy. Perhaps she would tell him later. Her instinct said that somehow it would do her harm now, would get between them.

"I thought I'd lie low after last night," Geoff said.

"Yes. It was wonderful. Looking after me like that. And then for me to behave like that, unforgivable."

"Have you seen anyone – anyone to tell about it?"

"Geoff, how could I tell anyone? Oh, how?"

"Have you seen anyone?"

"People in the office. Nothing for them to notice there. We did a superb clean-up."

"Nobody else? No phone conversations about it?"

"Geoff, please, idiot. Would I?"

206

"Good."

"Well, of course." She kissed him again. Her eyes were doing a little better in the darkness now and she could make out something of his face. He looked appallingly tense. She thought there was even a touch of savagery in his eyes and the set of his mouth, that same harshness of last night. But all this could be dispelled soon. "Geoff, I don't want to stay here. It's not because of last night – no regrets, no hang-ups about it at all. The opposite. I want to take you to my place."

"Oh?"

"Yes, all right, a big change. I've been stupid about that. Some daft mental block."

"Great."

"God, don't I owe you a proper bed for once, or more than once?"

"Grand."

They began to descend the stairs, arms around each other. "Leave your car," he said. "I've got one. A limo. Quite worthy of you. I don't want you out of my sight, not even for a moment. I've been going nuts today, thinking I'd lost you."

"What car?"

"Peugeot 605."

"Their biggie?"

"Exactly."

"How did you get it?"

"Ask no questions."

"Oh, like that. Right, then."

They shut the fire doors and Geoff climbed the wall to join her in the lane after bolting the yard door. "You'll have to tell me the way," he said, as they walked to the Peugeot, their arms still around each other.

Chapter 31

She pointed to her drive in Marine Parade, but he did not stop. "I'd like to find somewhere to talk first," he said.

She laughed. "We're not nomads any longer, Geoff. Can't shake the habit? We'll talk inside. Before, afterwards, even during."

"No. Somewhere close."

She did not understand but said: "A car park by the bistro on the cliff."

He pulled in there, opposite the coastguard building, dark now.

Julie said: "Yes, let's walk a little, look at the sea and the lighthouse. Listen to the tide's melancholy, long, withdrawing roar. We've got the time, have we? Must you get home, though? You're on short-term loan, as ever? But that's all right, too."

"Wait a bit," he said.

"All right. I don't mind where we are." She nestled against him.

"This was his car," Dilsom said.

"Naturally. It'll be OK for now, but you won't hold on to it, will you, Geoff? It will be on the computer, if it's stolen, and I should think so. Would that slob own a 605?"

"You know, you've got a police mind."

She hated that, and the tone frightened her. Suddenly her joy ebbed. Why were they out here? "No, no, but when you said 'Ask no questions', I—"

"So damn sharp."

She straightened up in the seat, moved back from him a little, but slowly – no suggestion of revulsion. There *was* no revulsion. Just terrible puzzlement.

He said: "Yes, the car's a liability, the car's a convenience."

"Well, at least it's got us here."

"You know about me, do you?" he replied.

"Some things about you. Some lovely things."

"Brade talks to you about the born-again scheme? The background?"

"What scheme? Born-again? Like the New Testament?" Perhaps it would be idiotic to pretend Brade's name meant nothing to her. "I don't know any background. All I know is what I see, Geoff. What I saw last night was – If that's from your background, I'm glad you've got it, or we'd be dead."

"Except, no background, no visit by Rick Cole."

"You knew him?"

"You thought so, did you? Spotted that, too?"

The mental distance between them seemed huge. He was worrying Julie badly now and she began to gabble. "It makes sense, that's all, doesn't it, surely – if someone comes gunning for you, and I have to assume he was after you, not me – I just happened to be there – it happened to be my office – if he's stalking you it's because he knows you from somewhere, doesn't he, some grievance, so I'd assume you knew him, too?"

"What grievance?" he replied.

"Search me. Is that what you mean by background?"

"You get no gossip? Not just Brade – there has to be gossip around. Of course there is. You're treating me like some fool, Julie."

"Why should there be gossip about you? If there is, it's not come my way, believe me. What did you say the name was? Cole?"

"Why?"

"For absolutely no reason. You mentioned it, that's all." She bent forward and pushed her face lovingly near his. Christ, it did look like the time for wiles. Or it was too late for wiles? That remoteness. That savagery. The hard suspicion in the nonstop questions. "Geoff, darling, what's the matter? You look terrible – and, yes, oh, I don't know – cross?" Jesus, if only that nursery word were enough. "I saw it before, on the stairs. Sort of – oh, I don't know – full of doubt, recriminations. I wanted to make all that disappear. And I know I still can."

"You scare me."

She yelled a laugh. "*I* scare *you*? Such rubbish. Come on, walkies." She put out hand to him, but he did not take it. "Well, I'll go alone." She knew she needed to be out of the car. Anywhere. The car would make it easier for him. Someone else's car. She had come to grasp what he meant when he said the Peugeot was convenient. Wasn't she dealing with a complete tradesman? Turning away, she felt urgently for the door handle.

"No, don't," he said.

"The view will calm you, set us up." She tugged hard at the handle and had the door opened a couple of inches. He reached across her and grabbed at it, trying to pull it shut again.

"Please, Geoff," she said and swung her legs around to kick with both feet at the door, abandoning all playfulness, all pretence, frantic to force a way out and get clear. In her memory she had only the devilish competence he showed last night. Geoff was lying across her, his weight flattening her into the seat. Even if she got the door open, she would not be able to make a run. They fought, she struggling full out now, trying to scream but doing not much better than terrified gasps. Half the time her face and head were against his coat, anyway, and any noise was stifled. In the end he won, of course, and pulled the door closed again. She sat hunched and crying, her head bent forward.

"Can't trust you, Julie, that's all," he said. "The things you said."

"Geoff, that was—"

"You don't say things you don't mean. You're a bloody clever girl. You'd polished it all up. It's what you feel, underneath all this. And, look, it made sense. Oh, yes. There's part of me, the Geoff Dilsom part, that says you were correct. Obviously, I'm all wrong for you. Not just the married bit – everything. You were bound to see it."

"No." But she knew now he had it so right.

"I'm Dilsom and I'm something else altogether. Dilsom's make-believe. A package made up in committee."

"What? How?" she said. God, he should not be telling her this. Why didn't he care that she knew? It had to be bad. Or was he squaring with her, so everything might be for ever open

210

between them after this? She clutched at the hope and came nowhere near believing it.

"Vale's my other name."

"What other name?"

"Hector Vale. You've never heard that?"

"Vale? How should I?"

He giggled. "How should you?"

"Yes."

"Apart from conversations with Brade? Well, some publicity in the old days." He sat for a minute gazing at the hedge ahead of the car. "Listen, Julie, I'm not a bloodlust idiot. Anyone would tell you that, even Brade or the Met, who knew Vale. Or Rick Cole would tell you, if he was talking, or any of his clan. And it's been a treat with you, I mean it – you really helped me hold this new life together for a while. New town, new person. But it's pick me up, put me down. I know the drill. I do it myself, of course. With you, though, it could be pick me up, put me down, talk about me. Perhaps not right away, but eventually. Inevitable. Someone like Hector Vale can't wear that, just can't. Against everything he ever learned, and Hector knows a hell of a lot."

He spoke as if Vale were someone else, and acted as if he wasn't. Julie saw that without her noticing he had brought the Ruger out and placed it on his lap, perhaps when she was crouched over, crying. He had placed the automatic almost as if inviting her to grab at it. Could he only shoot in self-defence? She was shaking too much, could not risk it. But what risk, for God's sake? The risk was to let him keep it.

And then the chance was gone. He had picked up the gun.

"Geoff, for God's sake." Now, she could manage some volume, almost scream level. "I could have talked to him tonight, if that's what you're afraid of. He was there. I wouldn't listen to a word, and didn't give him a word." Tears hit her lips as she pleaded.

"Brade? At your office, this time of night? What I mean, he's always going to be there."

"No, no, he'll get the message."

"Which message?"

"He'll give up."

"They don't give up, Julie." And then he seemed to switch and talk to himself. "I'll never get another chance like this."

"You never cared?"

"I cared. But now—"

She heard a car at speed, or maybe it was cars, very close, then hard braking. Two sets of headlights suddenly tore into the Peugeot. The blaze grew stronger, whiter, more direct, as if spotlights had suddenly come on as extra. Holding the Ruger up, Geoff turned urgently to squint into the glare towards the nearest car. She saw Dave Brade come running from behind the lights, nimble, haloed by good wattage, mouth wide open and obviously shouting what had to be the "armed police" rigmarole, though he carried nothing she could see, and though she could not hear through the glass.

"Jesus, you told them, Julie," Geoff said. "How? How?" He raised the Ruger and Julie threw herself on him from the side as the gun roared. And then there were two more roars, but from further off and the driver's side window shattered. A spread of innumerable tiny, burning pains ripped her right cheek, and her neck and nose and she thought, Christ, what sort of a sight will I be at meetings with a face pitted like this?

Chapter 32

"Well, of course, wonderful, wonderful," Raging Bullfinch declared, "and I've always known it would come out like this, because you are notably, in fact, supremely, someone of will and durability. The kind of officer we need. Plus magnificent family support."

"Thank you, sir," Glyndwr replied. "And on behalf of my parents and partner. At some stage, possibly when I get into the convalescent home, I would like to discuss my future career profile, if you have the time. I've made some notes."

"Yes a brilliant recovery, Glyndwr. And of course we can talk about your prospects. Later. Things here might have settled down a little by then. But, at the moment, I have to tell you, and Dave will bear me out on this, we have an unspeakable mess on our hands."

Brade, sitting on the opposite side of Glyndwr's bed, said: "Tricky, certainly, but it could be worse, sir." Then he thought this might sound blasé, so added, "Cover operations for junked grasses are the most difficult jobs we get. The permanent bend in Glyndwr's skull would bear me out."

Bullfinch stood in a sharp, fierce movement and paced nervously back and forth at the end of Glyndwr's bed, occasionally flapping his arms in gestures of suffering and confusion. You could spot clearly now where the bird nickname came from. When Bullfinch was facing away from the bed, Brade saw Glyndwr move his hand slowly back and forth, as though scattering bread crumbs. Bullfinch had on a broad lapelled navy pinstripe suit that did everything superior cloth could do for a man, and the buzz was that he had had four of these made in London as soon as he landed the post and was still paying. A garment of this nobility could contain a man's panic until the most

213

extreme moment, like Vesuvius abruptly broken up by eruptions.

Bullfinch said: "I can't see yet where to apportion blame on this, nor, naturally, am I concerned only with the mere negativism of blame, but by God, I will discover who's at fault here. We're facing all-round repercussions, Glyn – by which I mean from as far as the Home Office. Grassing's meant to be a growth industry, and we've done it no damn good at all. This is a man we were ordered to protect and one of our own people blasts him in the head. His child goes dangerously missing for hours when we're supposed to have the whole family under guard. Loose guard, admittedly, but under guard. And, Christ, when Dilsom's found he's with a woman who –. Well, Dave, I have to say your part in this – I have to warn you that in the apportionment of blame I shall be – I hope I always am – I shall be thorough to the point of exhaustiveness – yet entirely fair – as indeed ever. I don't think anyone could dispute that."

"Absolutely, sir," Brade replied.

Bullfinch swung his head about and up loosely on his neck, periodically gazing at the ceiling of the hospital room. It was an action Brade had seen before when Bullfinch grew feverish, as though he were looking for some high perch where he could settle, blessedly, clear of all those bringing him evil and worry, yet from which he could let fall his spatter of odium.

Free now of the head bandage, though still confined to bed, Glyndwr said: "I've been out of it all, in a sense, sir, vegetabilising at my leisure in the land of Nod for so long, but whom did you give Dave as replacement for myself in this operation? That really interests me. I like to know who's treading on my heels, as it were, in the tacit yet significant unofficial rankings."

Bullfinch came to rest and sat down. "This fucker told you to ask me that," he replied, pointing at Brade. "His filthy hall- mark on it. Is the suggestion that I understaffed this job? Come right out and say it if that's what you think. Don't imagine you can get away with damn innuendo because you're an invalid, bunkering under a counterpane."

"My curiosity only, sir," Glyndwr replied. "Dave and I haven't ever discussed it."

"There'll be no dodging out of liability on that alleged account, Brade. Dare you question my policy on personnel? This was a task that could easily have been handled with available resources, if it had been treated with basic skills, and without the – Well, my God, Dave, a woman moving from one of my senior officers to a piece of nark grease like Dilsom? Do you suppose that could happen in any other force? Why do I have to—? I intend to examine this in depth, believe me – the implications as they reach out to you, the way it could have come about. And how is Julie now a wonderful girl?"

"She'll be fine. Glass fragments only. They say she won't be scarred. She could have been dead, so really she's laughing, isn't she?"

The nurse who had allied with Brade for talks to Glyndwr during the dream trek came in. "His uncle's on the ward phone again, Dave, asking about his condition," she said. "Did you mention something about not letting him know Glyndwr had come round? I think the hospital wants to proclaim it – as a success. So, what do I say?"

"I'll say it," Brade replied.

The nurse looked very uncertain: "Oh, I don't know about that. If one of the administrators, or even the Secretary himself, heard there'd be—"

"It will be OK," Brade said.

"No, no, she's right," Bullfinch chirped. "You'll damn well drop me further into it, Brade." He rhythmically thumbed behind both fine lapels, for comfort.

"It will be OK."

"Ask him which of my dear uncles he is," Glyndwr said. "One would like to show gratitude for his long-term, caring attitude. Maybe *I* should talk to him."

"What? No. I won't have this, Dave," Bullfinch cried. "Neither Glyndwr nor you. The wrong words and – further repercussions. Hospital ethics. Department of Health involved. I have enough, surely."

"I'll take it gently, sir," Brade replied. "We can't push the responsibility on to nurses."

"Push? Who'd push? Push anything? No, certainly not, but – I hope I don't need instruction from you on responsibility, Brade, but—"

"Show me where the phone is," Brade told the nurse and followed her out.

"Very discreet, damn it, Dave," Bullfinch called.

When he picked up the receiver Brade said: "The University Hospital of Wales announces that Glyndwr Jenkins has made a complete recovery and is talking like the Nine O'Clock News, healthy as a Swiss bank."

"This is grand, grand. Will they be keeping him in the hospital for a while, in that same room, or moving him to convalescence?"

"Are you missing anyone up there?" Brade replied.

"How's that, man?"

"A lad popped up in the dock here early today all meanly wrapped in a make-shift shift or winding sheet. Three bullet wounds. Carrying a Ruger. Are you still there? You've gone quiet."

"Who is this speaking?"

"Where's your black accent gone, man?"

"Which lad?"

"Twenty-fiveish. Great teeth. Probably a fine smile, previously, but rather stretched now. Joke haircut. I wondered if probably one of the kin. Our preliminary identification, done on prints and Met pictures only, says a Richard Cole or Rick. Probably travelling – I mean, when he was – in a stolen Peugeot 605. Some form, obviously. South London address. Brother of Brydon Maurice of very fixed abode for some years yet. Your name Cole? Or possibly Linacre the Yard tell us. Nunky, we'd very much like you down here, you see, but not to detongue Glyndwr. A bit late for that, in the circumstances, wouldn't you say? No, just to identify this water-sports lad. And then there's funeral costs."

When Brade returned to Glyndwr's room, Bullfinch had gone. "*Could* it be worse?" Glyndwr asked.

"Not much," Brade said. "Dilsom will live. Poor shooting, really. Boris Simpkins – but he was running at the time, a Walther, and only the head in view, when we're trained for the chest."

"You weren't carrying the Magnum?"

"Yes."

216

"But didn't – oh, I see – kept it holstered, afraid you'd kill him for the wrong reason?"

"Something like that."

"But how scrupulous, Dave. How existentialist."

"I thought so, yes. Dilsom will be sick for a long time, and in jail for longer – attempted murder on Julie, and perhaps he did the lad in the dock. Or more than perhaps. I hope Dilsom's family will stay here, though. They could be an asset."

Glyndwr said: "Dave, do you think Bullfinch was fobbing me off – about the career discussions? My future does need structuring, you'll agree."

"There's a lot to Carmel, you know," Brade replied. "Oh, knees, yes, but beyond, as well. Sure, her ancestors loathe us, but she might not be irrecoverable. And the boy's great. Real flair. I went back to see him after he'd been missing yesterday and he's still sitting up in bed, going over all of it. I don't think he minds talking to me now. He'll lie, obviously, but not the whole time, and you can't say fairer than that about most people, child or adult. Jeremy told me he had seen his father earlier in the day on the marina, pretending to be someone else, driving a Peugeot and wearing a hat. Playing Cole? Probably the boy had met Cole and was hoping to meet him again, by arrangement. Cole could reassure him about who he really was, couldn't he? Anyway, the boy had the car's number. That's what I mean, flair. Well, I put out a call because we're supposed to be nursemaiding daddy and we spot the car, just in time at Penarth. As you'd expect, we were concentrating there, and around her office."

"You're talking to yourself, as if I was still deep under." Glyndwr lay back and closed his eyes.

"Well don't relapse," Brade said.

"I tire easily now, Dave, especially of people talking about their triumphs."

"Fuck you, then."

"Julie?" Glyndwr replied.

"We put frogmen down in the dock and they came up with what could be a sinker that broke free. Possibly from a Senator."

"Ah. This is an executive vehicle often."

"She's not at her best, but I asked her if she's missing

anything, obviously. She says not, and there's no way of linking these things with a particular car, I gather."

"Ah. Accessory? Julie? Never."

"That's my feeling, too. Maybe. We've got a tangled situation. Two Rugers. The car. She seems still very fond of Dilsom, regardless. Wants to sick visit him, although he's under guard."

"Has to come to you for permission? Dave this is piquant. Even poignant."

"Get lost."

"She's going to wait for him? I mean, ten, fifteen years? He tries to kill her and she's still drawn? They're like that, Dave. For the sake of a bit of intensity they'll forgive and forget. What does he say?"

"He's not saying anything just now, or for a month or two, they reckon. We bring you around, and then we've got another bastard at it."

Brade went home and spent some time on the stuff in *The Great White South* about erecting stables and kennels on *Terra Nova*. There had been no clowns or elephants or acrobats aboard, but the horses and dogs made him think of Andy Rockmain, so perhaps the recollection aids had worked to that extent, anyway. It seemed Rockmain would be moving on now, and there might be no more attempts to spirit the kids into a strange circus.

Cliffy knocked on the door later. He was alone and rather magnificent again in full gear, though no Good Shepherd's staff. "Just to say, Caspar Indicay has had a stroke, Dave. Apparently some undisclosed recent incident of acute stress. Cathedral clergy are implored to mention him in our prayers but I might forget. You know what memory is. I always say, if God wanted us to recall better He'd have issued better equipment."

218